9/18

Carousel Beach

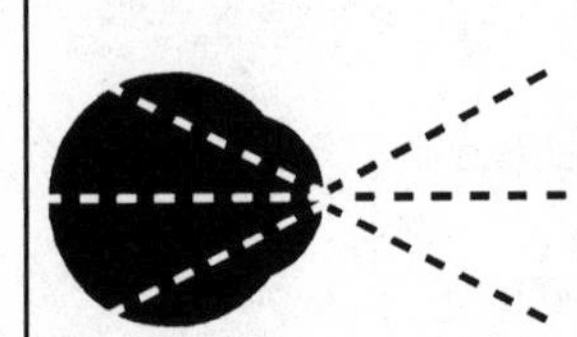

This Large Print Book carries the
Seal of Approval of N.A.V.H.

Carousel Beach

Orly Konig

THORNDIKE PRESS
A part of Gale, a Cengage Company

Farmington Hills, Mich • San Francisco • New York • Waterville, Maine
Meriden, Conn • Mason, Ohio • Chicago

This is a work of fiction. All of the characters, organizations, and events portrayed in this novel are either products of the author's imagination or are used fictitiously.

Thorndike Press® Large Print Peer Picks.
The text of this Large Print edition is unabridged.
Other aspects of the book may vary from the original edition.
Set in 16 pt. Plantin.

**LIBRARY OF CONGRESS CIP DATA ON FILE.
CATALOGUING IN PUBLICATION FOR THIS BOOK
IS AVAILABLE FROM THE LIBRARY OF CONGRESS**

ISBN-13: 978-1-4328-5710-3 (hardcover)

Published in 2018 by arrangement with Macmillan Publishing Group, LLC/Tor/Forge

Printed in Mexico
1 2 3 4 5 6 7 22 21 20 19 18

For Miriam. Forever.
For Alex. Always.

ACKNOWLEDGMENTS

This book has been six years in the making, with more revisions and starts and stops than I can count. Both the story and I have changed and matured since those early drafts, and I owe deep gratitude to the many people who helped shape both of us during that time.

Special thanks to . . .

My agent, Marlene Stringer, for your enthusiasm and guidance.

My editor, Kristin Sevick, for helping me fall in love with the story all over again. And to Bess Cozby and the amazing team at Forge for turning my vision into reality.

My early, middle, and almost-final readers. You know who you are, and you know I adore you for every bit of constructive advice and every kick-in-the-butt you provided over the many, many revisions. Extra love to Laura Drake and Kerry Lonsdale who've been with this story from day one.

The writing community — in particular, the amazing Tall Poppy Writers — for sharing knowledge and unicorns. And, of course, my heart is always with the talented and generous writers of the Women's Fiction Writers Association.

All my wonderful readers, for warming my heart with your enthusiasm and love for the characters I've created.

My parents, Lea and Peter, for always believing and cheering me on.

My husband, Philippe, for allowing me the freedom to pursue my dream.

And my son, Alex, whose love and encouragement brightens my world.

One

Everyone has secrets. Some are selfish, some necessary, but all have the potential to shred lives.

I should know. For the past year, I've been marinating two secrets. I don't know anymore if I spun them to protect others or myself.

For the past year, I've alienated myself from everyone who cares about me. I've sequestered myself in a repurposed garage with only wood animals to talk to and embraced the guilt. Well-meaning friends and family, even virtual strangers who know what happened, tell me it's time to move on.

They don't understand.

In forty-seven minutes, I'll be standing at the cemetery, commemorating the *yahrzeit* of my grandmother and my baby. People will tell me it's time to let go.

They'll never understand.

I pinch my eyes shut and attempt to breathe through the lump in my chest. I don't want to go to the cemetery.

My family was never religious. My mother could probably count on one hand the number of times she's been to the synagogue. My grandmother held on to a few traditions, although I don't think she had a frequent-visitor card to the local temple either. It was when my grandfather died six years ago that she seemed to find a new connection with religion. Okay, that's stretching it a bit. She still didn't go to services, but she became strict about observing the Jewish mourning practices and lighting Shabbat candles in honor of her late husband.

And she spelled out exactly what we were to do when she passed. My mother was not impressed. But my mother was also a stickler for appearances. She would enforce Grandma's request to the last dotted *i*.

So here we are.

"There you are. We need to get going." Vale stands in the door to our bedroom. He's ready to go; handsome in a dark-blue suit, a white shirt, and the yellow-and-blue tie my grandmother bought him our first holiday as a married couple. Back when everything still felt possible.

"Interesting choice of tie." My left eye twitches. I try to soften my tone but the words escape, unchecked. "She gave it to you."

Vale's shoulders tip back almost imperceptibly, just enough to make the crease across the front of his shirt pull smooth. "I know what tie I have on. I thought she'd like it. That you'd appreciate the sentiment." His right eyebrow pops up, challenging me.

"I didn't think you believed in that *spirit stuff.*" I mimic his tenor. His brown eyes darken.

"Really, Maya? Today you want to pick a fight? Over a tie?" His jaw juts left, the set of his mouth leaving no question where another mistimed comment from me will lead us. He turns and moves toward the stairs. "I'll be waiting in the car."

In the bedroom, I stare at the black dress hanging on the back of the closet door, still wrapped in the clear plastic from the dry cleaner. I walk past it, turning slightly so my shoulder doesn't brush the bag. The last time I wore it was to their funerals. I grab the hanger and shove the dress behind the hanging clothes at the back of the closet, then reshuffle my other clothes to hide it.

It's just a dress. An expensive one, I'm sure, since it was my mom who bought it.

But it's tainted. It has the invisible stains of their deaths.

The horn blares. I yank a maxi from its hanger. It's a soft, flowing fabric, really more of a beach dress, especially with the waves of blues, from light to dark. Grandma and I bought it together two summers ago.

I slip on a pair of high-heeled sandals and tuck my hair into a quick French knot. A swipe of mascara and lip gloss, and I'm done. It's the most I'm capable of.

I ease into the car and catch Vale's pinched expression. I know my comment about his tie is coming back.

"Interesting." He turns away and starts the car.

He doesn't approve. Mom won't approve either. But Grandma will.

We drive to the cemetery in silence. Music doesn't seem appropriate, and conversation seems to be something neither of us has the energy to tackle.

He turns the car into the driveway and through the large gates of the cemetery. He hesitates at the first fork, the silent question sizzling between us.

I suck in air and look to the right. "Not today."

He doesn't state the obvious. It's been "not today" for a year.

I visit Grandma's grave regularly. With her, I can wallow in my grief, then unleash my anger. I'd told her to take it easy. But she was a stubborn old lady and had overruled me. She was an adult. She made her own decisions. She didn't need my protection. It wasn't my job to mother her.

But it had been my job to protect my unborn baby. And I'd failed. I can't visit his grave because I'm afraid of the guilt, and I'm drowning in the grief.

"Not today," I repeat.

"Of course." It's barely audible over the rumble of the engine as he pushes on the gas pedal. The car lurches forward, and my stomach plummets. I sneak a look at Vale and wonder how we got here.

What happened to the young us? The couple we were? The couple that found humor in almost everything and comfort in each other?

I need to say something.

"Remember Crazy Stan's funeral? I'm still amazed there isn't a poster with our faces and a big red line through them at the front gate."

Vale chuckles. "True. Do you even remember what got us giggling like that?"

I squint back in time until I capture the memory. "The Rottweiler with the *kippah.*"

"Oh my god, that's right." The corners of his mouth disappear into dimples and his eyes crinkle.

"What possessed them to do that?"

"And how did they keep it on him?"

Vale's smile deepens and the dimples that mushed my insides all those years ago, work their magic again. "We used to laugh a lot."

"We did." The dimples push out, the crinkles smooth away. And as quickly as it came, the moment flitters out the open windows of the car, leaving a gaping stillness.

I look closer, trying to find the man I married. The slightly too long hair that flopped when he got animated, the mischievous glint that was the innocent warning for one of his wicked jokes.

I reach and touch his right hand, which rests on the gearshift. My index finger glides over the ridges of his knuckles. I want to lace my fingers through his, hold the gearshift together the way we used to. I want to feel his comfort and know that everything will be okay. Vale turns slightly toward me and allows a slow smile to soften his face. But his attention stays on the narrow road and his hand tightens underneath mine as he shifts from third to second.

A line of cars stretches ahead of us, and

we park behind a black Tahoe. Our Audi sedan looks like a toy in the caravan of SUVs and minivans. One other lone sedan, my mother's Mercedes, sits at the front of the row.

Luckily our parking spot is under the canopy of a willow tree. I pull myself out of the car and inch closer to the tree. From here I can see Grandma's grave and my family standing awkwardly around it. They can't see me, and the only person who's noticed our arrival is my brother, Thomas. He acknowledges Vale then looks at the passenger side. I see the line deepen on his brow, and he looks back at Vale, who hitches his head in the direction of the tree.

Traitor.

Vale walks to where I'm hiding, encircles my waist and pushes me gently forward. "It's okay. Come on." His voice barely carries over the whisper of the breeze through the feathery leaves.

"I can see fine from here"

"But you're expected up there."

"They'll understand."

"Do this for her." Does he mean Grandma or Mom? He gives me another gentle nudge.

As I approach the group, my brother moves forward and gives me a kiss on the cheek. Mom turns and nods, the movement serving the double duty of a hello and scrutiny. I can just barely make out a perfectly shaped eyebrow behind the rim of her dark Chanel sunglasses. At least my diamond earrings and upswept hair aren't offensive. My father beams his welcoming smile but stays glued to her side. Assorted friends create a semicircle around the grave. A handful of Grandma's octogenarian friends fill in a few open spaces.

Vale leans close, kisses my cheek, then gives my waist a you-can-do-it squeeze before moving to stand with my brother and the rabbi by the headstone.

I linger a step outside the circle of dark, solemn faces surrounding the grave. I can't bring myself to close her escape route.

"Never block the path to the sea, Mims. It's seriously bad juju," she'd always say. The willow rustles, and I can't contain a giggle.

Mom notices. She always does. She takes a half step back and mouths, "It's a memorial, Maya. A little respect please."

I shoot a desperate look toward my husband. He gives me what I'm sure was meant as a reassuring smile. It only succeeds in making me feel more isolated.

The rabbi begins reciting the mourner's kaddish and the respectful hush becomes a somber silence.

By tradition, tonight we should be lighting candles and sharing stories. Mom will light the candles, but there will be no sharing of stories, no reminiscing.

My relationship with my mom is challenging on its best days. But her relationship with her mother was outright belligerent. Mom was closer to her dad — one of the few things she and I have in common. When Grandpa died, her already tenuous relationship with her mom was stretched like an old rubber band.

I steal a look at my dad. He winks in return. He'd better be around for a good long time. I don't think our mother-daughter band has much stretch left.

I turn away from the assembled crowd and look at the view. Grandma picked this spot herself. When we buried Grandpa six years ago, she purchased the plot next to him and the plots on either side, then had it written in the contract they would be laid to rest facing the cliff and her beloved ocean.

The rabbi drones on, his voice merging with the background noises — the rustling willow, the crashing surf below, the impatient gulls, the utter stillness of a cemetery.

How can it already be a full year? My hand touches my belly. I try to cover the move by pulling on my dress, feigning a tug-of-war with the wind. I back away from the grave and the crowd. My mom lays a small, smooth stone on the newly placed grave marker. My dad bends to do the same.

I take a few steps closer to the cliff and will the wind to snatch my grief and dump it into the sea.

A voice cuts the lulling song of the breeze, "At least you made the effort to be here." Mom's curt tilt of the head closes the subject on my choice of attire. "You're just like her. She wasn't much for tradition either. Until recently, at least." I bite the inside of my lip. No need to point out that six years is outside the definition of "recent."

A gull squawks. A wave crashes. The willow shimmies. *"Ah, don't pay any attention to her, Mims. She was born uptight."* Grandma's words tickle the back of my neck. As long as I can remember, it was "us" against "them." Them being Mom and Thomas. Dad refused to take sides, at least openly. Grandpa was the familial Switzerland.

"I will expect you at the reception." Mom turns and walks off, not waiting for an answer.

I release the clip holding my hair. Curls blow across my face, whipping the tears away. I shut my eyes and count to three. I hear my mother thanking someone, then someone else, her voice getting farther away with each count.

Car doors slam behind me, signaling that the memorial is over. Tires crunch the gravel.

I take a half step forward. The wind grabs at my hair, twisting curls high then dropping them to thump against my back then up and around my head. Through the tangled mass, I look out at the ocean. The delicate fabric of my dress twines around my legs, and a parade of goose bumps prickles my arms.

"Where did I go wrong, Grandma? Oh god, I miss you. I need you. I don't know how to get past this." I push the words past bottled up emotions. The wind picks up again, drying the salty drops on my cheeks.

"It's time." Vale touches my arm and the goose bumps reverse direction. "Are you okay?"

I squeeze my upper arms in a protective hug. "I don't think I can stomach going to Mom's. Can we go somewhere? Just the two of us?" I turn, hopeful for a reprieve.

"She'll be mad if you don't show."

"She'll be mad if I do show. We both know I can't live up to her expectations." I wave my fingers open to indicate my less than perfect appearance.

Vale watches the cars slip over the hill. He turns back, his mouth drawn, but the softness in his eyes gives him away.

"Thank you." I release the stranglehold on my nerves.

We sit at a table on the patio outside the Sugary Spoon, our favorite coffee shop, a block from the beach. A seagull hippity-hops around the tables, eyeballing every occupant in turn, looking for the next person who will give him a tasty afternoon snack.

The summer season hasn't started yet so the main strip is still pretty quiet, especially on a Thursday afternoon. It's warmer here, without the cliff breeze, and I'm glad for my summery dress. Vale shifts in his dark suit, removing the jacket and tie with a relieved sigh.

The seagull hops to our table, his black beak open, his beady eyes sizing us up.

"Are you going to finally talk about this?" Vale tosses a chunk of his croissant to the gull, then turns to look at me.

"What *this* do you want to talk about?" I cringe inwardly. He's trying to be supportive. I know he is. They all are. But if one more person tells me to put it behind me, to let it go, I'll lose what's left of my mind.

He's watching me. I blow into my mug, even though the liquid isn't hot anymore, and watch the white froth of milk swirl into a muddy brown mess.

"It's time to move on, Maya. For your sake. For our sake. It wasn't your fault."

I force my gaze up and make eye contact.

How do I move forward when I destroyed everything? How do I tell him that it was my fault? That I killed them both?

Two

Vale maneuvers the car down the crowded street and the neighborhood unfolds in slow motion. Large pickups and vans create a maze. It's the annual presummer frenzy. Owners who don't live here year-round arrive to spruce up their houses before the summer rental season kicks off. Year-round residents tackle touch-up projects and landscaping.

Our house sits toward the end of the street, just a few houses short of oceanfront. It belonged to Vale's grandparents, once upon a lifetime. When we decided to move back to Kent, Delaware, four years ago, they happily signed the house, and its mold, over to us.

My grandparents lived three streets away. The house was sold a few months ago. I don't go by there anymore. Not since she died.

My parents live farther down the beach.

Technically, it's a different town, but if you blink, you'll miss the sign. I always use the town name when talking about going to visit them. It's my immature way of pretending we don't live fifteen minutes apart.

Vale pulls into the driveway, letting the car roll to a stop inches from the garage. Or what used to be the garage. We transformed it into a studio for me not long after moving in. The house itself is a typical old beach bungalow with small rooms that didn't leave much space for me to spread out. The smell of solvents and paint clung to our clothes, and it wasn't long before we were finding X-Acto knives, paintbrushes, and even a chisel mixed in with the silverware. But our first test in compromise came when Vale found his ratty fraternity T-shirt wrapped around a can of shellac primer. That's when the car moved out of the garage and my restoration projects and I moved in.

"Do you want to go for a run with me?" He leans against the car, his right palm taps on the roof, fingers splayed. He reminds me of a horse anxious to have the halter removed so he can bolt free to the other end of the paddock.

"No. You go. I want to get back in there." I tilt my head toward the garage.

Vale's gaze twitches in the direction my

head is angled. "You can't work all the time. Some fresh air will do you good."

I nod. He's right.

"Next time, okay?" I close the car door as gently as possible, afraid a loud slam will sound like an exclamation mark.

He doesn't say anything, just taps the top of the car one more time before turning to the house. I wait for the back door to slap shut, then count to ten before following. I can't work in this dress, but I'd rather avoid another lecture about holing myself up in the studio.

I step into the kitchen, careful to catch the old screen door before it bangs behind me. Vale is standing in front of the refrigerator, drinking from the bottle of orange juice.

"Glasses are in the cabinet to your left."

He lifts one eyebrow but doesn't stop drinking. When he's downed half the container, he recaps it and puts it back on the top shelf, closes the fridge door, and leans against it, arms crossed, watching me. "You don't even drink this orange juice."

"So?"

"So, what's the difference if I drink directly from the bottle? I'm saving having to wash a glass."

I shrug.

The corners of his mouth twitch up into

an amused grin.

"What?" I match his stance although I'm not leaning against anything, which makes my attempt less causal. I'm also not grinning.

"You're sexy in that dress."

"No wonder my mom gave me such a dirty look."

"Don't bring your mom up now. I'm trying to seduce you." He arches his brows suggestively.

Heat zips up my neck, and I fight the urge to turn and flee to the safety of my studio.

Vale takes a few steps forward, his left hand open, ready for me to slip my hand into his. I imagine my feet superglued to the floor so I can't bolt. My hands drop to my sides and I grab the fabric of my dress.

"How about it, gorgeous?" He's standing in front of me, his left hand tracing a slow path up my right arm. I shiver. His hand retraces the path down until he reaches my hand. Goose bumps race up my arm. His fingers lace through mine, forcing me to release the bunched fabric.

"I can't." I pull my hand away.

"Come on, Maya. It's been too long." I hear the catch in his voice. I can feel the tremor of effort on his part. *Stay calm, don't spook her. She'll soften eventually.*

"I can't." I press back into the kitchen door then sidestep around him, careful not to make contact. Behind me, I hear the soft thud of an I'd-like-to-slam-the-hell-out-of-this-door. I hate hurting him. I hate the distance between us. I hate that he doesn't understand.

He's been trying to bridge the physical chasm for six months. We've had sex once in that time. It was awful. One more failure to add to my guilt pile.

"How much longer, Maya?"

How do I answer that? It's not that I'm not attracted to him. I am. It's not that I don't want to be intimate with him. I do. But I can't. My body refuses to cooperate, and my mind refuses to forget.

"I don't know. It's not like I have this planned out."

"Well, fuck. Maybe it's time you started planning. Because I'm done waiting." He brushes past me.

I stay rooted in the middle of the kitchen listening to the creaking of the floorboards as he moves around above me. The squeak of the dresser drawer. The thump of a shoe dropping. A few minutes later, he brushes past again, wearing his running clothes. He grabs the extra key from the bowl on the counter, adjusts his earbuds, and jogs down the back stairs.

No good-bye.

He disappears from view and I close my eyes, leaning into the counter for support. I picture him stretching against the car. One leg bent at the knee, fingers circling his ankle while he tips up on the ball of his other foot.

My upper body instinctively leans forward and I tip up on the balls of my feet. I should have gone with him. We used to run together. Even though his long legs stretch him past the six-foot mark, he always adjusted his stride so I could keep pace. And we were always in step.

Until . . .

No. I'm not doing this. Not now.

I change into a pair of old jeans, the ones with all the paint splotches and rips, and a tank top, then pull on Vale's old Cal Berkeley sweatshirt, inhaling the mixture of his cologne and my paint. I burrow into the comfort, even if it's only a temporary one.

I step into the studio and exhale the tension. There's no room for it in here. I walk to the table, flip on the electric kettle, and the music. Chris Botti welcomes me with his soul-touching trumpet. While an orange-chocolate tea bag steeps, I turn my attention to the mummified shape of a wooden carousel horse. He's the last of the menagerie from the historical merry-go-round on the boardwalk. He's also my favorite. He was *our* favorite. Mine and Grandma's.

The city stopped operating the carousel almost five years ago, not long before we moved back. Funds for its upkeep had dried up. The salt air and years of only moderate maintenance left the carousel in sad shape.

When we moved back to town, my former boss at the museum in Kansas City pulled in a favor and secured me a freelancing job with a friend of his who owned a handful of antique stores. The work kept my hands busy and a trickle of money dripping into our bank account. But while I loved restoration work, those projects never captured my heart. None of the pieces that came through my studio had the history of the museum artifacts, and none of them held secrets that they wanted divulged. It was almost like they wanted to remain anonymous. Which is fine for them, boring for me.

A few months after we moved to Kent, I'd joined Grandma for one of her morning walks to Carousel Beach as the locals called it, and we found ourselves in front of the old carousel pavilion. There we were, holding our paper cups of coffee, listening to the memories of a working merry-go-round, when Grandma turned with a look I hadn't seen in her eyes for too many years.

"You're going to petition the city to restore our carousel."

"Are you crazy? I can't do that. I don't know anything about restoring carousels."

"You're an art restorer, Mims. This is art."

"Giant art. With moving parts."

"Vale can help connect you with people for the moving parts." She'd waved dismissively. This was not an idea she was going to let go. "Think about it. This is perfect for you."

And I had thought about it. A lot. I was equally intrigued and terrified. The excitement won out, and five months later, I approached the city council with a proposal that included a fundraiser, as well as several individual investors. It was one of the few times having wealthy, connected parents in the community paid off.

My proposal had included pictures of myself as a little girl riding my favorite horse, with my grandma standing next to me. I'd also submitted pictures from the early days of the carousel and a picture of the carousel builder, a local boy who, according to what little information I could dig up, had left town several years after the merry-go-round was completed. Grandma was uncharacteristically evasive when it came to those early days of the carousel. She blamed it on old-lady brain. I kept asking, and she'd answer in spurts of excitement and sputters of don't-remembers.

The council had been swayed, though, and the carousel was mine to restore. The ugly chain-link fence surrounding it was replaced by a wood fence with strategically placed "windows" for passersby to see the progress. Signs were placed around the perimeter on how to contribute to the renovation.

To my surprise, people donated. And left notes about what the carousel meant to them.

I'm not sure why it surprised me. Clearly, Grandma and I weren't the only ones who loved the carousel. But to us, there was something magical to it, something personal. Whenever we'd go ride it, Grandma would get a just-between-us glint in her eye and whisper, "These animals know things, Mims. They'll never betray a confidence."

And she was right. Which is probably why I find them easier to talk to some days. Especially lately. They have their secrets, and so do I. But while I unravel their secrets, they keep mine. And that suits me perfectly.

I sip the tea, wincing as the liquid scalds a trail down my throat. I have just two months before the grand reopening on the Fourth of July. There's always a big party on the boardwalk, and the city has already started promoting this one as extra exciting, with the return of the beloved merry-go-round. *No pressure, Maya.*

Except for this one horse, the animals are done. The drum panels and ceiling panels are almost complete. The machinery and gears are in the final stages of installation. This handsome guy is the last holdout.

I rest my hand on the large, wrapped form in the middle of my studio. He brings with him memories of summer fun.

Memories of love and discovery.

Memories of old friends and promised dreams.

A sigh like a slowly leaking tire pushes the last thought away.

"Let's get you out of there." With the loving tenderness of a mother unwrapping the blanket of a newborn, I peel the layers of packing off.

Finally free, the carousel horse stands among the discarded packaging. He's rough, worn, tired. Magical. I run my hands gently over the faded colors of his saddle and trace the once-vibrant pattern on the breastplate.

I flex my fingers, letting them slip into the waves of his wooden mane, then rub his ears and run my hands down until they cover his eyes. I cup his muzzle, waiting for his warm breath.

I step back to admire him. Dust particles, captured in the rays streaming from the skylight, dance around like tiny fairies casting spells. I ease up onto the worktable, crisscross my legs, and pull my notebook closer.

Ding, right front hoof.

Gash, base of left ear.

Chip, flank just above tail.

Seventy years of secrets to uncover and thirty years of memories to reminisce. And the clock is ticking.

"How many times did I ride you?" I rewind my brain to those summers so long ago, when my only worries were getting to the carousel early enough to be the first on my favorite animal, and if I wanted a chocolate-vanilla swirl ice cream or a pretzel after the ride.

It was always Grandma who took me. When I was very small, she'd stand next to me, a steadying hand on my leg as the carousel went round and round. When I was old enough to ride alone, she'd climb on the animal next to me, her head back, happy, carefree. She told me stories about the beach and watching the boardwalk transformed from a stretch of sand and shells into a thriving summer getaway. She'd get a faraway look in her eye and a nostalgic smile talking about the big excitement during the summer of 1943, when the carousel was installed.

It must be true that some traits skip a generation. Grandma loved the carousel. My mom abhorred it. She claimed motion sickness just watching the wooden animals blur by in a nauseating mosaic of color. For me the carousel was magic. Still is. It's one more thing that links me with Grandma and splits me from Mom.

I glance at the diagram of the carousel. "Do you miss your ostrich friend?" I ask, my finger on a drawing of a horse on the outside row, an ostrich chasing behind him as the carousel picks up imaginary speed. "Don't worry, you'll be together soon."

The horse stands patiently. Even faded and weathered, he's beautiful.

The once-brilliant colors of his saddle and breastplate are rubbed to an almost unrecognizable color. The left ear hints of the reddish brown that made this horse stand out as the leader of the herd. His once-polished black hooves are now mostly gray. The raised tassels around his saddle pad are worn almost flush with his body, and their brilliant blue is now more muddy creek than sparkling ocean.

Where other people might see old, I see mystery. Secrets. The good kind.

Restoring the beauty of the past always intrigued me. While my friends were falling asleep in the back row of the darkened auditorium of the eight A.M. art history lecture, I was in the front row, leaning forward, wishing I could crawl straight through the vinyl screen on the stage. I wanted to enter the world that created such beauty, talk to the artists whose imaginations reached through the centuries to tickle mine.

There's always a story. The eighteenth-century stoneware from England with the letter *C* carved into the bottom. The artist's initial? The third batch of jugs he created? A clue to where he lived? Or a thirteenth-century sword with a spiral inlay in the blade — the swordsmith's signature? A promise to a fair maiden? A warning to an enemy?

"And what stories do you have to tell, my friend?" My face relaxes into the faintest of smiles. "Remember the summer Simon kissed me for the first time?"

That was the summer I turned fourteen. Simon was fifteen and so mature. His parents had just bought the house five streets down from Grandma and Grandpa's. When he showed up on the beach, all the girls would tug at their swimsuits, making sure their assets were properly displayed. I didn't have any assets to display back then. Still don't.

That was also the summer I fell in love for the first time. To the frustration of every girl on that beach, Simon had shown interest in me — the tomboy. We played beach volleyball and had corn dog eating contests. I had a mean spike and could inhale corn dogs with the best of the boys. These days, however, the smell of corn dogs gives me an odd mixture of nostalgia and nausea.

Somewhere between corn dogs and beach volleyball and endless hours on the merry-go-round, I experienced why those girls on the beach primped and posed. I discovered the quivering stomach flutters of seeing someone walking toward you or turning and smiling at you.

Simon, with his shaggy, dark-brown hair and shimmering green eyes. The smile that always started with the left corner of his mouth.

A sigh breaks loose. Why did I indulge that

skip down memory lane?

I twirl a curl that refuses captivity. I tilt my head to get a better look at my old friend and blow a puff out of the corner of my mouth, the loose strand of hair taps my cheek and scatters the lingering images of a first love.

"Enough. Let's get busy." I hop off the table and take a couple of steps toward the horse.

First, I'll make a drawing of him, diagramming every detail, from the large planes of the saddle and his body, to the intricate shades in his mane and tail, and the elaborate decorations of his bridle and breastplate. I walk around him, jotting notes, squiggling details, roughing out general shapes.

I'll take photographs, too. They're invaluable for checking details and documenting the stages of the restoration. But graphite to paper is where I build the emotional connection.

I pull a piece of paper from a giant sketchpad and sink to the floor by the horse's legs. I like to start with the legs. You can tell the character of the animal by the way it stands. Perfectly square, he's solid and steady. Hind legs slightly forward, he's ready to leap away. Right front angled, he's easy to ride. Left front snapped up in a perfectly parallel line, he's your leader.

The crisp bell of the trumpet teases the mournful violin, and together they envelop me in a world of highs and lows, joy and heartbreak. My hand moves across page after page of gleaming white sketch paper. I've redrawn his raised left front leg three times before I get the exact ninety-degree angle of the bent knee.

A song ends, and I catch myself out of breath. The floor around me is covered with sketches, each page revealing another curve, a deeper angle, a sharper contrast. I stare at the drawing I've just finished. The hoof is detailed. The angle of the knee precise. But the intertwined hands resting on the bent knee of the horse as the carousel speeds up and the music gets louder are as soft as the memory. The tingle of that first touch with Simon and the memory of us, huddled between the carousel animals, ripples up my spine.

I crumple the drawing and toss it into the trash can, then glare at the horse. "Look at what you started."

I force my thoughts to fast forward, my left hand in Vale's as he slips the diamond band onto my ring finger, his hand trembling with emotion. His hand splayed on my belly and the look of awe on his face with each ripple from the occupant inside.

My stomach constricts, strangling the memory.

I glance at the clock above the door. It's almost eight P.M. Yet again, I've managed to spend almost eight hours without noticing time passing. My stomach grumbles. Okay, part of me has noticed time passing.

I roll my head in a slow circle, hoping to loosen the knot lodged at the base of my neck. I pull my shoulder blades toward each other, relishing the momentary ache of sore muscles being forced out of their slouch zone.

I close the studio for the evening, saying a reluctant good night to the horse, and walk to the back door of the house.

There's a light in the kitchen, and the smell of pasta welcomes me in.

"Vale?" He's not in the kitchen, and the house is quiet except for the *thump-flop-thump* of clothes tumbling in the dryer. I'll have to thank him for doing the laundry. Again.

"Vale?" I call once more, even though it's obvious he's not home.

A sticky note on the microwave door calls for my attention. *Couldn't wait. I was hungry. Didn't want to disturb you. There's a plate in the microwave. Meeting Thomas for drinks. V.*

A whoosh of air escapes from my lungs — relief?

That's not fair. The last year has been hard on both of us. But we'll get through it. Somehow. I hope.

I crumple the note and drop it in the trash on my way to the wine bottle. The notepad and pen rest on the counter next to the wine. My fingers strum a silent chord on the accordion of yellow sticky notes. It's a thin cube, not the one I bought a couple of weeks ago. Or have we used that many notes already?

I pour a glass of wine, grab the plate, and ease into my regular seat at the table. It's a good thing Vale likes to cook. That was never one of my strengths, and even though I've managed to master a couple of simple recipes, I'm more than happy to turn over kitchen duties.

The long, floppy pasta reminds me I need to put an order in for leather straps. I'll need them for the reins.

There's a yellow legal pad on the table, a pen clipped to the side. I reach for it and an envelope slips out, gliding to the floor at my feet.

It's addressed to Vale, the return address an architectural firm in Seattle. I shouldn't read it; it's not addressed to me. But I'm curious.

I slip the paper out. It's short, to the point, and delivers a karate kick to my gut.

Dear Vale,

It was a pleasure meeting you last week. We're all looking forward to welcoming you to the firm. . . .

Three

The paper crinkles in my fist, loud in the quiet of the empty house. "What the hell?" The words reverberate through the kitchen. Not even the clothes dryer answers.

We're all looking forward to welcoming you to the firm.

He's leaving? A jab of fear jolts me out of my chair. He can't leave me. I know things haven't been great, but there's a reason. He said he understood. He said he'd be there with me. That we'd get through this together.

My legs turn to limp linguine, and I sink back onto the chair.

I grab for my phone, then slap it down on the table. What do I say? "Hi honey — when will you be home so we can discuss the fact that you're leaving me and moving to the other side of the freaking country?" My phone buzzes angrily as I hit the wrong password again. Tears stream down my cheeks and my teeth chatter. I want to scream at him, at myself, at the world.

I finally unlock my phone. I can't call him. I don't want to scream, and I don't want to sound hysterical.

Instead, I type, *"When will you be home?"* and hit send, then strangle my phone waiting for a response.

"Ten-ish. Your bro says hi."

"I don't give a crap about my *bro,*" I yell at the phone. I do. But I don't. Not now. Now I only care about my imploding marriage.

Breathe, Maya, Breathe.

Ten-ish is still an hour away. I'll lose my mind waiting.

How did he never mention this? Seattle? That's the other side of the world. He hates rain. It rains there. A lot.

The ice maker spits out a fresh batch of ice into the internal container, the sound sharp and unsettling. A shudder barrels through me.

Was the seduction attempt earlier today a final test?

I stand and walk to where the bottle of wine sits next to an empty wineglass. He had his glass with his dinner. Alone. While I was in the studio. Alone.

I pour myself another glass. I need to do

something. I need a plan. I need a bath.

Clutching my wineglass, I make my way up the narrow stairs. At the top, I turn left and into the small bathroom. I hate this bathroom. It needs to be gutted. And it's been the "next project on the list" for the last three years. The only thing I want to keep is the old claw-foot tub. It's luxuriously deep and one of the few tubs where I can actually keep chest and knees under water. But the rest has to go. From the wobbly toilet with the tiny round seat to the miniature Tums-yellow tiles on the wall and the not-so-white-anymore tiles on the floor.

What happens to that project list now? Who will renovate this bathroom? We should have made the time.

I turn the hot-water knob as far as it goes and give the cold-water knob a nudge, just enough so I don't shriek like a boiled lobster the moment my behind hits the water. Then I pour eucalyptus bubble bath into the waterfall plummeting from the faucet. When the room is sufficiently steamy, I ease into the tub, catching my breath at the initial scorch of hot water. A sip of wine, an inhale of the eucalyptus aromatherapy oil, and I sink in deeper, the water warming the tension from my back.

Don't think about it. Relax. Think about the

horse. Think about the beach. Relax. Dammit, why didn't he say anything to me?

I lurch forward, wine slopping over the rim of the glass and bleeding into the fluffy white bubbles. "Shit." I lick the side of the glass.

Footsteps on the hardwood stairs give me just the warning I need to slip back under the protective bubbles. With my foot, I nudge a snowy white peak where my midsection lies submerged, just in case.

When was the last time my husband saw me completely naked? Four months ago, when he walked in on me in the shower. He'd wrapped the towel around me when I got out but didn't let go. I was wet and trapped. He was aroused. I wanted to be. I tried to be. For a few delicious moments I was. I'd gone through the motions, then apologized. The kiss of death to intimacy.

Standing at the altar you repeat the words, "for better or for worse," and looking into the eyes of the person you adore, it feels like "for worse" will never happen.

Then it does.

"Hey," Vale says, easing the door open.

"Hey," I answer over the lip of the wineglass.

"Thomas says hi."

"So you said in your text."

He narrows his eyes, probably wondering if that was an invitation for a fight or an awkward attempt at a conversation. I'm equal opportunity for both these days.

Deciding on the latter, Vale continues, "He wanted to know if you'll be coming out of your studio long enough for your mom's big summer barbecue."

I groan and scoot lower into the tub. My hand juts out of the water to capture the snowy mountain before it escapes and exposes my chest.

Mom's annual "Summer Fun" barbecue that's anything but a casual, fun barbecue.

I shrug, causing a fluffy white cone to relocate. "What's the point?" I keep my eyes on the dancing bubbles.

I hear him inhale sharply. "Because," he draws out the word, "they're your family. And we go every year."

"You're not even planning on being here, though, are you?"

"What are you talking about?" Our eyes meet and his face becomes a conflict of emotions. His mouth tightens to a thin, don't-go-there line. His eyes soften, revealing a sadness that all but guts me.

"Why didn't you tell me about the job offer?"

"I tried."

"When?"

"Too many times. Not that you would remember, because it didn't revolve around your mourning or your carousel."

"That's not fair." My insides clench.

"It's not. But it's also true."

"Were you planning on telling me, or was I going to find out when your suitcases were packed? And what about me? Or am I not included in your plan?" My heart beats in my ears. "Or should I be on alert for a courier with divorce papers?" I prattle on, aware that my voice is rising in pitch and volume.

"None of the above."

"Then what, Vale? You have a job offer that I didn't know was even a seedling of an idea."

Confusion and frustration war for dominance in his expression. "I told you I was meeting with Ed. I told you that they were trying to recruit me."

I toss through the recesses of my memory and come up empty. "When?"

"Two months ago. A month ago. Last week." His shoulders slump in defeat.

I don't remember. How can I not remember something this critical? Two months ago I was in the middle of restoring the lion. A month ago I was rebuilding the jumper rabbit from the inside circle. And last month would have been Grandma's birthday. Last week I was fighting with my mom about details for the *yahrzeit.* And preparing the studio for my new arrival.

"I'm tired, Maya. I'm going to bed." He rolls his shoulders and takes a step out of the bathroom.

"No." I startle us both.

He does a quarter turn but doesn't fully commit. "No, what?"

I swallow, hard and loud, the words fighting their way to freedom. "I don't want you to go."

"To bed? Or to Seattle?"

I can't find the words to answer.

"I don't want to go either, Maya, but I need a reason to stay."

I push forward and onto my knees, my soapy, exposed upper body stopping us both. Vale's eyes travel from my face to my breasts. With one blink, his expression turns from beaten to hopeful. I skid along the porcelain base of the tub and scoop bubbles over me, the movement louder than any words.

"That's what I thought," he mumbles. He turns, leaving me to decide if I can give him a reason to stay.

He takes slow, small steps across the hall.

It shouldn't take more than seven normal strides to go from the bathroom to the bedroom. But he seems to be stalling. I hold my breath and squeeze my eyes tight. I hear the dresser drawer squeak open and then shut with a knock.

We need to fix that. Or better yet, get a new dresser. The bedroom set was a gift from Vale's grandparents. "Set" is a misleading word. Most of the furniture came with the house. We bought a new couch for the family room and what little furniture I needed for my studio. Everything else is a mishmash of left-behinds. What's here works, and best of all, it was free, so I can't complain. But I wish we'd made more of a mark on this house.

There's only one room we started personalizing. We yanked out the old musty furniture and painted the walls a fresh spring-morning-at-the-beach blue with fluffy white clouds on the top third and the ceiling. The smell of paint still oozes from the crack between the door and floor, even after all these months. Or maybe only in my mind.

I turn to put the wineglass down on the back of the toilet and gasp as a wave of cold water slaps against my stomach. The suds have all moved on, leaving a murky film skittering around the top of the water. I wrap a towel around my body and tiptoe down the hall.

The slow, deep breathing from the bed tells me he wasn't waiting for me to make the next move. He's lying along the edge of the bed, a clear "your side/my side" distinction. His body forms a lightning bolt, and his hands are tucked under his left cheek. I'm rooted at the door, the light from the hallway reaching around me and highlighting the expression on his face.

He seems so peaceful. No "should I accept the job?" angst. No "what's happening with my marriage?" worries. Not a care in the world. I wish I could lose myself in sleep.

I pull open the dresser drawer and cringe at the creak of the old runners, twisting quickly to see if the sound woke him. He tugs at the blanket but doesn't wake. I don't know if I'm relieved or disappointed.

A year ago, I would have shaken him awake. We would have talked or argued, but we would have reached some decision, and then we would have made love. Or we would have made love then talked it out.

But tonight, I slip quietly past the foot of the bed and ease under the blanket as gently as possible. I lay on my back for a minute, listening to the *thwank-thwank* of the ceiling fan, and try to stir some emotion that will move my left arm to reach for Vale. In the end, I turn, my body curling into a question mark, my hands tucking under my right cheek.

I'm no closer to having a plan than I was two hours ago, and I'm no closer to keeping my marriage together. I've taken a giant leap backward in moving forward.

Four

The curtain flutters and my dream scurries out the open window. Seagulls bicker outside, and a lawn mower kicks over. The smell of freshly cut grass tickles my nose. I roll to my side, feeling a bit disoriented, like after a ride on the carousel when I've been looking up at the ceiling panels.

Vale isn't in the bed next to me. I listen for sound inside the house. No water running in the bathroom, no footsteps in the kitchen below.

I push myself out of bed, straighten the T-shirt I'd slept in, pull on a pair of shorts, then pad down the stairs barefoot, careful to avoid the creaky fourth step. I stop at the bottom and listen.

The only noise in the kitchen is the tocking of the wall clock. I pour a cup of coffee and glare at the clock. Vale's mom bought it for me a couple of years ago thinking it would be a "colorful addition to my studio."

It certainly is colorful, with its rainbow numbers and glow-in-the-dark hands. I hate it. Not because it's from my mother-in-law, mind you. The incessant tock, tock, tock of every passing moment makes me absolutely toddler-tantrum crazy.

I finish the coffee, grab a banana, and head out the back door toward the studio, where there are no noisy clocks.

The studio snoozes under a hazy blanket of morning light. The sun is still too low to wake up the dust fairies living in the skylight, and without the overhead lights, the daylight filtering in from the windows creates deep shadows around the carousel horse.

As usual, I flick on the music and electric kettle. It's become reflex. And it's become my work quirk. I only drink tea while I'm in my studio. Outside of these walls, I'm a die-hard coffee-bean supporter.

When the water has boiled, I pour it over the tea bag and inhale the deep chocolate aroma as it mixes with the tangy orange. It's an acquired taste. My best friend Sam introduced me to this concoction. Vale hates the smell, so, like my paint supplies, the tea has been banned from the house.

I stare at the horse standing majestically in front of me. He is a "stander." Standers are larger, more elaborately carved and painted than their jumper brethren. Some people may think they're not as much fun as the horses that go up and down, but I always loved them. This one most of all.

My vision blurs, a combination of steam from the mug pressed against my lip and memories crowding teardrops onto my eyelashes. Grandma and I would race to the carousel for the honor of riding him. If I got there first, Grandma would stroke his head, then run her hand along his shoulder. Her hand would rest on his belly before she'd concede and move on to the next animal in line. Then she'd wink and whisper, *"If you listen carefully, Mims, he has some great stories to tell."* I hear Grandma's cackling laugh in the washed-out notes of a fading memory.

"Okay, big guy, I'm listening." I set my mug down and approach the horse. I start at his tail and walk along his right, or "romance," side. It's the side facing out, more elaborate in its decoration, to entice riders. The details are vivid in my memory, even if nature and the years haven't been as kind.

"You're in better shape than a lot of your friends were. Lion was the worst. Do you know I had to completely replace one of his legs? Poor guy." I flick a look at the horse's head.

"Remember Angie's tenth birthday when stupid Robby Morgan pushed her off the lion because only boys were supposed to ride 'The King of Beasts'?" I drop the tone of my voice, mimicking Robby, even though his voice had been as high as mine back then. "Wonder whatever happened to him? He was such a jerk."

I push away the memory of Jerky Robby and crying Angie, her dress ripped from getting caught on the metal stirrup, and her knee bloody from landing on the wood-plank base of the carousel.

"We used to have fun, didn't we?" I pet the horse's wooden neck.

I return to the table and jot a few thoughts on my notepad. The song fades into a momentary hush. There's a rustle behind me, and what sounds like the gentle knock of a hand with a ring tapping hollow wood. I feel a prickle on my neck, the fine hairs shifting.

I squeeze my eyes shut and turn. The prickle melts into a shiver. I force my eyes open and walk back to my friend. It's not fair that she isn't here to share his restoration with me.

I run my hand over the saddle, at the

once-raised sections worn down by years of riders. My index finger traces the outline of the saddle and the delicate swirls barely visible on the painted saddle pad.

My hand slides along the curved wood of the horse's shoulder until my palm is cupping his belly. The same movement Grandma used to make, her greeting and good-bye to a special wooden friend. "Oh, Grandma, I miss you," I whisper into the horse's hard mane, my forehead pressing into his neck.

"I miss you both."

This should have been the perfect summer. The summer with my baby. The summer Grandma and I got to see the carousel come back to life. Now only one of the three will be alive.

Absently, I rub the raised strip of the girth. My forehead scrunches, and I rub the spot again. "What is that?" I squat to get a better look at the rough lines on the horse's belly.

"Did someone ding you when they removed the pole? And you didn't kick them for doing this to you?" I look closer. My finger traces the marks. That's not a ding.

"Let's get you on the table." I wrap my arms around the horse's middle and carefully lift him from the stand in the middle of the studio. He's not heavy, but I walk slowly, conscious of his size as I near the table and ease him up.

With the horse on his side, I get a better look. It's absolutely not a ding.

For Meera. Forever.

Meera? That's what everyone called Grandma. She hated her given name, Maria; she claimed it was too formal, too stuffy. It was the only name her mom ever used, and from the stories Grandma told, her mom was a tough enforcer of rules and proper behavior.

"What in the world?" I squint and read it again.

For Meera. Forever.

"Grandma? What's the story behind this?"

I trace the carving with the index finger of my left hand. The diamond of my engagement ring zaps a bolt of light at me. I try to picture my grandfather contorting to carve this inscription. My grandfather the lawyer. Not likely. Grandpa was as honest and straight-arrow as they came. *Predictable* is the word Grandma used.

I squint at the horse's belly, trying to picture a young version of my grandfather twisted under the horse, carving the love note to his bride. Nope, still don't see it.

So if it wasn't him, who could it have been?

Who else can I talk to about this? Grandma was my go-to person. She was the one I went to when the girls at school teased me for my "baby boobs," and she'd taken me to buy my first bra. She was the one I went to when I had my first period, and she'd walked me into the drugstore for my first box of pads. Mom was never there for such things. She was always busy being perfect. And I wasn't perfect by any pretzeling of the imagination.

I tap Vale's name on my phone but get his voicemail. I try Sam, but she doesn't answer either.

I pull a chair closer and sit. Now I'm eye-to-belly with the horse and the mystery inscription.

For Meera. Forever.

What story would Grandma weave? She was brilliant at making up stories when I was young. I'd name an object, and she'd spin an amazing tale. Even when I lacked the creativity to find a new subject, her imagination never faltered. Each story was unique. And magical.

I indulge a pout as I return the horse to the middle of the studio. I miss those stories. I'd fantasized about the three of us

— Grandma, me, my baby — curled up, laughing, and lost in the magic.

I stand and return to the table, but my mind can't settle into work mode. I try Vale again, but the call again goes immediately into voicemail.

There has to be someone out there. I know who's out there, but I'm not calling her. Mom and I never did agree on anything Grandma said or did. I accused her once of being jealous. I'd expected to be grounded, waited for the wrath of my mom, but she'd only looked at me, then turned and walked away, leaving me to swallow the unsavory stew of guilt for hurting her feelings, and adolescent smugness for delivering a direct hit.

I call my brother. He picks up on the third ring.

"Hey, little sis. To what do I owe the honor of this call?"

"Can't I just call my brother?" I try for a light, breezy tone.

He laughs. "Of course. And yet you rarely do."

He's right. Even though we're close in age, we've never been that close.

After a too-long pause on my end, Thomas prods, "So? What's going on? Vale said you were more obsessed than usual with your wood friend."

"He said that?" My voice squeaks in surprise. Vale teases me for talking to my charges, but he's also been my biggest supporter. Biggest after Grandma.

"Nah, those are my words. He just said you're working too hard."

"Oh. I'm not obsessed." I hear the childish pout in my voice. Even as an adult, my brother manages to bring out the little kid in me.

"So, Maya, why did you call?"

I take in oxygen reinforcement. I called him to talk and now I'm wishing I hadn't. *But I did, so . . . Talk, Maya. Tell him.* "I found something on the carousel horse that's wigging me out. You know the horse Grandma and I both loved so much?"

"Ummm." I hear typing, and the slightly muffled response tells me he has me wedged between his shoulder and ear. My time is running out.

"There's an inscription in his belly made out to Grandma," I rattle forward, hoping to regain his attention and a smidgen of enthusiasm.

"Graffiti?" It's half question, half dismissal.

"No, it's deliberate."

"So?"

"So this is huge." I bite back frustration. Why had I expected more from him? He's just like Mom.

"Why?"

"Seriously? Come on, Thomas. This isn't Grandpa's style."

"Your point?" The background typing starts up again.

I tighten my hold on the phone, wishing the pressure would somehow transfer through the line and strangle my brother. "My point is . . ." I swallow hard, the sound echoing in my ears. What is my point? "Oh forget it. Why did I think you'd understand anyway?"

"Typical response. Why don't you ask Mom?"

"You think she'd know?"

"Probably not."

"So why suggest it?"

He sucks in a dose of patience. "I got nothing, Maya. I don't want to fight with you, and I really need to get back to work. Maybe Mom remembers a story Grandma once told her, or knows someone who remembers when the carousel was built. She has tons of old-people connections."

"Now that is brilliant."

"Hello? Helloooooooo? Who is this? Can you please put my sister back on the line?"

"Ha, ha. Seriously, I give credit where it's due. That's a brilliant suggestion, Thomas. Thanks."

"Good luck."

We hang up, and for a brief hiccup of a moment, I wonder if he was wishing me luck in finding someone who can answer my questions, or luck in dealing with my mother. I inhale, exhale, inhale, and tap Mom's name in my phone directory.

"Hello, Maya." Mom's formal tone is a sharp reprimand for blowing off the reception yesterday. Well, that's probably not exactly true. It's a sharp reprimand for pretty much everything I've ever done in my life.

"Hi, Mom." I can't bring myself to apologize, and idle chit-chat doesn't suit us. "Did Grandma ever talk to you about the old merry-go-round?"

I hear something suspiciously similar to a snort. "The merry-go-round? Really, Maya. When did you ever know me to take an interest in that thing?"

That *thing.*

I pinch the bridge of my nose. "Do you know anyone who lived here during the time it was built who I could talk to?"

"Not that I can think of."

"What about the builder? He was local.

Do you know if anyone from his family still lives in town?"

"Why would I know this?"

"You're on the city arts committee?" I try to change the sarcasm into an ego stroke.

It doesn't take.

"*Arts* committee. Paintings. Photographs. I don't know anything about the carousel."

I want to argue that historical carousels are considered art, that collectors pay a heavy bag of coins for well-restored animals, that there are museums dedicated to carousels. But I don't.

"Thanks for your help, Mom." I don't try to check the edge in my voice. There's no point.

"Always a pleasure, Maya." She doesn't try to check the disapproval in her voice. There's no point there either.

Now what?

I turn on my laptop and, while it powers up, flip through the pages in my project notebook until I get to the section on the origins of the carousel. H Creations is the company on record. In addition to the official documents from the historical society, I've included a few old newspaper articles. Hank Hauser was the mastermind and master-hand. A picture in one of the articles catches my eye — a young man stands proudly next to the merry-go-round, holding one end of a banner that reads "Grand Opening." The other end is in the hands of then mayor of Kent, Alfred Tate, according to the caption. I squint at the faded photocopy of the article, hoping a hint will jump out.

For as much as Grandma talked about the carousel, she didn't say much about Hank. She'd said they were friends. Passing friends, whatever that meant. She'd said he moved away a couple of years after the carousel was completed and that she didn't know what had become of him.

I type "H Creations" into a search engine, but the results are too varied. I add *Kent, Delaware,* and find more of what I already know. I change the search to *Hank Hauser, Kent, Delaware.* There's a nice write-up on the man behind the merry-go-round, a wedding notice, a few more articles about other installations he built. But nothing current and no obituary. It's as though the man moved to another planet.

I turn back to the carousel. *For Meera. Forever.* Who would have done that? And why?

Five

The Audi is parked in the driveway, but I don't remember hearing Vale return. Seeing the car gives me an extra bounce as I make my way to the house. He always has good advice; he can help me piece this together.

The sharp crack of metal hitting ceramic stops me at the door. Another crack and the vibrating clang of metal on metal, followed by a string of curse words, propels me forward.

"Vale?" I trot up the stairs and come to a dead stop at the entrance to the bathroom. "Whoa, what happened here?"

He flicks an annoyed glance in my direction and slams the hammer into a tile next to the sink. It cracks and shoots slivers at him in protest.

"Want to tell me why you're destroying the bathroom?" I try again.

"There's a leak," he says between gritted teeth, slamming the hammer into another row of tiles.

"So you decided to demolish the entire bathroom?" The tank has been removed from the toilet and the tiles behind it have already been torn from the wall. There's a jagged line of damaged drywall and stubborn tiles running to the base of the pedestal sink. A mosaic covers the floor in a wide arc around Vale.

"Would you rather have it leak into the kitchen?" He yanks at a tile that clings to the drywall like a frightened child clinging to its mother's leg.

"Okaaaay." I use a proceed-with-caution tone. "So what's the game plan?" I take a hesitant step into the bathroom, careful not to step on ceramic shards or cracked nerves.

Vale releases an exaggerated sigh and twists to face me. His right hand flips the hammer around while his left hand pushes a flop of hair out of his eyes. "The game plan? Fix it." His gaze flicks over my face before turning around.

Last night's stalemate slams into my chest, shoving the inscription into the irrelevant-topic pile.

"Vale . . ." I shift my weight, unsure what to say next, or what to do. There's a crunch of a tile under my heel. Vale's body tightens at the sound, but he doesn't turn around.

Instead, he resumes his pounding.

I should offer to help, a sort of olive branch with a wrench.

The idea is chased away by a muffled string of curse words and a shattering of tiles.

I back step until I'm in the doorway. The pounding stops and the dusty air hangs heavy with the words we both want to say but can't.

Olive branch, Maya.

"Can I help?"

"No, it's fine. Thank you, though."

"Do you want to see if George has time to help? I can give him a call."

"No. Thank you, though."

Snap goes the olive branch.

"This looks like it's going to be a big project. You don't have time for this." I try to sound encouraging, supportive.

"I took the week off."

"Why?" The word ricochets off the tiles, an accusation more than a question.

"I need time to think. And the bathroom needs to be fixed." He nods, apparently agreeing with his assessment of the situation.

"Think? About staying? About us?"

"Yeah." His voice is barely more than a whisper. He sounds tired, almost defeated, and I feel a twinge of dread grabbing at my throat. He turns and looks at me, really looks at me, like he hasn't seen me in a long time. He studies my face, makes eye contact.

There are new lines at the corners of his eyes, and the mischievousness that usually sparkles in the deep brown is missing. I blink at the few gray hairs that dance over his left ear as he moves his head. When did those happen?

I take a half step forward. "Vale," I start, but my mouth clamps shut as he shakes his head.

"Not now, Maya."

I retreat half a step. We've defaulted to "not now" as the standard answer for any uncomfortable discussion or feeling. It won't fix us, it won't make things right, but neither one of us knows how to break the "not now."

I retreat another half step. "Do you need the car?" The instinct to escape claws at my insides.

He scans my face, his jaw moving left then right, and I wonder if he's going to change his mind, accept my help, agree to talk.

He doesn't. "No. But we'll need to go the bathroom-and-tile store later." He picks up a shard of a green porcelain. "Unless you'd rather stop on your way home?" It's an innocent question on the surface.

I hesitate for a skip too long. Vale's lips pull tight, and he turns back to the demolition, leaving me, once again, off balance.

Renovating the house was supposed to be our project — together, as a couple. We'd spent the first night in this house moving from room to room, plotting the demise of certain walls, planning the renovation of others. In our heads, we had the entire house remodeled and looking sharp.

Then reality kicked in. Vale got busy with designs for turning an abandoned convenience store into a modern new restaurant, and I won the contract for the carousel restoration. Instead of fixing up our own run-down piece of the world, we both threw ourselves into bringing new life to other run-down places.

Until fifteen months ago, when we started redecorating the extra bedroom. Suddenly, all of the dreams we'd discussed seemed within reach and the excitement to make this house really ours was reignited. We spent hours on the floor of that room talking about how to paint it, what furniture it needed, what window coverings would be best. Even the house seemed to catch the mood. Steps didn't creak as loud, faucets didn't drip all night, and the latch on the screen porch started latching again.

For four glorious months we schlepped old furniture out and shopped for new, we peeled moldy wallpaper and painted fresh colors on the walls and ceiling.

"Can we go together?" I ask over the pounding.

He nods. Or at least I think that's a nod.

Maybe that will be the seed to the olive tree.

Six

Today my car is the only one navigating the narrow roads of the cemetery. I ease to a stop next to the willow tree, even though there's plenty of room closer.

The breeze tugs, and I allow it to guide me closer to the edge of the cliff and the vast view to the horizon. The sun pirouettes off diamond sparkles as the waves roll into each other. The wind stills, dropping a suffocating stillness around me.

I breathe in the salty air, then turn. The air punches out of my lungs at the sight of the gray marble, Grandma's name etched in black. Around the base are the stones visitors placed yesterday during the ceremony. Everyone except me.

Yesterday was for them, for the formality. Today, it's me and her. Today, I don't have to share her with anyone.

I pick up a flat, oval stone by my feet and smooth it between my thumb and index finger. A fluttering pulls me forward. Tucked under a large stone is an envelope.

I cross my ankles and lower until I'm sitting face-to-letters with Grandma's name. I trap my shaking hands between my butt and the soft grass.

Twenty-six stones of varying shapes and sizes and colors rest around the headstone. I stare at the collection, wondering who placed each stone and what words they whispered in parting.

The envelope jitters as the breeze picks up. Who would leave a letter on a grave?

I shift left, releasing my right hand from captivity. I flick at the corner of the envelope. Is it wrong to open it? What if the person who left it wants it to be read? But what if it's private?

I roll the stone gently with the tips of my fingers. It's not like Grandma will be reading it, so what's the harm? The stone thuds over, exposing the one word on the front of the envelope. *Meera.*

Curious, I slip the envelope loose, slide a finger behind the triangular back flap and pull the folded paper out, afraid that if I blink it'll disappear like the last leaf in a winter wind.

My dearest Meera,

It seems we were just sharing stories. Not a day goes by that I don't miss you. I wait for the day we're together again. I suspect it won't be long now. And this time, forever.

Yours, H.

The pounding of my heart echoes in my ears. The carving in the horse flashes through my mind.

For Meera. Forever.

Forever.

I read the letter again, my attention jerking between the paper in my hand and the marble headstone in front of me.

"Oh, wow." That inscription on the horse obviously wasn't done by my grandfather. His first name was Alexander. No *H* there.

"Grandma? What secrets were you hiding?" I don't, of course, get an answer.

The air around me is so still I can hear a blade of grass groan under the weight of a caterpillar.

Why didn't H sign his name? I flip the paper over, hoping there's more. The only thing there is an embossed logo, upside down. Whoever H is, he was either in a hurry or absentminded. I twist my head before my senses catch up, and I turn the paper instead.

"Tower Oaks?"

Tower Oaks is the retirement community on the other side of town. Grandma never mentioned visiting anyone there. I try to think back to yesterday. Was the shuttle bus from Tower Oaks here during the service? Could H have been right here, and I didn't know it?

I pull into a visitor parking spot at Tower Oaks. A hunched lady shuffles past, moving her walker a quarter-inch at a time while a nurse walks patiently beside her. By the entrance, a younger old man sits on the bench reading a book. From a balcony two stories up drift the tormented sounds of a daytime soap opera

It's been over a year since Simon moved back to town. Grandma mentioned running into him and that he told her he'd taken a job at Tower Oaks. She'd obviously omitted the fact that she ran into him *at* Tower Oaks.

Don't jump to conclusions.

After she told me he was back, I'd look for him everywhere. My heart would stutter any time I saw someone who resembled him. But it was never him. I thought I saw him walking through the grocery store shortly after he returned, but I was with

Vale and pregnant. Not exactly the ideal chase-down-your-ex scenario. My future was next to me and inside me, not in the produce section.

Since that sighting, nothing. As though he weren't living in the same town at all. Or, more likely, as though he were avoiding me.

I get out of the car and slam the door harder than necessary. How could she have kept something so huge from me? I walk past the old lady and her nurse, ignoring their stares.

The electric doors whoosh open. A blast of sterile air assaults my nose and sends goose bumps scampering up my bare arms. The heaviness of anticipated death clashes with the overtly cheerful décor.

A barely twenty blonde smiles up at me as I walk to the reception desk and pops an invisible piece of gum in greeting.

"I'm here to see Dr. Riley." I try what I hope is an authoritative tone even though my nerves are pinging like an arcade game. I've just opened the door to my own soap opera. Here to see the man I was certain I'd grow old with then walked away from on the night he proposed. The man who may be the link to a secret my grandmother wanted to hide.

"Are you family of one of his patients?"

An eyebrow lifts with the register of her voice.

The phone on the desk in front of her chirps, and she raises a finger in a "one minute" request. She transfers a call to a Mrs. Fowler and turns back to me.

I still owe her an answer.

"No. A friend." *Friend.* I doubt Simon Riley would classify me as a friend.

The receptionist assesses me for the length of two gum pops.

"Is he . . . ?" I start to ask, but stop at an extra loud pop of her gum.

She picks up the phone, her expression unimpressed and unconvinced. "Dr. Riley, please come to the front desk. Dr. Riley to the front desk."

She darts a look sideways at the swoosh of automatic doors opening. I turn in the same direction. A green plaque with white letters reads *West Wing.* Above the door, in elegant stenciling, are the words *Tower Oaks Memory Support Center.*

A man in plaid golf pants and a yellow polo shirt walks through and the doors squelch shut behind him.

"You can wait over there." The receptionist points at the grouping of uncomfortable-looking chairs by the windows.

I perch at the edge of a chair, my attention jerking with every opening of a door. I try focusing instead on counting the up and down of my right knee, but it's moving too fast.

"Maya?" The voice reaches my ears a split second before the brown tips of dress shoes enter my vision.

I close my eyes, count to three, and lift my head. On three, I open and look straight into Dr. Simon Riley's confused face.

"Hi, Simon." My voice sounds croaky, as though I've just woken up and haven't cleared my throat yet.

"What are you doing here?"

He's standing with his legs slightly apart, arms crossed over his chest. Not the most welcoming of hellos. Although I really didn't expect anything else. Did I? If he'd wanted to see me, he would have found me.

You didn't look for him, either.

"How've you been?" My left eye twitches. *Lame, Maya, very lame.*

"Fine. But I don't think you're here to inquire about my well-being. Not after all this time. So?" He shifts his weight.

I pull the envelope out of my pocket. "It was left on my grandmother's grave. It's on Tower Oaks stationery. And it's personal."

Simon's gaze drops to the paper flapping wildly in the space between us. "And?"

"It's from someone whose name starts with *H.*"

"That narrows it down, doesn't it?"

I want to shake the answers out of him. Because suddenly I'm absolutely convinced he knows so much more about my grandmother than I do. And that stings worse than a flu shot. I focus on movement at the other end of the waiting room. A family walks by carrying bags and balloons. The balloons are depressingly cheerful and a stark contrast to the pained look on the face of the man carrying them.

"You know who wrote this, don't you?"

"Why is it important?"

So we're going to play the answer-a-question-with-a-question game.

"Who's 'H'?"

"We're not playing this game, Maya."

My face flushes. He could always read me. "I'm not playing a game, Simon." I sound about as convincing as I feel.

"Then tell me why you're here, blazing mad. It's been sixteen years. No hi, how are you?"

"I asked."

He gives me his don't-bullshit-me look. It was a meet-an-acquaintance-at-the-grocery ask and we both know it. He inhales and, with a practiced patient tone, says, "I'm great, Maya, thanks for asking. I'm happily married with three kids, a puppy, and two guinea pigs."

I sneak a look at his left hand. No wedding ring. I twist at mine with my thumb until the diamond is tucked in my palm. I knew he'd gotten married. Not having a ring doesn't mean he's not anymore. And what does it matter either way?

"Truce?" I put my hands up in a peace offering.

"Truce. Now tell me what this is about." He sits in the chair next to me, body angled, our knees almost touching. I shift my weight to the opposite butt cheek, giving my knees an extra half an inch of don't-touch-the-ex space.

"It's about my grandma. And the carousel. You know how special they both were to me. And secrets. Secrets she kept, and secrets that I think you have an answer to."

He tips his head and looks at me from under the brown forelock. I'm oddly comforted that he's still wearing his hair shaggy. He releases a puff of air and the forelock flutters. "I guess I'm not surprised you put it together."

I sag into the back of the chair. I'd been waiting for the confirmation, but I wasn't ready for it. "You obviously know more than

I do. Care to share?"

"I'm not sure it's for me to share."

"Well it won't be her telling me, so it's either you or H."

"H is Hank," he indicates at the letter. "He moved back to town years ago. Your grandma used to come visit him."

"Hank?" I feel the creases deepen on my forehead as the information collides with reality. "Hank Hauser?"

Simon nods.

"My grandmother has been visiting Hank Hauser?"

Simon nods again, his eyes searching my face, tugging at my soul.

"Hank Hauser the carousel builder? The man she told me she barely knew and didn't know where he was?"

Simon shrugs.

I want to scream. I want answers.

"For how long?"

"A couple of years, I think. Every Tuesday, Thursday, and Friday. Teatime. Or cocoa time actually. Hank likes cocoa."

Tuesday and Thursday afternoons were her book-club meetings, although I don't think they ever actually read books. *Of course not, there wasn't a book club.* Friday was knitting group. I have scarves and a hat as proof that she went to those. *Doesn't prove anything, Maya.*

My body deflates. "Wow. What else was she lying about?" It's not really a question though, and Simon only shrugs in response.

We're quiet for a few minutes. Simon acknowledges a doctor walking past and an older couple walking arm-in-arm toward the sliding doors to the back garden.

"She was here the day before she passed." Simon swallows hard and looks away. He'd always liked my grandma. And she adored him. She'd save a stash of Rice Krispies bars just for him because she knew they were his favorite. "Her death has been very hard on Hank."

I remember the envelope, still clutched in my right hand. "He was at the memorial?" I try to force my memory back to the faces surrounding the grave.

"No. After. He didn't want to intrude. Said he wanted to say a private good-bye."

"Did you know he built the carousel?"

Simon nods.

I shake my head. All these years he's been right here, in the same town. All these years, Grandma has been coming to see him. So many years of lies. How could she?

"Can I see him?" All the questions I wanted to ask him, all the questions I peppered Grandma with instead. Why didn't she tell me?

Simon's eyes dart to the doors of the West Wing as they slide open for a slow-moving procession of two. I watch as the old man maneuvers his walker, the nurse walking slowly by his side, one hand on his back.

The words above the door to the West Wing pull at my eyes like magnets. "Memory Support Center," I read aloud, and then turn back to Simon. "Can he . . . ?"

Simon's head bobbles left then right in an uncommitted response.

"What does that mean?"

"He has good days and not-so-good days."

"Is it just age or does he have some form of dementia?" A sense of dread rattles through my insides.

"Alzheimer's." The word drops out of Simon's mouth.

"What does he remember?" The butterfly in my stomach has reverted to an uptight caterpillar, the slithering feeling leaving me queasier than I'd been with morning sickness.

"Some, yes. Come on, he'll appreciate the company."

I let Simon lead me across the lobby and through the secure doors into the Memory Center. What memories will I find in there?

We walk down the hallway, past doors

propped open, revealing the intimacies of those unable to care for themselves. I cringe involuntarily as we pass a room with a woman crying softly.

"Some days are harder than others," Simon says as we round a corner and start down another long corridor. "Here we are." He stops in front of a room.

"Julie, this is Maya Garrison." Simon turns and I suddenly notice the nurse's station behind us. "She's here to visit with Hank. How's he doing today?"

Julie flashes a smile at me and a broader grin at Simon.

"Brice. It's Maya Brice," I mumble as a flush of heat sears my cheeks. "Do you think he's up for company?" I look between nurse and doctor.

"A short visit should be fine," Nurse Julie responds. "But if he gets agitated, I'll have to ask you to leave."

"That's fair." I take a hesitant step forward, aware that both Julie and Simon are watching me. I take another less-hesitant step and tap gently on the brown wood door propped open by a rubber doorstop. I'm answered by the soft, sad sounds of a trumpet muffled by a pair of old speakers. Contrasting smells of lavender and hospital antiseptic assault my nose. And in an oversized brown leather chair sits Hank Hauser, hands resting on the armrests, eyes closed. He doesn't move when I knock again, harder this time. I turn anxiously toward Simon and Julie. Simon tips his head in a *go-on,* and I rap a third time on the door.

"Mr. Hauser?" My voice squeaks with sudden apprehension. "Hank? May I come in?"

The song fades to a crackle. I look to where the noise is coming from and my mouth forms an O as I realize he's listening to a record player. Vinyl records. My grandmother used to play her favorite old vinyls for me over and over on the sweltering summer days when we hid inside under the gentle movement of the ceiling fans.

The record player rests on a desk by the window, a handful of books and picture frames sit neatly on a chest-high bookshelf. Next to the desk is the hospital-issue bed, saved from its sterile appearance by a quilt in burgundy and forest green checks. An Oriental rug covers the cold tiled space between the bed, desk, and chair. Having finished my visual tour, I turn to the two armchairs in the middle of the room.

Hank is watching me.

I open my mouth to speak, but no words form. The look on Hank Hauser's face has stolen them away.

"Meera. You're here."

Seven

Hank's words are as soft as the air escaping from his lungs. His eyes glisten with unshed tears; his gnarled hands grip the armrests.

An electric current zips down my spine.

He thinks I'm her.

I came because of an inscription carved into the belly of a carousel horse and a letter left at a grave. But the answer to whatever questions I have is beaming at me in full wattage.

My legs wobble and a hand grips my elbow, steadying me. "Are you okay?" Simon whispers into my ear.

"Doc, help the girl in." Hank waves his hands animatedly, gesturing for me to sit in the chair beside him.

Simon retains his hold on my elbow but doesn't move.

I tug my arm free. "I'm okay."

"Hank, hi." I take a couple of tentative steps forward. "I'm . . ."

"Oh, Meera." Hank tosses his head back and lets out a deep belly laugh. For a split second I can picture him as a young man. Strong and handsome. Commanding. "My memory may not be what it used to, but I'd never forget your angelic face. Come sit with me."

I perch on the edge of the chair, keenly aware that both men are watching me.

Hank reaches forward and traps my hand between both of his. I look down. The heat from his hands is both comforting and claustrophobic. I want to say something but I'm afraid of breaking the spell, of crushing the joy on his face.

"It's been so long, Meera. What . . ." He thinks for a minute, head tilting as though to catch the memory. "Twenty-four years, right?" He grins like a child pleased to have found the correct answer to a challenging question.

"Twenty-four years?" My voice chirps with confused surprise.

I sneak a look at Simon, still standing in the doorway. His shoulders lift in a slow not-sure-where-this-is-going look.

Hank laughs again and pats my hand. "You never were great with numbers," he teases. A shadow of recollection darkens his face, then passes with a blink. "Well, I'm just delighted to see you now. Tell me how you've been. Have you moved back or are you just visiting your folks?"

I'm trapped in a past that didn't include me, yet insists on sucking me into its depths. My palms feel clammy and my heart slams against my rib cage. I'm sure everyone in Tower Oaks can hear the pounding.

Hank pats the top of my hand, bringing me back to the present. But whose present? Mine or his? His with me, or his with my grandmother?

I ease my hand out of his grasp and shift in the chair. I have so many questions that I'm ready to burst, and yet I'm at a complete loss for words. My right knee jiggles and I catch a smirk on Simon's face. I was always a nervous jiggler. So was my grandmother.

Hank's warm hand stops an upward bounce. "I've made you nervous. I'm sorry."

I force my legs still and slide my hands under my thighs. "I'm fine. Tell me, how've you been?" I smile, hoping my nonanswer will slip through the time warp of our conversation.

"Ah, you know me, I'm always good. Strong as a horse." Hank flexes his right arm to show what must have once been an impressive bicep but is now an old man's thin arm in a blue button-down shirt.

My brain stumbles over what to ask next. I want to know about the man who was obviously closer to my grandmother than just a passing friend, as she'd insisted. I have so many questions for the man who built my beloved carousel.

All questions are scratched away as the needle reaches the end of the record. I pop up from the chair, suddenly itchy to move, and walk the handful of steps to the record player. I pick up the album cover.

"Maynard Ferguson," I read aloud, then place the needle on the black vinyl disk. Suddenly I'm six again, wearing a frilly dress and sequined sandals and dancing with Grandma in the open-air ballroom by the beach as Maynard Ferguson and his big band send summer off with a rollicking party.

"Remember that concert he gave in the old Spanish ballroom, Meera? That was the grand opening for the carousel. We danced so long we had to put our feet in the ocean after, to stop the aching." Hank chuckles at the memory and sways to the music. "We had some good times back then, didn't we?"

I turn slightly toward him, wondering how to respond. He's not waiting for a response though. His eyes are closed, and he continues to sway in time to the music, a small figure in an oversized chair. The ancient player behind me skips, and I turn quickly to rescue the precious record from getting scratched, blinking away a sudden tear.

"Tell me about the carousel."

"The carousel." Hank's face crumples into the past. The serene memory of dancing gives way to something more complex. Nostalgia. Sadness. Love.

Caught in the swirl of emotions, I'm pulled back to the chair next to him.

"Ha." He lets out a laugh from deep inside a memory. "Remember when we helped old lady Marsh onto the ostrich and she almost tumbled off the other side? Or when we got caught in the storm and waited it out in the engine room?" He smiles, and I swear I catch the hint of a blush flash across his cheeks. "We were so afraid your parents would come looking for you."

The portal into the past is wide open, and I want more. "What else?"

He pats my knee. "You always were crazy about that merry-go-round. Just like me."

And just like me, I add silently.

He looks up, the radiant smile fading like a bulb on a dimmer switch. "You know, it's not running anymore. They shut it down." A lone teardrop escapes onto his check, and I choke down a lump of emotion.

"I know. But it's being restored. That's actually . . ."

"I hate to break this up, but the kitchen will be cleaning up from lunch soon. Hank, you should eat something," Nurse Julie says from somewhere behind me, cutting me off. She walks past Simon and comes to kneel in front of Hank. Simon follows but stops a few paces from us.

"Oh, okay." Hank looks from the nurse to the doctor, then at me. "Oh, okay," he repeats. The eyes that moments ago sparkled with memories are now glistening with confusion.

"I'll come again when we have more time to talk," I assure Hank, who's looking from me to Julie like a child unsure which parent to follow. His hands grip the armrests, bulging veins winding their way to the sharp ridges of his knuckles. I squeeze his hand. "I'll come back very soon."

I stand, and Hank grabs at my hand, a silent plea not to be left behind.

"I'll see her out for you, Hank. You go with Julie and get something to eat," Simon says, smiling at him. He puts a hand on the small of my back, and I instinctively lean in to the touch.

"Oh, okay. I am a bit hungry," Hank agrees, somewhat reluctantly. He releases his grip on me, then pulls himself up from the chair, with Julie's steadying hand on his elbow. "Well, thank you for stopping by." His tone is suddenly stiff and formal. He narrows his eyes, assessing me, placing me.

My breath hitches, and I sink deeper into Simon's side. I watch the snail-pace progress as Hank and Julie make their way out of the room and around the corner, toward the dining hall.

"Come, I'll buy you a coffee. Although by the look on your face, you could probably use something stronger." Simon's words chase away the eerie sound of rubber-soled shoes shuffle-squeaking on tile.

We walk down the hall, and I focus my attention into a narrow tunnel, hiding between imaginary blinders like a carriage horse. I know if I look to the side and into any of the rooms, I'll lose what little composure I have left. Simon steers me down the hallway and to the waiting room. I jolt at the hiss of an espresso machine. I hadn't noticed the kiosk in the corner when I came in.

A smiling gray-haired lady with a nametag that reads *Barbie* hands Simon a latte and asks what she can fix me. He grins sheepishly.

He leans to pretend-whisper. "Barbie fixes the best lattes around. But she keeps me in line. Three's my limit. Unless I can sneak one from her replacement when she goes on break." He winks at Barbie and flashes a grin that makes her giggle like a teenager, and twists my insides like it used to when I was a teenager.

Barbie hands me a latte and bats her eyelashes at Simon. "I'm on to you," she says revealing a clipboard from next to the register. On it are a handful of names with check marks. I glance at the sheet and smile. Simon, two checks. Dan, one check. Tim, three checks. Robert, four checks and a big "No more today." Barista Barbie obviously has a thing for the men.

Simon laughs and gives Barbie a last wink. He gestures for me to follow, and we step outside into the bright heat of midday. A handful of bistro tables are scattered around the flagstone patio, and park benches are tucked into nooks of bushes or under trees. A few birds chirp, but otherwise the patio is deserted. We find a bench in the shade and sit.

After a few minutes of sipping our drinks, he angles his body to face me. "Is that what you were hoping to find?"

I take another sip. Simon was right: Barbie really does make great lattes.

The hot wood of the bench warms the

back of my knees while the intensity of Simon's scrutiny burns through to my core.

"I didn't know what to expect. But it wasn't that." Hank's face when he saw me — saw *her* — fills my vision.

I shift on the bench so I'm looking directly at Simon. "Why did he think I was her? Where does he think he is? When?"

Simon pushes a hand along his thigh, ironing out an imaginary crease in his pants. "Alzheimer's is an ugly disease. For his age, he's doing quite well, though. How much do you know about it?"

"I've watched movies and read books where a character has it. And I have friends who've talked about relatives with Alzheimer's. But this is the first I've come in direct contact with anyone who has it." I watch a squirrel scurry across the lawn, his tail waving hello. Or good-bye. "What am I supposed to do when he thinks I'm her? I can't be her. That's wrong."

"I understand how uncomfortable it can be, but that's his current reality. And trying to talk him out of it will only agitate him and make it worse."

"I can't do that. I can't play games with him."

Simon is slower to respond this time. "It's not a game, Maya. And I'm not suggesting you pretend to be her. What I am saying is that when he's confused about what year it is and what part of his life it is, you engage him about what he remembers of that period. Ask him a question about something he's just mentioned, or something neutral."

"How often does that happen?"

"More in the last few months. The disease is progressing."

Hank and Julie come into view through the large windows. She has her arm linked through his. They could almost be a couple on a date. Hank says something and Julie laughs. I wonder if he's telling her about old lady Marsh or commenting on the lifeless lunch.

I picture my grandmother and Hank together, talking. Talking about what? What did his family think when they saw the two together? "Is his family around?"

Simon is also watching Hank and Julie's slow progress inside.

"Not anymore." His voice drops and I know he's thinking about her. My grandmother adored Simon. She called him Doc, just like Hank had. For as long as I've known him, Simon insisted he would be a doctor. "He has a few friends at the facility. Rowdy group. They're fun and good for him. Most of the time."

"Is it okay if I come back to see him?" I lean forward to gauge Simon's reaction.

"Just check in with one of the nurses first." His expression gives nothing away. So unlike the man I knew, who couldn't hide a feeling with a ten-count head start. Is it a skill learned in medical school or from years of heartbreak?

I push a tall weed around with my toe and watch it sway. "I need to go. Thank you for the coffee. I . . . I guess I'll be seeing you around then." I stand and walk to the back doors of Tower Oaks. I feel him watching as the glass doors suck me in. And I feel Barbie watching me as the front doors spit me back out.

EIGHT

I glance at my watch and push down on the gas pedal. It's been three hours since I left on my errand. Vale must be getting itchy to go to the tile store.

I park the car in the driveway and fight the urge to tell the carousel horse about meeting his dad. *Good grief, Maya, you need to get out more. Talk to your husband, not a wooden horse.*

Inside, the house is quiet. No smashing of tiles, no TV, no clothes dryer thump-thumping.

"Vale?" My voice bounces through the house, sounding loud and out of place. When did this house take on a hollow, unloved echo? I reach for the doorknob. Maybe I'll wait for him in the studio instead.

A sticky note loses its sticky and flutters to the floor. I shouldn't be surprised that the house feels abandoned when my husband and I have resorted to communicating through notes. Maybe not exactly abandoned, but unloved-in.

Don't forget dinner at Thomas and Bree's. Went early to shower. Come when you get this. p.s., Our shower doesn't work. p.p.s., It's 4:45.

Shit, I forgot. He left forty-five minutes ago. Fabulous. Dinner with my brother and his family isn't exactly what I had in mind for tonight. Not that I had much in mind, but I'd hoped to talk to Vale about Hank and the horse. I can't do that amidst the commotion that is my brother's life.

I trot up the stairs to change. Bree serves dinner at six P.M. sharp. No exceptions. Ever. If I hurry, I'll just make it and avoid another "you need to re-engage with the outside world" lecture.

I like my sister-in-law; I'd even go so far as to call her a friend. But Bree subscribes to the same philosophy as my mother: Perfect on the outside is perfect on the inside.

Her house is perfect, her kids are perfect, she's perfect. And her marriage is perfect. Why wouldn't it be? She's always there for Thomas and the kids. She's *given* Thomas kids.

Everything Bree is, I'm not.

I kick off my tennis shoes and pull my

socks off. Case in point, botched pedicure. Two weeks ago, Bree treated me to a "girls' day." Lunch, pedis, shopping. It was an intervention, she'd said. Lunch had been a stiff affair at the country club. Mom and Bree both loved going there. I, of course, was like a bowling ball on a golf course. But I'd smiled and chatted and didn't spill anything on myself. The perfect pedi with the stylish teal nail polish hadn't made it out of the pedi chair before I smudged four nails. Bree, on the other foot, had waddled expertly to the drying station, mumbling about me being a lost cause. I'd begged off the shopping portion and I think Bree had been relieved.

I wiggle my toes with their smudged polish. Probably better not to wear sandals tonight. I get out of my dirty clothes and pull on a clean pair of yellow capris and a white T-shirt. I spray perfume on my wrists, neck, and chest, then another quick spray into each armpit for good measure.

My hair stays in the messy bun I'd shoved it into when I got in the roasting car. I put in the diamond studs Vale bought me for our one-year anniversary. They're the only hint at anything resembling perfect. The matching diamond pendant winks from the velvety drawer of the jewelry case. I reach for it, but my hand stalls midair. Instead, I push the lid shut. The pendant had been another present from my husband. He'd placed it on top of the first sonogram image of our baby.

I swipe at a rogue tear. This is not the time to fall apart. If Bree sees me with weepy, red eyes, she'll pounce. I still haven't told her that I canceled the appointment she'd made for me with her therapist friend.

I rush out of the house, dreading what's waiting for me, but anxious to escape the ghosts in my own house.

Before I can get the car door open, two kids and a puppy tumble down the steps of the house, shrieking and barking and running toward me.

"Aunt Maymay, you're here!" Eight-year-old Megan throws herself at my legs.

"Aunt Maymay, we got a puppy!" Alex, older by just over a year, grins at me.

"I see. Hey." I touch his chin, tipping his face up. "You lost another tooth. Meg, show me your smile."

Meg shows her teeth, all intact. Alex's grin spreads, and he makes a sassy face at his sister. "Yup. The tooth fairy brought me a puppy."

"Wow, that must have been one strong

tooth fairy to carry that puppy." I eye the ball of fluff, rolling in the grass next to us.

Alex giggles and takes off running, the puppy barking at his side. Megan rolls her eyes, the wiser-than-her-years younger sister.

Bree and Thomas had wanted a two-year gap between the kids. Guess Bree isn't perfect at everything.

"Kids, back inside." Thomas walks out of the house to corral everyone for dinner. "You just made it. Saved us all from a lecture." He kisses me on the cheek, then gives me a gentle push toward the house.

We follow the kids and puppy. "When did that happen?"

Thomas exhales. "Two days ago."

"He's cute. Looks fancy for a shelter dog though."

The kids had been begging for a pet for years. Bree had been adamant that she would not take care of a smelly, messy dog. But Thomas had crafted a deal: If the kids kept their rooms clean for four months, they'd go to the shelter and adopt a dog. A soft spot for animals was one of the few things we had in common.

"It's a goldenpoo. Or something. Bree heard they don't shed and are good with kids."

"Doodle."

"What?"

"Goldendoodle."

"Fucking expensive is what I call him."

I glance at my brother. I'm the one with the mouth, inherited from my grandmother, according to Mom. Thomas rarely curses.

"Kids obviously love him." We watch as the three jockey for position in the kitchen.

"Yeah, he's cute. Just wish she'd stuck with the plan." He turns to me. "Where were you? Vale said you took off on some secret errand and have been MIA all day."

I quirk an eyebrow, trying to think where the secret part of my errand came from. "No secret."

"So where were you?"

"I went to visit Grandma."

Thomas turns in exaggerated slow-mo.

"Oh stop." I turn my back on him and dump my bag on the bench by the front door. "I wanted to see if I could learn anything more on the inscription."

"Oh. And what did Grandma have to say?"

"Funny."

"Seriously, Maya. What did you think you'd find at the cemetery?"

"Who was at the cemetery?" Bree weaves her way out of the kitchen, a salad bowl held over her head as she sidesteps around small and not-so-small bodies.

"Maya went for a heart-to-heart with Grandma." Thomas doesn't soften the disgusted-big-brother tone. I feel twelve again.

Vale follows Bree out of the kitchen, holding a platter of hot dogs and burgers. The kids bring up the rear, each carrying a platter — Megan has sliced tomatoes, pickles, and lettuce, while Alex has a plate of buns.

"Daddy and Uncle Vale cooked," Megan announces with an accusatory tone. Her new best friend is a vegetarian, and Meg announced that she, too, would no longer be eating meat. Except that she can't resist burgers, and Thomas makes the best burgers.

"Guilty as charged." Thomas grins at her. "Come on." He indicates for me to walk ahead. "Let's get in there before they devour everything."

For the next half hour, I'm spared the inquisition as food is passed, kids are reminded not to feed the dog, and Vale is reprimanded for feeding the dog.

The puppy scratches at my calf, adding a sad whimper in case I need more convincing.

"Don't do it," Bree scolds, waving a knife at me. "He has to learn that people food is off limits."

The two adult males and the two kids are suddenly deeply engrossed in what's on their plate.

"Nothing from me." I raise my hands in surrender, even though I hadn't been the one feeding him all along.

"What's his name?" I reach down to pet the fluffy head, and open my palm to give him a bite of hot dog.

"Dov," Alex announces, giving the *V* an extra edge.

"It's Hebrew for bear. Because he looks like a bear," Megan adds, with full foreign-language authority.

"Cute." I wipe the puppy slobber from my hands onto the napkin, hoping I won't get busted by Bree.

"What did you find out at the cemetery?" Vale looks skeptical. Or is that suspicious?

"A lot actually."

"Grandma was chatty, eh?" Thomas smirks. Bree shoots him a warning look.

I make a face at him and Bree turns the warning look on me. "Turns out, the old man who built the carousel was a close friend of hers. He lives in town and left her a letter yesterday, after the memorial ceremony."

Megan looks up. "But she's dead, she

can't read."

"Does she need glasses? Mommy got glasses to read with last week," Alex offers helpfully.

"No, sweetie, glasses won't help. If you're done eating, clear your plates and go play." Bree's cheeks are pink and I can't help think it's because she was outed for needing reading glasses. Perfect people have perfect eyesight.

"You were gone a long time for just a visit to the cemetery." Vale isn't suspicious, he's annoyed.

"I went to Tower Oaks after. Hank, the guy who built the carousel, lives there."

"Tower Oaks?" It's part question, part accusation. He knows Simon works there. He also knows I haven't been in touch with Simon since he moved back. Until now.

The tension hangs between us, thicker than the ketchup Alex dumped all over his plate and lap.

"I'm going to get the kids into the tub. Thomas, clean the kitchen please." And in two blinks, Vale and I are alone. Even the dog scatters, yelping after the kids.

"I wanted to ask him questions about Grandma and the carousel." I answer the unasked question.

"What did you learn?" He leans back,

arms crossed, right leg over left. Vale has never been the jealous type. I've never given him reason to be. Then again, our relationship has never been on such unstable ground.

"Not much. He has Alzheimer's. Today wasn't what the doctors call one of his better days."

Vale's face softens a little. "Sorry."

I want to tell him more, tell him about Hank thinking I was Grandma, tell him that it was awkward and uncomfortable seeing Simon. But I don't. I let the conversation fizzle into a stew of half-truths.

"Aunt Maymay," Megan yells from the top of the stairs. "Will you come tuck me in?"

"Excuse me?" I look to Vale before pushing out of the chair. We're in a shaky enough boat; last thing I want is to tip it over. He nods, but his posture doesn't change.

At the top of the stairs, I turn into Alex's room to say good night. He's in *Star Wars* pajamas on top of his *Star Wars* blanket, one arm around a giant stuffed bear I bought him two years ago, the other around his bear puppy. He looks up and gives me a toothless, sleepy smile. I blow a kiss, not trusting that I can keep the lump in my throat from bursting out.

Megan's room is across the hall. She's sitting on her bed, waiting, watching. "Are you okay, Aunt Maymay? You look funny, like Mommy does when she watches one of those sad movies."

I wipe at a tear trickling down my cheek. I lean down to give her a kiss and inhale the sweet smell of kid shampoo.

I'd bought several bottles, along with diapers, lotion, and wipes. The smell took over the house the moment I'd unpacked the bags. It's the smell of innocence and love. Now it's the smell of loss.

"Into bed with you." I pull the tie-dye comforter back and wait for her to slip under, then tuck the blanket around her, sealing her in like a mummy, with only her head poking out. I give her another kiss, then stand before the tears spill out. "Sweet dreams, sweetie."

I turn to leave, slowly so as not to upset Megan, but as fast as I can before I come undone, again.

NINE

It's early when I slip out of bed and put on my running clothes. Vale rolls over and pats the empty space.

"Where are you going?" He's looking at me with one eye, the other buried in his pillow.

"I can't sleep. Thought I'd go for a run."

"Want me to come?" The words are partly muffled by a yawn.

"Nah, go back to sleep."

"Sure?" He yawns again.

"Sure." I sit on the edge of the bed to put my shoes on.

Vale rubs a slow circle on my back. "You could come back to bed." His hand falls to the bed, and I twist to look at him. He lets out a gentle snore, the offer rescinded.

I latch the back door behind me and whisper a good morning to the carousel horse in my studio, then turn toward the ocean.

The sun is a fiery ball playing peek-a-boo with the ocean. I stretch my hamstrings on a bench along the boardwalk, watching the early crowd of runners, walkers, and seekers. The runners are focused, enjoying the still-crisp air, their strides long and confident on the packed sand. The walkers huddle in their sweatshirts, hands circling coffee cups as they watch the dolphins dance around the waves. The seekers take tentative steps this way and that, heads bowed, eyes squinting at anything that might prove to be a treasure they can display on their mantel back home.

The sound of waves and gulls calls me, and I make my way to the edge of the water. A Weimaraner bounds up to me, nudging at my hands.

"Hey you." I squat and rub his ears. His tongue slurps across my cheek and nose. "Well you're friendly."

"Max, get back here." The dog's owner arrives next to us in a pant from his sprint down the beach. "I'm so sorry. He has personal space issues." He grabs for the dog's collar, but I wave him away. For the first time in months I'm laughing — really laughing. Max continues to lick my face, his stump of a tail wagging furiously.

I fall onto the sand and wrap my arms

around the dog's neck. "No need to apologize. Actually, that's exactly what I needed today."

Max's owner smiles and offers a hand, which I willingly take. "Sorry again. He's very excited to be at the beach."

"I get it." I brush sand off my butt and give the dog another rub behind the ears. "I'm always excited when I'm let loose on the beach." I turn to Max's owner. "Are you here on vacation?"

It turns out that Max and his owner, Brian, are renting a place on the other side of town for the summer. We chat for a few minutes about places to eat in town, the best times for running on the beach, and avoiding crowds. With a final lick, Max follows Brian down the beach in the direction of their rental.

I slip into the stream of runners, finding my pace. The morning breeze tugs at my ponytail, and suddenly I'm as free as Max. I hear the waves and the slapping of my tennis shoes on the wet sand. I hear my breathing getting raspier as each swallow beats at my eardrums. My arms and legs propel me forward, past walkers and slow joggers, past seagulls and sightseers, past an old couple holding hands and a dad chasing his toddler. Faster, harder.

I stop and double over, forcing the salty air through my lungs. What the hell possessed me to take off at such a speed after months of no running? Ghosts, that's what.

Vale had tried getting me to talk after we left my brother's house last night. Thomas and Bree had both called and texted and called again. I overheard Vale talking to Bree on the phone. He thought I was in the tub and couldn't hear. *"It's been a tough year, Bree. I don't know what to do anymore. . . . I know, Bree, it's been difficult on me, too. . . . I've tried that. But she keeps shutting me down. And shutting me out."*

Anger rolls through me, sudden and unexpected. I shut my eyes, willing my body to move, to get me as far from these feelings as possible.

"Hey, you okay?" I watch the toes of dark-gray running shoes as they pop up and down in place. They twist to the side and a neon green Nike swoosh dominates my vision. The shoes continue to run in place. The voice above me sounds more urgent. "Maya?"

I suck in a lungful of air and force my eyes from the bouncing sneakers, up sculpted calves and taut thighs. Thank god the shorts are long. "I'm fine, thanks." I force my body upright and I'm eye-to-eye with Simon.

Just like that, I'm fourteen again. The new summer hunk is leaning against one of the umbrella sheds, a swarm of giggly girls surrounding him. He's captivating them with stories of life in Hollywood. I'm standing at the back of the circle, sure beyond my wise years that he'd never actually played basketball with Rob Lowe or mowed Harrison Ford's yard.

My friend Sissy pokes me in the ribs with her sharp elbow and swoons — literally swoons, like we'd seen actresses do in the old movies her mom liked to watch. I roll my eyes at Sissy, at the rest of the swarm, and at Hollywood Hunk and his stories. That's when he caught my eyes. He'd been watching me, his expression amused by the challenge of the hard-to-impress girl.

"I'm outta here." I shouldered my way out of the baby-oiled, glistening mass of girls and trotted to the volleyball net, where a handful of kids were ramping up for a game.

"One more," the already familiar voice of Hollywood Hunk comes from behind me. Our team won that game. And since we banded together for the rest of the summer, we won pretty much every other game as well.

"That was some pace you had going." Simon pulls in a long draw of damp sea air.

"I'm obviously too old for those sprints, though."

I blink myself forward twenty-some years. Simon is leaning forward, pushing down on his thighs with the heels of his hands. I stare as the muscle in his right thigh ripples.

"I . . . I have to go," I stammer, feeling a flush in my cheeks that has nothing to do with my ridiculous attempt at a morning run. After all that's changed, nothing has changed. Simon still gets to me.

He can't get to me. I'm the one who left, I'm the one who walked away — no, ran away — the night he proposed.

"Wait, Maya, we should talk." He catches up easily, his steps matching mine. Left, right, left.

"About what?" I spin to look at him.

"About us."

"There is no us."

"There should have been." He's got me there. But if there had been, then I would never have met Vale. Or lost a baby.

When I don't counter, he continues, "I saw you a few times. Once you were with him. Another time with your grandma. You looked beautiful pregnant. I saw you at the grocery store a few months ago. You were staring at canned vegetables. You looked so sad."

My mouth opens, then closes. Simon saw me with my husband, saw me pregnant. I try to imagine how I would have reacted if I'd seen him with his wife. Even worse, if she'd been pregnant. I remember that day in the grocery. The sight of pumpkin puree had unraveled my barely stitched-together nerves. I'd fled right after that, leaving my cart in the middle of the canned goods aisle. Milk, ice cream, tampons, apples, toothpaste. Abandoned.

"Simon . . ." I look around as though people are all around us, listening, when the truth is, there's no one remotely close enough to hear, nor would they care. What was I going to say? What can I say?

"Why?"

I look up, unsure if Simon asked the question or if it was a trick of the wind. He's watching, waiting.

"Why what?" I know, I just don't know how to answer.

"It was our dream. We'd talked about it for years. So what the hell happened? And what was so awful that you vanished? Poof." He makes an exploding fist gesture.

"I got scared." It's the lamest answer I can give, but it's also the most accurate.

"Of what?"

"Of us."

"What does that mean?" His voice vibrates with frustration.

"We were too young."

"What? It's not as though we were considering running off and getting hitched by an Elvis impersonator."

I watch a jogger go by. She adjusts her earbuds and taps at the phone strapped to her bicep. I want to join her. I want to sprint away from this discussion and the memories frothing to the surface.

Simon takes a step to the side, blocking my view. "If you weren't ready, you could have said something. You should have said something. You were leaving for a year in London. I wanted you to know I'd be here, waiting."

"I knew you would be. I never doubted you." I can't meet his eyes.

"I don't get it." His hands shoot up, the frustration threatening to crash over both of us like an overzealous wave.

I shrug. I know before my shoulder hits the peak of the arc that I've sealed whatever friendly terms we could have moved forward on. Simon was not a fan of my excuse-for-everything-and-nothing shrugs. Neither was my mom.

"Seriously, Maya? Twelve years and the only explanation is a lousy shrug?"

We'd been together six years. We'd had all our firsts together. And I'd never once imagined myself with anyone else. Not even during the various college parties when guys asked me out, or during our all-night study sessions, when my boyfriend was halfway across the United States and everyone around me was hooking up on one-night stands or collegiate flings.

I never doubted we'd be together forever until he asked me to be his forever.

"I guess the finality of the commitment freaked me out." I still my body, denying my shoulders their freedom again.

"Commitment issues? After everything we went through together?"

"We were kids."

We glare at each other, a game of emotional chicken.

I'm the first to cave. "And yet six months after proposing, you married someone else." The memory of the wedding announcement stings my eyes. Mom had sent it with a "thought you should know" note. *Thanks, Mom.*

"It was a mistake."

"Looked like a pretty glamorous mistake." I'd smudged the newspaper image beyond recognition, trying to dissect every nuance in the photo. Simon in a tux standing next to a model-perfect woman in a slinky designer gown, slit up to her hip, and stilettos that brought her to Simon's shoulders. Her arms were wrapped around his torso, his right arm draped around her shoulders. His left hand shoved into his pants pocket. I'd wanted to see the wedding ring. I sneak a quick glance at his left hand. There hadn't been a ring on it yesterday. Still no ring.

"Yeah, well you disappeared with only an 'I'm sorry' note left on my car. And ignored every letter after that. What was I supposed to do?"

"Not rebound so fast?" I have no right to be jealous. I didn't back then and I certainly don't now. Like a slow-motion cartoon, his last comment slams into me. "What do you mean I ignored your letters? I didn't get any letters."

"It doesn't matter." His posture is defiant, but his expression is defeated. "I don't know why I thought talking now would help. Forget it. Good-bye, Maya." He turns to leave.

A sudden chill races up my spine. Is he saying good-bye for now, or is there more finality to it? Does that good-bye include Hank?

"Simon," I reach for his arm, but he's faster and moves before I make contact.

"Can I still come see Hank?"

He studies me for an unnervingly long couple of seconds. "Suit yourself. Just don't break his heart as well."

TEN

The undercurrent of heartbreak propels me to the edge of the water, where the remnants of a wave chase me back. I toe-out of my running shoes and pull off my socks. The wet sand is wake-up cold. I shiver but walk forward anyway.

Excited voices behind me call attention to a dorsal fin swimming close to shore. A woman squeals as her kids run to the edge of the water. The crowd has grown to the size of a small mob.

"Relax, people." A man in a tracksuit and floppy fisherman's hat announces as he leans on the metal detector he's carrying. "It's a smooth dogfish shark. Only dangerous if you're a crab or a clam."

Despite the assurance, the squealing woman doesn't release her death grip on her kid's hoodie. If I were that kid, I'd unzip and make a run for it. But this one doesn't, he just looks like a bulldog straining against a choke collar.

The shark swims away and the crowd disperses. I head in the opposite direction from the flow of beach walkers until I'm almost even with my street. I look up at the top floor of the houses on prime oceanfront lots. I can just make out the top of the street sign. The dune cuts off half of everything, including the bodies of people walking along the boardwalk.

I should be getting home. The carousel horse needs my attention.

My phone buzzes in the pocket of my sweatshirt.

"Hey, bathroom store is open now. I'll even buy you breakfast on the way. How about it?"

It's not just the carousel horse who needs my attention.

The first time I met Vale, I was twenty-four and the bike I'd borrowed from Grandma's garage punctured and bucked me off. Not one but two flat tires, and a nasty case of road rash on my right arm and leg.

Luckily, it had happened on this street, a street I rarely took back then, and in front of a house I'd never paid attention to until that day.

Vale had seen me go down and came to see if I was okay. He tossed the old bike into the bed of an older pickup, thankfully better maintained than the bike, and drove me back to Grandma's.

"Can I buy you breakfast on the way?" he'd asked. Breakfast at the Robin Hood Diner became our special time. When was the last time we went? The promise of French toast makes my stomach gurgle.

I turn back to the ocean. A woman, maybe my age, probably younger, jogs by with a shaggy dog of miscellaneous breed. She looks fresh while the dog looks like he's ready to flop over and be carried home.

"Can we get a dog?" I text Vale.

"Breakfast and tiles first?"

My stomach gives a reminder kick, but my legs don't move. The feathered end of a wave tickles my toes and the soles of my feet. I brace myself as the sand shifts with the receding water.

Just don't break his heart as well.

Good advice, even if he hadn't meant my husband. I type, *"On my way,"* and turn for home.

By the time we get to the bathroom-and-tile store, I'm hopped up on four cups of coffee and ridiculously close to a breakfast-food coma. I should have stopped after the third slice of French toast, but the fried eggs and bacon had smelled so good.

"Think you can get out, or should I come around and haul you out?" Vale grins as he turns the ignition off and opens the driver's side door.

"Ha. Ha." I pull at the latch and the door pops open. A groan helps propel me out of the bucket seat.

"Elegant."

"Oh, kiss my ass."

"Happily."

"You'll have to catch me first."

He laughs. "That's not much of a challenge right now. You can barely get out of the car."

I give him the nastiest face I can muster before his laughter becomes contagious. We get a few curious stares as we walk into the store, which only kicks off another wave of giggles. Vale winks at me when we finally catch our breath. In this minute, we're the old us.

"Okay, okay, time to get serious. How about looking at sinks first?"

"Toilet is more important." I grab his arm and pull him to the row of toilets. I sit on one, announce it's too small and walk to another, shaking my and head muttering, "Too big."

Vale laughs. "Okay, Goldilocks, over here. This one is just right."

He's almost right. We compromise on the one next to it, with the more modern shape and handle. And the slightly higher price tag.

"Sinks." It's Vale's turn to lead me across the store. "That one is nice and should fit in the space we have." He's pointing at a mahogany-stained cabinet with a glass bowl precariously perched on top. I run my fingers around the lip of the bowl, then lift the handle for the water, turning it left and right and left again.

"You do realize you can't make water come out of the faucet, right?" He leans over my shoulder and together we stare at the lifeless faucet.

"Yeah, yeah. I like it. Isn't it too modern though?"

"Too modern for what?"

"The bathroom? The house?"

"You're the one who wanted the most modern crapper in the store. It's perfect, Maya, come on."

I stall, slowing his walk to the tile department with my lead feet. This is all going too fast suddenly. We can't make these big decisions faster than a finger snap.

"Too expensive. What about this one instead?" I break free from his hold and walk to another mahogany-stained cabinet.

Still modern lines and with open space at the bottom, but the basin is square porcelain.

"Nice. Fine."

"What kind of answer is that?" I turn on him with a burst of aggression like water erupting from a long-unused faucet.

"Whoa." Vale holds up his hands in surrender. He turns and, without another word about the vanity or my outburst, walks to a row of tiles.

I want to pull the nastiness back into the bottle, cork it, throw it into the ocean. But once released, the bitchy genie doesn't want to be contained. "Hey, don't walk away." I march after him like a petulant child.

"I'm not going to fight with you, Maya."

"I'm not looking for a fight." Except I am, and I don't know why.

Yes I do.

"What are we really looking for, Vale?"

He stops midway down a row of tiles. "Everything that's now missing from the bathroom. Which is pretty much everything." He tries for a light tone that falls heavy.

"No. What are we looking for?" I don't back down. With the spigot open, I can't let it go. "Are we fixing or remodeling?"

His face hardens. "This isn't the time to

have this discussion."

"It wasn't the other night either."

Vale scans the tiles around us. I cross my arms and wait for him to look at me.

"Remodel."

"For us or a buyer?" My heartbeat hammers in my ears.

"Let's start with us." It's more a question than a statement though.

Thoughts and questions trip over each other, but none escapes through my clenched teeth.

Vale pivots to face the row of tiles behind him. "How about these tiles?" He points at shimmery rectangular glass tiles. They seem to change shades of blue and teal with each twist of my head and sideways step. They're gorgeous. And perfect.

"Nice. Fine." I'm being a brat. I feel it. I can't stop it. "I prefer these." My finger traces the wave pattern along the edge of a light blue tile. I see us from above, and I'm appalled. A couple of hours ago, I stood on the beach wanting to do the right thing for my marriage. An hour ago, we were having a great time over breakfast and the right thing was right there in my grasp.

"A bit cliché, isn't it?"

A couple walks past, the man pushing a stroller, the woman cradling an infant in a purple kangaroo pouch strapped to her chest. It's an ugly purple, not the color I would have chosen. I'd turned my nose up on those when we used to go to the baby stores. I'd give anything for one strapped to my chest right now.

I turn back to my husband. "Like wanting a dog?"

"What? Where did that come from?" He looks at me, confused.

"You ignored my earlier question about getting a dog." I hold up my phone with the text exchange glaring from the screen.

"I wasn't ignoring. God, Maya, you're giving me whiplash. And no, cliché as in decorating a beach house with a beach theme." His words carry a measured, don't rock-the-overemotional-lady cadence.

And that only fuels my unprovoked anger. The burning in the back of my throat reaches my eyes.

"Oh, honey." Vale pulls me into a hug. I'm acutely aware of strangers staring as they walk by, a salesman clearing his throat and skirting around us. Vale steers me out of the store and down the sidewalk, away from the parking lot and our car. I want to protest that I need to get home. I need my studio, my work, my horse.

Vale tightens his hold on my hand and

leads me to the park. We find a bench by the koi pond and sit, quiet, neither of us ready to poke the volcano of my emotional state.

Two young women sit on a bench across the pond. The brunette is absently pushing a stroller back and forth while she regales her friend with a story.

The movement of the stroller hypnotizes me. Babies everywhere. Everywhere but in my arms, in my life.

Vale clears his throat and squeezes my hand. "You need to let this go, sweetie."

I yank my arm back, elbowing myself in the ribs in the process. "Stop. Stop telling me to get past this. Don't you get it? I can't. I can't move on. Not without them." My throat closes around the word *them,* making it thick and ugly.

Vale exhales, slow, deliberate, and with the released air, it's as though his whole body shrinks. "I lost them, too. I loved them, too."

"But they weren't your responsibility." I choke on a sob.

"You and our baby were my responsibility."

Except I was carrying him. I failed him. I was selfish and caused this.

The baby in the stroller lets out a wail

and the ladies stand and walk away.

I'm suddenly aware of the commotion surrounding the early afternoon playdate crowd. I watch the various minidramas unfolding around us. In the sandbox are two boys at odds about the height of their luxury sand hotel. *What happened to the days of sand castles?* A game of soccer turns into a meltdown when another boy insists that the goal his "no longer best friend" clearly made doesn't count because he kicked with his left foot and everyone knows the rules say you have to kick with your right foot. And on the sidewalk, a little girl stomps in protest over the unfair allocation of drawing space, her fists digging into her hips, pigtails bobbing menacingly, face turning a shade of red deeper than her *Life Is Good* T-shirt while her friend continues drawing chalk flowers, unperturbed.

Would our son have been the kid in the sandbox? Would he have been chasing sticks with a dog? Drawing on the sidewalk with giant chalk?

Vale puts his arm around my shoulder and pulls me closer. "You may just have a point about getting a dog," he says, kissing the top of my head.

Anger and guilt puddle into sadness. Sadness for what we lost and sadness for what I'm losing.

ELEVEN

The afternoon sun melts into the concrete of the parking lot. Hard to believe that just this morning I'd been running in a sweatshirt. If this is any indication of what Mother Nature has in store, summer will be brutal.

I shut off the engine and savor the last bit of comfortable air-conditioning before stepping into the bone-chilling air of Tower Oaks. No wonder everyone inside is always huddling in sweaters.

I walk the handful of steps between my car and the front doors. A bead of sweat trickles down my cleavage, whether from the heat or anxiety I can't tell. I wonder if Hank will remember my previous visit. Another step and the doors slide open with a whoosh, the blast of cold sucking me in like a riptide.

Two faces watch my progress. Out of the corner of my eye, I catch Barista Barbie. A young brunette, hair pulled into a loose knot on the top of her head, smiles from behind the reception desk.

"Good morning." She stretches painted lips even further, exposing brilliantly polished teeth.

"Hi. I'm here to see Hank Hauser." I look past her to the painted *Memory Support Center* sign.

"Your name?"

"Maya Brice." My scalp tingles as the receptionist consults a piece of paper. Could Simon have put me on a no-admittance list? I shift my weight back, ready to bolt for the door if she calls security. Which is ridiculous, because he wouldn't do that. I hope.

"If you could just sign in please. West-347." Her head dips forward, indicating the sign-in sheet on the counter, then bobs right toward the West Wing. I have the strongest urge to tweak her bun the way you would a pom-pom on a wool beanie.

"Thanks." I mumble, flexing my fingers at my sides.

Muffled sounds of television programs seep out of partially open doorways, interrupted only by the squelching sound of rubber shoes on tile floor as nurses and doctors walk past. A doctor in a white lab coat dips his head in a hello. A woman in business attire clicks past on impossibly high heels without acknowledging me.

At the nurse's station I see Nurse Julie, but she's busy talking to another nurse.

The door to Hank's room is open. My tentative knock is swallowed by the saxophone solo coming from the old record player.

"Hello? Mr. Hauser? Hank?" I rap my knuckles on the door again, hoping not to startle him.

He turns from the desk, squinting at me. "I'm sorry dear, I didn't hear you knock." He lowers the volume of the music, his eyes never leaving my face. "Can I help you?" His voice has the warble of age.

I feel my face slacken with disappointment. I'm a stranger to him today. Well of course I'm a stranger. He's never met *me.*

"Umm, yes, I'm Maya Brice."

"Well, Miss Brice, come, come. It's not often I get such lovely company. What can I do for you?" He indicates the two armchairs, inviting me in with a shaky wave of a hand.

I allow a quick look over my shoulder, half expecting Nurse Julie to jump me before I get another step inside Hank's room. But she's still busy, her back now turned to me. I suck in a quick breath and step forward with the exhale.

"I, um . . ." I hesitate. "I, um . . ."

"Come, come, Miss . . . what did you say your name was?" He stands and walks to the armchairs. "Come sit."

I move deeper into the room and stop, face to frame with a photograph of the carousel. My carousel. Our carousel. In it, Hank is standing next to a horse — my horse, our horse — and beaming at the photographer. In the crowd behind him is my grandmother. It's a different angle from the image in my binder. That one didn't show much of the crowd, just a smiling Hank and a glistening carousel.

Unlike the tiny faded photocopy in my binder, this photograph shows the magnificence of the original carousel and a radiant Hank. The man, captured on glossy paper, fills the space with the assurance of youth. Happiness radiates from him to the crowd surrounding the carousel. My grandmother's face betrays a tenderness that inspired a secret message carved into the belly of a wooden horse.

"The carousel." My voice carries a hushed awe and my heart flutters.

"Yes, the carousel. You know it?" Hank asks.

An icy wave threatens to choke my lungs and I wrap my arms around myself in protection. It's a valid question, there's no reason he would know about my affiliation with the carousel. I'm a stranger to him. Just some person who's come to visit. Except I wasn't a stranger two days ago.

"Yes, I know it."

"Come sit, Miss . . ." He narrows his gaze. "What did you say your name was?"

"Maya Brice," I answer over my shoulder, my eyes glued to the picture. "The photograph, has it been there all along?"

"Of course. It's always been there." Hank dismisses it with the flick of a brittle wrist.

I look from the man in the room to the man in the picture. The facial features are the same, edgier in the photo. The hair is still full, white and thinner in real life. I touch the frame. "How did I not notice it?"

He looks as surprised as I feel. "You were here before?" A flutter of agitation crosses his face. "Probably while it was being reframed. My daughter's idea. You're interested in the carousel?"

"Yes." I cross the distance to the chairs and sink into the one I'd occupied last time I was here.

A big, childishly satisfied grin pulls at the wrinkles on his face. "I designed her."

A shudder barrels through my insides. "I know."

"You do?" The wrinkles on his forehead unite.

I force a clementine-sized lump down my throat. "I've been working on restoring that carousel for a couple of years now. I'm down to one horse, the big bay stander in front of the ostrich."

Hank settles deeper into the chair next to me, both of them grunting with the effort. "You're restoring the carousel? How is the old girl?"

"Still beautiful."

The flicker of a memory passes over him, like a cloud that muffles the light for just a blink. "Do I know you?"

My heart hammers, blocking every sound except the painful swallow of anxiety. I lean forward in the chair, the creak of the old leather startling me still.

"I'm, um . . ." I force another lump down my throat. Do I tell him I'm Meera's granddaughter? He thought I was her last time. How will he react if he finds out who I really am? "We were talking about the carousel. I'm restoring her." My voice cracks with anxiety.

"How is the old girl?"

"Still beautiful." I suppress a shudder at the echo of our conversation.

"You know, I designed her. I can tell you

all about her." He flashes a grin.

I scoot forward in the chair, ignoring any further protest by the upholstery, ready to hear the story straight from the horse-carver's mouth.

Hank leans back in his chair, eyes closed. Laughter from the nurse's station pings off the walls and my nerves.

I suck in a cold dose of strength and prompt Hank, "There wasn't much detail about previous restorations in the background material the Historic Trust Foundation gave me."

I look expectantly to Hank, hoping he'll jump in with the offer to hand over his notes.

I'm rewarded with a nod. And my hopes are promptly dashed with a shake. "I didn't take notes. Every inch of that carousel lives here." He taps his temple with the index finger of his right hand. "And here." The finger moves down, pushing gently on his heart.

"You don't have notes? Colors? Do you know about any of the restoration work done in more recent years?" My voice hops with anticipation.

Hank's bushy white brows scrunch together in thought, the lines at the top of his lips multiply as his mouth pulls in. "Nothing big. Normal wear, and that's what you want to see in a carousel. It means she's loved. Although the sea air isn't terribly kind."

I've come too far to let this fizzle like bath salts. "I found an inscription carved into the belly of one of the horses. I'm hoping you can shed some light on it?"

Hank stares at me for a minute, long enough that I think I've lost him and begin to rephrase my question. "The inscription in the horse's belly . . ." I let the rest of the sentence fade, then grab for my phone. "I can show you pictures."

Hank waves me away. "I don't need photos. She's perfectly documented in my memory."

I bite the inside of my lip.

"That horse is perfect." He sighs.

"It's not a gash," I jump to explain.

His face transforms into a long-ago memory. "No, it's not a gash. That horse was the last one I made, and I made him for the most beautiful girl I'd ever seen."

"Tell me about her." A prickle travels up my spine. I should tell him who I really am. He's studying me, looking through me, actually, and I wonder if he sees the connection.

"She looked like you a bit. Same hair,

same color eyes. You're a beautiful girl. Your husband is lucky." He pats my hand.

Tell him, Maya.

I don't. I mumble thanks and fight the heat of a blush.

Silence swirls between us. I inch forward in the chair, anxious for him to continue.

His eyes refocus on me and he smiles. "What brings you to see me, young lady? Are you a friend of Diane's?"

I force the corners of my mouth to relax and silently curse myself for not asking Simon more details about Hank's family. "No, I'm not. I'm here because of the carousel."

"The carousel? Why?"

For the briefest moment, I wish Nurse Julie would get in here and force me out. I'm not equipped to handle this.

Hank pushes himself up and shuffles to the bookshelf by the desk. His fingers walk along the spines of a handful of books before settling on a burgundy-leather album. He flips through a few pages, the memories playing in his features like a silent movie. I wait for him to come sit, to share the photos. He stops midway through the album and reshelves it.

He shuffles back to the chair and settles next to me. "You were asking about the carousel." It's half question, half recap.

I want to ask about the photo album. I feel oddly cheated.

"I designed her, you know. I had help, of course, with the big pieces around the engine and the mechanical parts. I'm not mechanical. I couldn't even change the oil in my car. And Annabelle, well, she has plenty of stories about my failed attempts at fixing things around the house." He chuckles at a memory. "She'd lie to me about things breaking just so I wouldn't try to fix them."

"But you handcrafted the animals by yourself?"

"Every last one."

"Which was your favorite?" I hold my breath, hoping the question pries open the memory gates.

"Favorite? Oh my. I loved them all. Each one came from a special place in here." He taps his heart again. "Lots of research, of course. I visited many carousels around these parts back then, and read everything I could about the carousels being built in Europe. They have some beauties over there. Have you been to Europe, Miss . . . ?"

"Brice. Maya. Yes, I lived in England for a year during college."

"England. Beautiful place. Lovely people.

My daughter, Diane, lives there, you know. Are you a friend of hers?"

I notice Hank's attention slide past me a split second before I hear the tap on the door. Suddenly self-conscious I tighten my tummy and reach to smooth the hair that's been tickling my cheek. I force my spine straight, proper posture shows confidence, my mom always said.

"I'm sorry to interrupt." The apology is accompanied by the sound of shoes on tile, but the voice isn't his. My bottom vertebrae give out and my posture collapses.

"Dr. Edwards, welcome." Hank gestures the apology to enter. "This is . . ." He falters, turning to me for help.

I turn, ignoring the grumbling of the chair. "Maya Brice."

"Yes, yes. Miss Brice is restoring the old carousel on the boardwalk, my old carousel." The beaming Hank is back. I've been with him for barely half an hour and I'm emotionally exhausted from the memory lapses and catch-ups.

Tap, tap. Hard-soled shoes close the distance into the middle of the room. How had I not heard him with those shoes? I look up, right hand following obediently, and shake hands with Dr. Edwards, mentally cursing my rolling stomach. I can't decide if

I'm disappointed or relieved it's not Simon.

"Lee Edwards. It's a pleasure to meet you, Maya." He pumps my hand, practically lifting me out of the chair with his enthusiasm. "I'm one of the doctors keeping Hank here out of trouble." He smiles at Hank, who chuckles and winks at me.

"I won't keep you," Dr. Edwards continues, turning his attention to Hank. "Just wanted to make sure you were feeling okay. Julie says you haven't gone for a walk yet today." It's as much a question as a comment, and I catch a slight grimace on Hank's face.

"I could use some fresh air," I offer. "Hank, would you like to walk with me and we can compare notes on the carousel?"

"That's a good idea, Hank," Dr. Edwards says, with the encouraging nod of a patient teacher.

Hank crosses his left leg over his right, his eyes riveted on his shoes as the left foot waves to its companion. Just when I think he's going to turn me down, the feet square, and Hank pushes himself up from the chair. He holds out his right arm and I lace my left arm around it, placing my hand on his forearm. Together we walk down the hall, Hank's rubber soles squelching, my flip-flops slapping. I laugh at his research stories, like the time he chased an ostrich around the zoo pen to get a close-up view of its beak and feet.

I marvel at the memories his brain contains and the details it can't retain.

Twelve

I lean against the fence and look through the opening at the "restoration-in-progress" carousel.

The ostrich is back in its post, restored to what I hope is almost the original beauty. I can't help but smile thinking about Hank chasing an irate bird to examine its feet and the irate bird pecking Hank on the head when he did finally catch it. At least this one wasn't mean and hadn't pecked at me when I worked on him.

There's an empty spot where the dominant stander goes. I should have gone straight back to the studio after talking to Hank but, somehow, I wasn't ready to face him. I feel like I've let him down in some warped way. The only thing I learned for sure is that Hank carved the inscription. But I already knew that.

Every question specifically about that horse had gotten lost in a memory hiccup. I can't help wonder if he was playing me to avoid the subject. *Don't be crazy, Maya.*

We'd spent over an hour in the Tower Oaks garden. Barista Barbie had fixed us up with a latte for me and a hot cocoa — extra whipped cream and a saucy grin — for Hank.

I smile remembering Hank's animated gestures as he talked about the animals, his hands sweeping through the air as he described each flourish and tassel, then stopping midair and sliding slowly down as he talked about delicate pinstripes.

I wish I could have seen her newly painted. I wish I could have known the young Hank.

The wind picks up and I give in to the pull of the ocean.

I twist my hair into a ponytail and hold firm while the wind grabs at loose strands and sends them whipping around my face. The sea, an ominous grayish blue, spits a briny mist at me, as if warning me not to come closer. The sky has turned the same color as the water, the only hint of a horizon are the frothy whitecaps on the waves.

Through the growl of the waves I hear a mom yelling to her kids to get moving before the storm hits. Once they're gone, I'm alone with the gulls and crabs and my thoughts.

I burrow my toes deeper into the sand and fold until I'm sitting, my shoulders hunching forward, chest pressing into my thighs, chin resting on my knees.

My thoughts swirl with the details Hank doled out, and questions about those he squirreled inside.

"What was he like, Grandma? What was your relationship with him? Why aren't you here to answer me?"

That's twice I've been to see him, and twice I've walked away with his letter still in the bottom of my bag. Twice when I've left with more questions than answers.

"You think I should have asked him directly, don't you? You would have shown him the letter and tried to get an answer from him. You would have gotten an answer. I'm not like you; I didn't inherit those mind-meld traits."

The air shivers around me, and a wave crashes onto the packed sand. I lick the salt from my lips. I should go before it gets nasty. Instead I push my toes deeper into the sand. There's something about the ocean during a brewing storm. Maybe it's the unpredictability, or the sheer force of nature. Maybe it's the fact that it drives everyone else away. Or maybe it's that my funnel cloud of emotions and thoughts pales in comparison to what Mother Nature can whip up.

The first time I visited, Hank was a fortysomething-year-old, reunited with an old friend. Today, he was a ninetysomething-year-old with a faulty memory, discussing a beloved project with a young restorer. Simon had warned me there were days Hank reverted to his younger self, when only his body stayed in the present. That there were days he couldn't remember how to get back to his room. And then there were days his mind was sharp enough to challenge the nursing staff with the hardest of crossword puzzles.

Today's Hank couldn't connect with who I was or why I'd come. But every detail of the carousel was perfectly preserved in his brain. I hadn't realized how much I missed talking about restoration practices until this morning.

The other Hank is endearing and my heart melts for him. Him, I want to protect him. This Hank, I want to syphon for information.

Fat, heavy raindrops dent the sand around me, stinging my arms and legs. The warning is short lived though, and before I have time to stand and brush the sand from my pants, the dark clouds release everything they've been storing.

I duck my head, laughing at the futile attempt to keep the rain from my eyes, and run for the boardwalk. A handful of people are huddled under the overhangs of restaurants or shops, waiting out the deluge. I trot past, careful not to lose my footing on the wet sand covering the wood boards. I straddle a puddle next to my car, my fingers digging into the wet fabric of my capris, the pocket refusing to release its stranglehold on my keys.

A car drives by and I squeal as water envelops my calves. Overhead, the storm gods clear their throats, alerting us crazy mortals standing in the rain to take cover. I pull at the keys, the sound of ripping fabric getting lost in a spine-tingling crackle as lightning slices through the clouds.

I yank the door open and tumble in as thunder booms around me. My left foot disappears into the cold, murky puddle as I throw my body into the shelter of the car. Water follows the squiggles of my curls, dripping down my back and into my eyes before dive-bombing the black leather of the car seat. The air-conditioning kicks in the minute I turn the key in the ignition, and my skin turns bumpy in the sudden chill.

From the safety of my car, I watch the waves leap up to meet the rain. The few trees along the side of the road sway, dropping even more water on the cars below.

A lone pedestrian sprints across the road, head down, clutching a briefcase above his head. He jumps over a puddle and onto the sidewalk. His dress shoes skid on the wet pavement and his shoulder makes contact with the wood fence protecting the carousel.

He loses his grip on his briefcase and I watch, helpless, as it summersaults over his head. He rubs his shoulder and bends to pick up his makeshift umbrella. I hope he doesn't have a laptop in there.

He stands and leans into the fence, catching his breath. Next to his head is the sign announcing the grand reopening.

Grand reopening.

There won't be a grand anything unless I get back to work.

THIRTEEN

I close my eyes as tendrils of steam from the tea tickle my nose, inhaling rich chocolate and tangy orange. The combination is soothing and stimulating at the same time. The studio is quiet this morning. For once, I don't want music. I want to hear what the horse has to say.

The rain stopped during the night, but the morning is still damp, and I can hear the drip from the gutters. I stare at the horse. He stares back.

"Well?"

He continues to stare.

"Lotta help you are."

Still nothing.

"Shall we start stripping you?"

I've made my drawings, taken photographs, cataloged every inch of him. It's been years since I last rode him and yet, standing here looking at him, I can feel the movement, hear the music, remember the happiness.

I think it's physically impossible to be unhappy when you're on or near a carousel. Maybe it's the vivid colors, the crazy menagerie, the loopy music. Whatever it is, merry-go-rounds have magical powers.

Whenever I was having a "poop day," as Grandma called them, she'd take me for a frozen custard and a ride on the merry-go-round. Even those times I wanted to stay mad or sad, like when Flynn Nelson picked Luann Waters to be his lunch club sit-with, or when Mom and I got in a fight because she wanted her hairdresser to give me a "chic bob" and I'd wanted to keep my unruly long curls.

The last raindrops from the tree outside ping a lazy beat in the gutter of the studio.

"Time to get to work." Time to release some of that old magic.

For the next few hours, I lose myself in details. He's no longer *the* carousel horse; he's a work of art, and I am nothing more than his restorer.

With the precision of a plastic surgeon, I remove one layer of history at a time, painstakingly documenting each color I encounter. When I'm done with the head, I pull myself up onto the table and scan the horse, from his erect ears to the high step of his front leg, to the rigid swish of his tail.

Restoration is a slow process, slower for some of the animals than others. It could be argued that I'm overagonizing; after all, these are not museum pieces. In two months, the merry-go-round will once again be at the mercy of the riders and the elements.

I'd spent two full days rebuilding the front leg of horse number twelve. Even with the metal stirrup, kids seem to prefer using his bent leg as their launchpad on and off. The leg had broken at the knee and been poorly put back together.

I've repaired chipped ears and tails. Hooves and legs. Dings and gouges. But mostly, I've reconstructed parts worn down by years of use. Saddles and bridles rubbed smooth under hands and bottoms.

For almost three years I've loved every one of the menagerie back to their, almost, original splendor.

A ripple races up my spine. I'll bring Hank to the reopening. I wonder what he'll think of the merry-go-round. Will it live up to his memory of the way it was when he carved those same animals? Will he be disappointed at some of the changes that have crept in over years of maintenance and renovations?

If only I'd known he was living here, I

could have collaborated with him from the beginning.

A bolt of anger jolts me upright. "Why, Grandma? Why keep the truth from me?"

Hours. We spent hours sitting in this studio, talking about whatever animal was in here at the time. Hours reliving memories and stories. Hours walking to the carousel house to check on the other renovation work. The Friends of the Carousel committee had hired, based on the research I presented in my proposal, specialists to update the mechanics, carpenters to rebuild the platform and surrounding structure.

"Oh my god." My fingers dive into my hair and I fist a clump of curls, the tug on my scalp stopping the rush of thoughts. The wasted opportunity. For me. For him.

Or maybe not for him. Maybe he didn't want to look back. Maybe they'd discussed it.

I don't buy it. He's so animated talking about the carousel. So why? Why did Grandma keep him a secret? Whom was she protecting?

My phone chimes with an incoming text.

"I'm baaaack."

Sam. She's been in New York on a buying trip for her boutique.

"How was the trip?"

"Awesome. Lots to tell you. Tonight!"

"Tonight?"

"Tonight. 7 P.M. Sharp. I'm coming to get you."

"I can meet you."

"Nope. I know you. I'm coming for you!"

"That sounds like a threat. ☺"

"It is. 7 P.M. Sharp. And change into something adult for once."

"Hey!!" I look at my sweats with the college name in block type down one leg, paint splotches everywhere, the frayed inseam and cuffs. My T-shirt isn't much more respectable. She has a point. Not that I'll admit that to her.

"Mwah."

"Only because you asked nicely," I type.

"I knew it." Sam's voice booms into the studio.

"Oh shit." I drop the X-Acto knife I've been picking at the layers of paint with.

"Hell of a welcome. Missed you, too."

"Sorry, you startled me. Is it seven already?" I twist to look at the clock.

"Nope. You still have twenty-three minutes. I couldn't wait any longer to see you." She skips into the studio and circles the horse.

I straighten and hug Sam when she finishes her inspection of the horse. "I'm glad. I've missed you, too."

"When did you have time to miss me? You've been a studio troll." She winks. I wince. It's a friendly jab, but it hits a bit too close to the not-so-friendly jabs from Vale.

I take in my best friend, stylish in a white T-shirt with a zebra face on the front. The zebra is sporting hot pink, oversized sunglasses with rhinestones. Her capris are a light blue, almost the same shade as the scarf billowing around the zebra's neck. On her feet are flip-flops, one blue with rainbow stripes, the other green with rainbow stars. Her shoulder-length brown hair is pulled back with a gauzy blue scarf.

"What?" She instinctively wipes at her mouth then checks her shirt. "Do I have toothpaste all over my face? Coffee stains on my boobs?"

"No, you look great. You always look great. Give me a minute to change." I grab her arm and lead her out of the studio, stopping only to flip off the lights and lock the door.

She pulls away to arm's length and makes a show of looking me up and down and back up. "You'll need more than a minute, sweetie. Take your time. I'll help myself to a drink." She walks to the fridge, surveys the contents, closes the door. "That's even more boring than your wardrobe."

I glare, she beams. I turn and sprint up the stairs. Two minutes later, I'm back in a mist of perfume, but at least I'm wearing clean clothes.

Sam wrinkles her nose at me. "You need to get out more. And not just to the grocery store."

"What's wrong with what I'm wearing?" I pull my T-shirt away from my body to check for stains. No stains. Do I clash? Pink shirt, white crop pants. No clashing.

"That's fine." She waves her hand, dismissing me from the neck down. "It's that." Her hand makes a circular motion over my head.

"What's wrong with my hair?"

"In a word? Crazy."

"Yeah, well, I washed it in the kitchen sink yesterday." I grab at a couple of long strands and let them drop.

"Why are you showering in the kitchen sink?"

"Vale decided to fix the leaky sink by demolishing the whole bathroom. He assures me we'll have a working bathroom by year's end."

"Speaking of . . . where is he?"

I stop and look around as if I expect to

find him in the kitchen. A note on the coffeepot catches my eye. I pluck it off and hold it up like I've grabbed the winning lottery ticket.

"He's meeting with his boss and a new client over dinner."

Sam pulls her mouth into a half frown.

"What?" Her expression sours my discovery.

"Sticky notes?"

I want to argue that we're busy, and leaving notes for each other is actually a good thing. I want to shake the feeling that my relationship with my husband is headed for the shredder.

I settle for snide. "At least we're keeping it spontaneous with color choice." I point at the various colored pads on the counter.

"Not funny."

"I know."

"So?"

"So nothing. We're trying."

"Try harder."

"After we eat. I'm hungry." I grab my bag and push the door open, sweeping a hand for Sam to go first.

"Fine, but stay downwind from me, please."

"Funny lady."

We walk along the boardwalk toward the

cluster of bars and restaurants tucked into the secondary streets. The Yellow Owl with its rooftop deck is our go-to spot.

"Ladies," a deep baritone welcomes us, and a hulking figure steps around the reception desk. Taylor Wheeler is the manager and sometimes bouncer at The Yellow Owl. At six foot six, he doesn't need to do much in the form of bouncing. For most people, finding yourself in his shadow is warning enough to stop any and all shenanigans. Taylor flashes his signature sparkling smile.

Sam stretches up to hug him. She positions her cheek for the welcome kiss and grins like a giddy schoolgirl.

With one arm around Sam's tiny waist, Taylor pulls me in for a group hug. "Always makes my day when the two of you walk in." He gives us both a squeeze then returns to the reception desk. "Dinner? Looks like it might start raining again. I'll put you inside if that's okay?" He taps at a hidden screen, securing a table for us, then pulls out two menus as a girl in a black halter top and flared black pants slinks to his side. "Lily will show you to the table. And I'll be over shortly to check that you're behaving." He winks and swats at Sam's exaggeratedly swinging rear.

Slinky Lily walks us to a booth along the

far wall of the restaurant. It's the perfect spot for observing the pickup attempts at the bar without being overtly obvious. I smile at the mix of people crowding the bar.

"Where did she get those shoulder blades?" Sam sticks her chest out and reaches to feel her own shoulder blades, then stares down at her chest. "Think they're fake?"

"Her shoulder blades?" My head whips from the retreating Lily with her protruding bones to Sam and her gyrations.

"No." The answer drips with *duh.* "Her boobs."

"Don't know. Ask Taylor." I flip open the menu but my attention is still on Sam, her left hand poking at her shoulder blades while her right hand pushes at her right breast. "Seriously." I laugh and lift the menu higher.

I order a blueberry martini and a salad while Sam dittos the salad but opts for sparkling water with lemon from a waitress who, Sam concludes after close inspection, doesn't have model shoulder blades and could use a boob job.

"Sparkling water?" I wrinkle my nose at her.

"It's all the rage in New York these days." She shrugs and diverts the conversation.

"What are you guys doing with the bathroom?"

"The original plan was just to fix the plumbing, change the tiles, and put in a new sink. Vale, however, has gotten ambitious and is now talking about rearranging the whole damn thing." A soft groan escapes me at the thought.

"What's the groan for? You've been wanting to redo the bathroom since I've known you."

"I just thought we'd plan it out before the demolition began, not after everything was already torn to shreds." *And not when there's the cloud of a move over us.* I stop myself from telling Sam about Vale's offer. After the sticky-note incident, I'd rather not open the door for deeper analysis of my failures.

"Vale is brilliant. It'll be gorgeous."

"I know. I'd rather hear about your trip to New York."

For the next hour Sam fills me in on the design studios she visited, the designers she schmoozed with, and the boutiques she's "borrowing" ideas from.

The first shipment of her purchases arrived yesterday and, in true Sam fashion, she promptly started rearranging the display windows. "I'll have to go back tonight and get more work done if I want to have the store in shape for opening tomorrow morning. Yes," she holds up her hand to stop an anticipated criticism, "I should have waited until morning. But oh my god, Maya, these T-shirts and shorts are the cutest things you've ever seen."

I stare at the sparkly zebra on her shirt.

Sam grabs at the zebra's ears and pulls the shirt forward. A man walking by our table stumbles and his female companion glares. I snort at the sight of his blinking eyes, her steaming face, and Sam's fingers pinching zebra ears that just happen to coincide with her nipples.

Sam's enthusiasm for reorganizing the boutique far outweighs her enthusiasm for her salad. I'm mostly done with mine, but Sam's looks like it's multiplied.

"Hey, don't look now, but we're getting checked out." Sam sits a bit taller and pulls her shoulders together in her prep-school posture.

"You're incorrigible." I shake my head and, as Sam's posture improves, mine sinks into the padding of the booth.

"The hottest of the two has eyes for you. Good thing he can't smell you from way over there. And he obviously needs to have his eyes checked."

I throw her a look. "Funny."

"I know, right?" She smirks and flops back into her seat. "Good thing we're not interested."

My eyebrows jump to attention. Since when is Sam not interested? In all our years as friends, she's never lasted more than three months with one guy. "*We're* not interested?"

Her shoulders curl, looking un-Sam like shy.

"Something you'd like to share? Did you meet someone in New York? And you didn't tell me? You're not moving?" I bolt upright.

"It's not someone in New York. I'm not moving." She shreds the paper napkin.

"But there is someone?"

For one blink I think my best friend is about to confess that she's finally settling down. And in that blink, I see a year that's passed; a year that I was so absorbed in my own world, I barely noticed what was happening around me.

She pulls herself together and, after a quick glance toward the front of the restaurant — probably assessing whether she can make a run for it or not — responds, "Nah, you know me." But the words lack the usual Sam sass.

Before I can question her further, she tilts her head in the direction of the bar. "The hot guys are leaving. You're the worst wing-man ever. Wait, one of them is looking this way. I think he's going to come over after all."

I look at the guy and our eyes meet. He stops midstep, then changes direction and follows his friend to the door.

Sam kicks me under the table. "You scared him with that evil death stare. What the hell was that about?"

"That was Simon."

"Who?"

"Simon."

"Simon?" Her eyebrows collide in confusion.

I nod.

"Simon." She exhales the word, as the name and the myth collide in her memory.

"By the look on your face, I'd say you and Simon finally ran into each other."

I nod again, one very slow up and down. "Twice in two days. Don't see him in the year he's been back, and suddenly he's everywhere."

"Back this pony up. Twice in two days?" Sam leans forward, elbows spread and hands tented, little-kid excitement coloring her cheeks.

"He's one of Hank's doctors at the retirement home. Then I ran into him on the beach."

"On the beach? Was he wearing a shirt? You never said he was *that* gorgeous."

"Seriously, Sam?"

"Okay, okay. Sorry. Distracted." She fans herself with a coaster and blinks innocently at me. "Who's Hank and why were you at the retirement home?"

"I haven't told you?"

"Told me what? You're moonlighting as a candy striper in an old-folks' home? Can they even eat candy?"

"Be serious." But I can't help laughing. *Serious* and *Sam* are not words usually linked together. "Hank built the carousel. And it appears that he and my grandma were friends." I air quote "friends," which makes Sam's eyes bulge.

"Oh juiciness. Tell me more." She bounces several times on the squeaky bench.

I lean into the table. "Someone carved the words *For Meera. Forever* along the girth of the horse I'm restoring right now. No name or initial. Nothing. Then I found a letter on Grandma's grave. It was addressed to 'my dearest Meera,' and said that not a day goes by he doesn't miss her. That they'll be together soon, this time forever. And it was signed *H.* Oh, and it was on Tower Oaks stationery."

Sam quirks her mouth in thought. "But if your grandma was friends with him and he's local, why didn't she tell you? I mean, hell, you've been working on that carousel for years."

"Yeah, I asked her the same question." I don't mask the snark.

Sam leans forward until the zebra ears are distorted by the edge of the table and whispers, "What did she say?"

I roll my eyes.

She laughs, sits back. "And he's one of Hank's doctors. Small world."

"Too small. Anyway, I talked to Hank. He's amazing. Oh god, Sam, he's exactly as I imagined he would be." I am suddenly sober, remembering our first meeting.

"Helloooooo." She waves a hand in front of my face. "What's that about?"

"He thought I was her the first time I met him." The air leaks from my lungs, and I slouch back into the hard vinyl of the booth.

"Whoa."

"I'm sorry for interrupting, but I have to ask where you got that T-shirt. I absolutely have to have one." A tall brunette in short-shorts and a teeny tank bounces up to our table. She's ogling Sam's chest while a table of men next to us ogle her back end. Sam shoots me a we're-not-done look before turning her most radiant I-can-sell-you-this-and-matching-boxers smile at the perky intruder. I half-listen while they discuss the other shirt designs and accessories Sam has been unpacking. The brunette promises to stop by the store the following day, then bounces back to the table where her friends are more interested in a basket of friend clams than zebra tees.

Sam turns back to me and pulls the cardboard coaster out of my hands. While they'd been talking, I'd been shredding the ears off the owl-shaped coaster. "There are laws against what you've done to this poor guy. Wait till Taylor finds out."

Despite myself, I smile. The waitress clears our plates and the shredded cardboard ears, and after inquiring about another round of drinks, which Sam waves away, leaves the bill, assuring us there's no rush.

Except that I'm suddenly feeling claustrophobic.

"I have to go, Sam." I slip money into the black plastic sleeve and stand.

"Hey, what just happened?" She grabs my hand.

"Nothing, I'm fine. Just suddenly tired."

"Bull. Two seconds ago, okay four, you were animated about the horse and your grandmother and her illicit affair." I glare at her. "Okay, her friendship. Then that bimbo shows up and you freak out."

"Really, Sam, I'm okay. It's been an emotional day and it all just caught up to me."

She sighs and pushes out of the booth. "Fine, let's go."

I lead the way through the restaurant and into the crowded lobby. We wave good-bye to Taylor and let the crowd spit us out the front door.

We walk home in silence, the unfinished discussion and the news I didn't divulge hanging between us in the uneven shadows of the streetlights.

When we get to my house, she envelops me into a bear hug. For someone so slight, she's surprisingly strong. "Come by the store tomorrow. I'll spruce you up." She makes me pinky promise I'll come, then gets in her car. She waves out the window as she pulls away.

There's a light in the kitchen and another in the bedroom, but the pull from my dark studio is stronger. I open the door and step into the mixture of past, present, and future.

FOURTEEN

"Hey." His voice startles me. The overhead light in the living room was off, and in the stillness of the house, I'd assumed Vale had gone to bed. I glance at my watch. It's well after midnight.

"Hey back. I wasn't expecting you to be up." I toe off my shoes and walk into the room, conscious that I'm on the balls of my feet, like the times I came home past curfew and was afraid of getting caught.

"I heard Sam's car leave a couple of hours ago."

"I know, I'm sorry. I wanted to jot down some notes on the horse before I forgot."

"Like you'd ever forget anything about the carousel." I can't decipher the thickness in his tone.

"Sorry."

"Sorry?" The light from a passing car flashes through the living room window, sending shards of light glittering from the highball in his hand.

"Sam says hi." I fold onto the couch, close enough that my knee almost touches his thigh but with a finger width between us.

"Thanks."

"How was the meeting? Where did you go?" I hope I sound less suspicious on the outside than the question sounded in my head.

"Good. Sushi."

"Yoshi's?"

"You know it."

An awkward heaviness settles in the crack between us. Yoshi was the first restaurant we went to when we moved back here, and we used to go at least twice a week. Then when I got pregnant, we stopped going. I'd told Vale it didn't bother me, that I was just as happy eating the cooked rolls or udon bowls. But we were in this together, he'd said, and so, together, we stopped eating sushi. After . . . well, after I couldn't stomach the idea.

"Listen . . ."

"I wanted . . ."

The awkwardness pushes me an inch deeper on the couch, an inch more distance between us, a chasm of emotional barriers.

"You first," Vale says. He takes a draw from his drink, the movement releases the sweet smell of the alcohol. Armagnac. My stomach flops, and I have to force my breath through my mouth.

I hate Armagnac. Hated it since I was thirteen and found a glass unattended on the coffee table. It was my father's aperitif of choice, the drink I always associated with him and Mom, elegant and sophisticated. I longed to hold the crystal glass, smell the golden liquid, murmur about its warmth. So when it was there, in front of me, I had to do it. I cradled the glass, I smelled the liquid, I took a sip. First one, then two. Tiny, tentative sips. The drink warmed my throat. I was sophisticated.

Then I heard a door slam upstairs, footsteps, a glass shatter. The footsteps came down the stairs, loud and mad. Another slam upstairs.

I downed the rest of the liquid expecting warmth. My eyes stung and my throat burned. What had seemed sophisticated a moment ago was pure misery.

I'd hidden in the powder room, swallowing bile and tears. My father had cursed at finding the empty glass but, no doubt, assumed he'd finished it and forgot. He hadn't heard me come home.

When he went to the kitchen, I snuck up to my room. Mom knocked a few hours later, calling me to dinner. I didn't answer. She came up later, another knock. I still didn't answer. She left the pizza by the door. It was the first time she'd allowed that. It wasn't the last. It had also been the first time I'd found my dad sleeping on the couch. It wasn't the last.

With the wisdom of my teenage years, I started picking at the hairline cracks I'd never noticed in our glossy life. Mom and Dad were the picture-perfect power couple. She was always polished, easily elegant in her designer clothes and weekly styled hair. She seemed to wake polished. Dad was tall, athletic, at ease in his slightly askew perfection. Together they were striking.

When he wasn't at the office and she wasn't at one committee meeting or another, they were playing tennis at the club, or entertaining, or attending gallery openings. Mom loved the arts.

Which is probably where I got my passion. Well, not exactly. She preferred modern art; I went for antiquities.

Vale takes another sip from his drink. The crystal glass was a wedding gift from my parents. Because everyone needs fancy crystal glasses that need to be hand washed and carefully protected.

"I hate those glasses."

I watch Vale turn the glass in his hand. The Armagnac releases its toxic bouquet.

"How can you drink that stuff?" I cover my mouth and nose.

"It's an acquired taste."

"That's one taste I wouldn't complain about you unacquiring."

"It's my thing with your dad and brother. You should appreciate that."

"How about picking up golf instead?"

"They don't play golf."

"Tennis then."

"I hate tennis." He twists to look at me in the dark room. A car inches past, its light illuminating his expression long enough to unsettle me. "I owe Ed an answer about the job." It's not a question or invitation for a discussion.

"And?" I don't think I want to know the "and," but I have to.

"It's a huge opportunity. He wants to develop a modern, old-world-charm community. And he's looking to me to take the lead."

I nod, but I don't understand any of this. "How did you not tell me you were interviewing for a new job? Especially one across the country?"

"I wasn't interviewing. Ed was in town for meetings, and we met for lunch. He wanted to bounce a few ideas off of me."

"Looks like one landed right in your lap. And you didn't think it was important to tell me?" The darkness takes on an edge. I want to soften it but I don't know how.

"I tried."

"You tried?"

"We've had this discussion." He looks out the window as the porch light on the house across the road comes on. "We don't talk, Maya. You don't want to hear anything that contradicts the reality you've spun for yourself."

Anger punches to the surface. "The reality *I've* spun for myself?" I inhale through my nose, fortifying for the next strike. Except nothing comes. He's right. I have spun a reality made from guilt and shame and defeat, and made myself a cozy nest in the middle. And from that cozy nest, I've avoided talking. I've hidden from hard discussions and uneasy topics. I've even hidden from the easy ones.

"You couldn't have tried that hard." Why can't I reach out to him? Why can't I forgive myself enough to forgive him?

We square off on the couch, neither one of us ready to dive into the deep end of the argument, but not willing to waddle to safety, either.

"Okay, Maya, let's talk. Ed has offered a once-in-a-lifetime opportunity. I didn't approach him, I wasn't sniffing around, it just happened. One minute we're brainstorming ideas, the next he's asking if I'll run with those ideas."

"Why Seattle?"

"Because that's where the property is."

"You hate Seattle."

"I don't hate Seattle. I hate rain." As if on cue, the sky opens with a crack of thunder and a deluge that muffles all other sound. "You'd probably like it there though. It's artsy."

"It's artsy here, too. And I don't want to leave."

"Why? What's here that we can't build somewhere else? Somewhere without the baggage? What's wrong with a fresh start?"

"You can't just move and pretend like the past didn't happen. The 'baggage' isn't an old couch that you leave by the side of the road for the trash guys to pick up. There's a lot here we can't take with us."

"What about us, though?"

"We're here."

"*We're* not. *You* are."

"That's not fair."

"No, it's not." He deflates into the couch. "None of this is fair. None of this was supposed to happen this way. But we can't continue like this. I can't continue like this."

A tremor starts from somewhere inside and builds until I shove my hands under my thighs to keep them still. "You've made a decision then." It's a statement. A statement doesn't require an answer, and I don't think I would want the answer if that had been a question.

He nods.

Shit.

"I'm not accepting the job, but I'm not turning it down either."

I look at my husband, the man I used to be able to read, used to know better than I knew myself. But sitting next to me is a stranger. "What does that mean?"

"It means that in two weeks I'm giving Ed an answer."

"Two weeks?"

"That's enough time for me to finish the bathroom and for you to get close to finishing the horse. And it forces us to address our situation. No more hiding, Maya."

The clock in the kitchen ticks in the darkness, taking Vale's side.

Two weeks.

"I don't think I can move from here." I whisper into the night.

Vale releases a slow, sad exhale. “And I don’t think I can stay.”

Fifteen

He had stayed, was staying. For now. At least for the next two weeks.

I wrap my hands around the mug. Vale is still asleep, or at least still in bed. He hadn't moved when I got up an hour ago. He usually rolls over and grabs my pillow, then pulls the blanket tighter around him. This morning, though, he was perfectly still. Too still.

"Good morning," Vale says around a yawn as he enters the kitchen. He stretches and I can't help but admire the taut stomach that peeks from between his T-shirt and the band of his shorts. When was the last time I noticed my husband as anything more than the person sharing space in my life?

"Good morning." I curl the coffee closer and rest my chin on the lip of the mug. It's no longer hot enough to send warming fingers to soothe my nerves. "What's on your schedule for today?" Such an innocent, everyday question, one I've asked so many times, and yet this morning it feels raw and insecure, prying and explosive.

"Bathroom." He pours himself coffee and drinks it looking out the kitchen window, his back to me. He turns, and my entire body hums with jittery energy, a live wire in a breeze. "You?"

"I was planning on visiting Hank before work."

Vale sets his mug down and crosses his arms, eyes locked on me. I feel the winds picking up, tossing my live wire nerves about.

"What will talking to the old man help?"

Everything. Nothing.

"He brings the carousel to life."

Vale's mouth pulls into a line. The winds are about to turn ugly. "Is this really about the carousel?"

"What else would it be about?" I keep my voice and my gaze steady.

His eyebrow quirks.

I bristle. He has a right to ask, I've given him reason to question. "If that were the case, why would I have waited over a year?"

"You were pregnant when he moved back. We were happy."

Were.

I wince, but Vale doesn't back down. "The

timing feels less than coincidental."

"Like a job offer?"

"Fair. Except I wasn't trying to keep it from you."

"I haven't been trying to keep it from you either." Not really, at least.

He cocks his head at my response, and heat sears my cheeks. I may not be able to read him anymore, but he sure can see through me.

"There's not much to tell." My eye twitches. I open my mouth and snap it shut. He tightens the cross of his arms across his chest. The clock is ticking. "I hate this," I finally blurt. "I hate that we don't talk, that everything between us is so hard."

He softens. "Me too."

I wait for more. Vale is the olive-branch carrier, the one who always knows what to say and when to say it. But not this time. This time he's waiting for me to be the first to extend the branch.

I know what I should say. Instead, I tell him about Hank. How Hank mistook me for my grandmother, how animated he gets when I ask questions about the carousel, how he can't remember who I am some days and asks my name every few minutes. I finish, breathless, exhausted.

I wait again for Vale to say something. He

doesn't.

"You know what pisses me off, though?" I'm surprised at the sudden stab of anger in my voice and the pounding of my pulse. "I'm pissed that she kept him a secret."

"I'm sure she had her reasons." That's what I get from him?

The answer fuels my temper. "She knew what the carousel meant and what it would mean to talk to him directly. All the questions, all the what-ifs — every single one was a lie."

Vale turns and fusses with the espresso machine, leaving me to fume about lies behind his back. A few minutes later, he walks to the table with two mugs. I set my now cold coffee on the table and happily accept the new offering.

"Not all secrets are lies." He pulls out the chair across the small table and sits.

I gawk at him. Of course they are.

"What did Hank say when you told him who you were?"

"I told you, he was excited to talk about the carousel restoration." I'm not answering the real question, and Vale gives me a pointed look. "It's complicated." It's a cop-out.

"So you lied to him." He watches me over the mug as he takes a few slow sips.

"No." He's got me.

Are secrets lies? Are they ever justified? Am I right keeping secrets from Vale? From Hank? Was Grandma right keeping her secret from me? I detour the conversation. "I'd like to include him in the grand reopening ceremony."

Vale's face hardens. He stands and dumps what's left of his coffee into the sink. With his back to me, he says, "Be careful what secrets you're hiding behind, Maya."

An hour later, I walk into the lobby of Tower Oaks, making a point of not acknowledging the open stare of the gum-popping receptionist. The hall toward Hank's room is mostly empty, but I'm hyperaware of every movement in the rooms I pass. Am I hoping Simon will come out of one of them, or hoping he won't?

Nurse Julie waves me into Hank's room. He's sitting in the wingback chair, legs crossed, a book balancing on his knee, his lips moving in silence. His airborne foot taps in time to a melody I can barely make out. I'm not sure for a minute if I actually hear music or if it's only coming from the movement of his foot. I rap on the open door, almost afraid of breaking into his private moment.

Hank looks up, his face opening, welcoming. "I'm so happy you came to see me today." He stands and drops the book to the chair.

I hesitate. Who is he happy to see? Who am I today?

Hank shuffles forward and grabs my hand. "Come, come, my dear. No need to stand in the doorway. I think we're old enough to be trusted in my room together." He winks playfully.

I follow him to the chair, unsure what to say or who I'm to be. "What are you reading?" I reach for the book, plucking it from his chair just before his rear makes contact with the cushion.

"Oh silly me." He takes it from me. "Thanks for saving my book."

In the immediate silence that follows, I hear the distinct notes of a trumpet. He really is listening to music, not just hearing it in his head.

"Meera? What's wrong?"

Today the part of Meera will be played by her granddaughter.

I close my eyes, tuning out everything but the music. The trumpet soothes away the tension and I turn to look at Hank. "Maynard Ferguson?"

He nods, his lips pulling into a reflective

pinch. "Remember that concert he gave in the old Spanish ballroom? We danced so long we had to put our feet in the ocean to stop the aching." He chuckles at the memory. "We had some good times back then, didn't we?"

Like a hot air balloon when the air below is turned off, I wither into a pile of colored fabric. Those are the exact words he used just days ago. I wonder if he remembers that I was here before.

As though reading my thoughts, he says, "But I'm repeating myself, aren't I? I was feeling nostalgic last time you were here as well. You must think I'm losing my marbles."

What the hell am I supposed to say to that? "Not at all," I answer and bite the inside of my lip.

I look up, sensing he's studying me, and force my smile a bit wider.

"Meera, honey, something is troubling you. Please talk to me."

I can't very well bring up the carousel reopening now. Simon had said that on days like this it was best to keep the conversation where Hank believed himself to be.

"I love this record." I pop out of the chair and walk to the table where the black vinyl disk spins.

"Me, too. We used to listen to it over and

over. I'm surprised it still plays after all these years. Remember how annoyed your mom used to get with this music?" He grins, and it looks just like the grin my father gave me and Thomas behind Mom's back, when she ragged on us about our music.

A silver picture frame glistens on the bookshelf next to the desk. The fluorescent overhead lighting reflects off the glass, blurring the photo tucked inside. I pick it up and tilt it from the glare. A woman stands in front of Big Ben. Her brunette hair is cut in an elegant bob. A red Hermès scarf, expertly tied around her neck, provides the only splash of color. I squint at the image, wondering if it was Photoshopped to make the scarf pop more. She's smiling in the direction of the photographer, but her eyes betray a desire to be someplace else.

"Is this . . . ?" I have no idea who it could be. I turn, holding the photograph in front of me.

"Ah yes, that's Diane."

"Is she still in London?" Tiptoeing through the minefield of someone's memory is a skill I haven't developed.

"Noooo." He draws out the word. "She was just here, actually. Maybe you saw her leaving?" He brightens, turning to the door as if she might be standing right there.

"I didn't pass anyone on the way in." I replace the picture frame on the shelf and make my way back to the chair next to Hank.

"Pity. You two would probably hit it off." His eyes flutter then close, his head tips back into the cushioned support of the chair. But his foot continues to bob to the beat of the music.

I fidget in the chair. It complains, and I force my body still. My hands refuse to cooperate, though, and I fuss at the creased hem of my shirt. I should have tucked it in. Mom would tell me to tuck it in, that looking sloppy makes you feel sloppy and be sloppy. I like sloppy. Sloppy feels comfortable. Except now. Suddenly it feels immature and out of place. Like me.

"Hank," I start then stop the words before they take us into the wrong decade. I don't know how to be my grandmother. I don't know how to be myself either.

"Oh, Meera. It wasn't easy at first. I knew we didn't have a future together, but I still hoped. I hoped the magic of the merry-go-round would be enough. Which was stupid, of course. But you can't blame a romantic for wishing."

He leans forward, grabs my hand and squeezes. "Annabelle understood me, she quieted me. She was so different from you. Where you were passionate and opinionated, she was tender and understanding. I loved her. And I loved you."

My mouth flaps open but there are no words. Hank squeezes my hand again. One of us has sweaty palms. I wipe my other hand on my pants.

"Hank," I finally manage, although I'm not sure what I want to say.

"We made the right decision, Meera. What we had was intoxicating, but it wouldn't have lasted. We wouldn't have lasted. And we wouldn't now have this friendship. I wouldn't give this up." He smiles, and I melt. "And, in my heart, I know it was the best thing for our Claire."

My hands turn from clammy to icy and I pull away from Hank. *Our Claire?*

Movement in the hall stalls the current speeding through my body. I twist to see who's there, who may have overheard, who else now knows yet another secret my grandmother was keeping.

There's no one there. I hear talking down the hall, muffled voices, someone laughing, a telephone ringing.

Our Claire.

"Meera, honey, I've upset you." Hank grabs for my hand, but I push off the armrests and walk to where the record player now sits idle.

It's one thing to know they had a relationship. It was even somehow comforting to know they'd found their way to each other again after all these years. But this? I don't know how to wrap my brain around this.

A knock on the door startles me. Apparently it startled Hank, too, because he bolts from the chair faster than I've seen him move during any of my visits.

"Excuse me for interrupting, but it's time for your physical therapy, Hank." A nurse leans into the room, enough to be present, not enough to intrude.

Hank is by my side before I've processed his movement. He leans close, left hand on my left upper arm, and places a whisper of a kiss on my cheek. "You'll come tomorrow?" It's part question, part command, part wish. He doesn't wait for my answer before shuffling to the door and disappearing with the nurse.

I stand in the empty room listening to the squeak of shoes on linoleum and the murmur of voices.

"Holy shit." I mumble into the quiet. "Any other secrets you're waiting to release on me, Grandma?"

My phone chimes with a meeting reminder. Time for the monthly mother-daughter lunch at the country club. I'd hate to keep "Our Claire" waiting.

Sixteen

At six minutes past one, I pull into the circular drive of the country club. I thank the eager boy in his blue shorts and white polo shirt as he helps me from the car and hops in. It takes only two steps before I hear the gunning of the engine and pebbles scattering behind me. In all the years we've been doing our monthly mother-daughter lunches, I've never arrived exactly on time. Well, I've never arrived at the table exactly on time. Last month, I sat in the car for twenty-five minutes so that I'd get to the table seven minutes late.

Mom is a stickler for timeliness. So am I. Except when it comes to meeting my mom.

She's already seated next to the floor-to-ceiling window overlooking the pond and golf course. She puckers brilliantly outlined rose lips and releases an air kiss when I lean to kiss her cheek. She doesn't bother getting up. But I do get a halfhearted tap on the back, a one-armed pseudo hug.

"You look beautiful as always, Mom." I settle into the chair across from her and fuss with the napkin as a waiter fills my water glass.

She studies me for a minute, a hair twitch of one eyebrow the only comment necessary about my decidedly un-country club appearance. At least I'm not in paint-splattered attire this time.

"So," Mom says after a respectful few minutes of squirming on my part. "Vale tells me you're remodeling the bathroom."

I stare at the glass of water she's just placed back on the table. There's not one smidge of lipstick on it. How does she do that?

Focus, Maya. "You talked to Vale?" *And I talked to Hank.*

Her mouth pulls into a satisfied smirk. My body tenses in response.

Well, Claire, *I bet I could wipe that smirk off your face.* No, not now, not here.

"Yes, we are," I say, forcing the edge from my tongue before continuing. "Then I'm sure he gave you the highlights."

"Umm." It's a nonresponse response, punctuated by an "I see" tip of her head. It makes me want to yell, "No, you don't see!

You don't know anything about what's going on!" But I don't. What would she say if I told her about Hank? How would she react? Hot like Grandma or reserved like Grandpa? I don't know Hank well enough to guess what he'd do.

"So, Mom." I chew on my pale naked lip and seesaw a fork between my left thumb and pointer finger.

"For god's sake, Maya, stop fidgeting."

I'm rarely completely at ease around my mom, and never at the country club. I look around, at the white linen-covered tables, the cut-crystal votive holders, the waiters in starched white shirts and creased black pants.

We'd gone against Mom's wish to have our wedding reception here. Vale had given it the old diplomatic "come on, Maya, this means a lot to her." Grandma had been less diplomatic with "stand your ground, Mims. A stuffy reception leads to a stuffy marriage. Just look at your mom."

The waiter arrives for our order, blocking my visual tour of everything I'm not.

"Spinach salad with poached salmon, please, Jaimi. And Perrier with a lemon slice. Please make sure there are no seeds in the lemon." She winks at Jaimi with what to him no doubt looks like a pleasant smile. I wonder if he realizes it was really a warning.

"Um, oh, same I guess." I hand Jaimi the menu I haven't opened.

As cool as a prosecutor assessing a shaky defense witness, Mom waits. I down an entire glass of water and watch as the busboy refills it. The entire time, Mom stays perfectly still, not even a hair waves under the air-conditioning.

She's reading me. It's what Grandpa used to do. It's also what Hank does.

"What do you know about Grandma's pre-Grandpa days?"

This was obviously not the question she was expecting. She reaches for the glass with its dancing bubbles and seedless lemon, and sips.

The waiter brings our food, and for a few minutes, we abandon our awkward attempt at friendly conversation. Mom takes small, elegant bites while I pull apart the perfectly cooked fish but don't eat.

"Did Grandma tell you about any boyfriends before she met Grandpa?" My heart hammers and I whisper "shhh" to it. *I could say something, I could crack this open. I can't. Not yet. Not until I know more.*

"Not much." She studies what's left of her salmon filet, flaking a few more pieces then rebuilding the mound.

"Didn't you guys talk? Weren't you interested?"

Mom's perfectly sculpted eyebrows distort. "You mean the way we talk?"

She's got me there. Except she's intimidating and unwelcoming. Grandma wasn't. At least not to me.

The waiter picks up an empty plate from a nearby table and walks to ours. "May I take anything? Get you anything?"

Mom dismisses him with a flick of her wrist. Hank would never be rude like that. Grandpa wasn't like that. Grandma would have invited him to sit.

"Your grandmother wasn't an easy person to talk to."

I take a larger than anticipated swallow of sparkling water and snort as the bubbles fizz up my nose.

"Maya." Mom's eyes bug then dart around the room. "Manners, please."

I cover my mouth and nose with the white linen napkin and wait for the tears to subside. This is why I rarely drink anything with fizz. Fizz and I don't play well together.

I gawk at my mom and dab at my eyes. "She was the easiest person to talk to."

"I guess we saw different sides of her."

"I guess." How were those sides so drastically different?

Mom folds a dark green leaf onto her fork with the tip of the knife, then flakes a piece of salmon. I'm once again mesmerized as the fork leaves her lips without a hint of smudged lipstick.

"Why are you staring at me, Maya?" She puts the fork and knife down and taps the corner of her mouth with the corner of the napkin. Her lipstick stays intact.

Because I know something that would blow your perfect rock to gravel. Because you're not who you think you are. Or pretend to be. Because I can't see how you came from two such easygoing people.

I swallow hard and reach for my water.

"I'm sorry, dear. I know how hard losing her is on you."

I may have caught her off guard earlier, but this knocks me flat on my butt. The sudden tenderness threatens to uncork my barely contained emotions. Navigating Mom's soft side is not something I know how to do.

Are all relationships between mothers and daughters cursed to bruised emotions?

The waiter comes to collect our plates, and Mom orders two espressos. I don't like espresso. I don't correct her.

There are so many questions I want to ask, so many sensitive spots I want to poke.

But she's disarmed me, and the weight I've been carrying for the last twelve months drops around me like an ancient, moldy blanket.

We sip our coffees and revert to safe topics: Megan's upcoming birthday and the lavish party Bree wants to throw, against Thomas's wishes. That Alex has started sleeping on the floor with the puppy because Bree won't allow the dog on the bed.

"I'd let my child sleep with the dog. I think it's so sweet," I mutter. For the briefest of heartbeats, our eyes meet and we're connected by the grief of a tiny coffin.

The waiter slips the white china plate with the bill on it next to Mom's left elbow. A gold pen anchors the paper against a sudden gust of air-conditioning. I shiver.

She signs her name and places her napkin on the table. Another monthly mother-daughter lunch over. Another opportunity for this mother and daughter to connect, missed. The chance to expose a newly discovered secret, gone.

The cars are waiting for us when we step out the front door. Mom leans left then right, her cheek barely making contact with mine. I'm not sure that even qualifies for air-kiss status. She waves and calls, "Bye, darling. Thanks for lunch," as she glides down the steps and into her waiting carriage.

I catch myself looking back to see who the "darling" is she's talking to. A man and his golf clubs return the confused look. I trot down the steps, head bowed to hide the flush of embarrassment, and allow the car to swallow me whole.

Seventeen

"Hand me those socks will you," Sam flips her hand in a general direction of four open boxes containing an assortment of socks, sunglasses, T-shirts, and bracelets.

After yesterday's lunch with my mom and a marathon session in the studio, I welcomed Sam's invitation for mindless-busywork therapy and girl talk. Even her bossiness is a relief. I haven't had the time to think about Hank or my grandmother or my mom in over an hour.

"Which ones?" I push my left hand into a box of ankle socks and grab a pair of knee socks out of another box with my right hand.

"Those. There." Sam points.

Again my eyes follow. I reach for a third box and pull out a pair of light-gray slippers. The left one has spots with blue trim around the opening and the right one has stars with green trim around the opening.

"These?"

"Yes. Finally."

"These are slippers."

"Okay?"

"You said hand you socks. These are slippers."

Sam turns in slow motion, partly because she's standing on a ladder, but I have no doubt it's also for full attitude effect. She flops her hand, palm up and waggles her fingers in a hand-it-over motion.

"Okay, spill," she says. "What has your panties wedged up to your armpits?"

"Nothing." I hand over an armful of slippers. "Ooh, these are my size." I set them on the ground and slip a foot in.

"Feet out of the merchandise, missy. Seriously, Maya, what's happening? You're totally off your merry-go-round." She guffaws at her own joke and points at the box again.

I hand over more slippers, this time with a bit more attitude. Sam chuckles.

"Do we need to play thirteen questions?" She folds onto the floor next to me. Sam's favorite number is thirteen. Even the store address is 1313. "Double lucky," she'd said when she signed the lease.

"It won't take three questions to get to the heart of this." I reach into a box and pull out a bangle bracelet. I slip it on and twist my arm to make it rotate from left to right. The enamel colors catch the lights, and I'm suddenly watching a merry-go-round spinning around my wrist.

Sam grabs at my hand and removes the bracelet. "You're making me seasick. Considering that yesterday was the country club lunch with mummy dearest, let's start there. It has to do with your mom?" She dumps a handful of T-shirts in my lap and a pile of plastic hangers in front of me.

While we hang the shirts, matching size to the small red letter at the neck of each hanger, I replay the lunch discussion.

When I've hung the last shirt and gotten to the awkward good-bye, I look up. Sam's staring. "What?" I snap, avoiding eye contact.

"You're keeping something from me."

"I'm not. Anyway, it's your turn. You said you have something to tell me."

She puckers her lips. "I did, didn't I? But by the color of your cheeks, what you're trying to hide is way better. Damn, Maya. You know I live vicariously through you and your family dramas. Gimme more."

My family may not be the happy, close-knit ideal, but compared to Sam's family, we're a '50s TV family.

Sam's father is the CEO of a multitrillion-dollar company known only by an acronym. Her mom is a dean at an Ivy League college. One of her brothers is a high-priced attorney in New York, the other is a big-shot CFO in Boston, and her sister is one of the leading plastic surgeons in Los Angeles. Sam, on the other hand, dropped out of college after her sophomore year, took the money her grandfather left her, and spent two years in Italy.

When the money ran out, she came home. Her family didn't welcome her with open arms or open wallets. Not even an open guest room. So Sam did what they expected of her: She moved to the beach and got a job as a waitress.

That's when we met. Fins had always been one of my favorites, and whenever Vale and I came to visit our families, it was the first place we went. And somehow, Sam was always our waitress. Two years later, when she turned twenty-five, her trust fund kicked in and Socks-A-Lot was hatched.

She tosses a pair of mismatched socks at me and gives me a come-on gesture.

"Remember I told you about Hank's memory glitches?"

She nods.

"Well, I went to see him yesterday morning and he was having an off day." I air quote *off.*

Sam scoots on her bottom until she's facing me, glowing with anticipation.

"The inscription and the letter were pretty clear that they were more than the passing friends she claimed. But they weren't even friendly friends. Sam" — I wrap my fingers around her forearm before I bounce out of my skin — "he referred to my mom as 'our Claire.' "

Sam's forehead creases and the corners of her mouth quirk. "You sure he meant your mom?"

"Who else could he be talking about? And the timing is not inconceivable."

Sam gives me a dubious look.

"Okay, think about it. They had a romance of some sort. We know that. Grandma and Grandpa got married after dating for a month. Mom was born barely nine months later."

Sam puckers in thought. "You think?"

"I think."

"I don't know, Maya, this seems like a stretch."

"You wouldn't say that if you saw him when he's talking to her."

Sam gives me a skeptical eyebrow.

"I know, I know," I jump to defend myself.

"But what if I'm right? What if Grandma and Hank had a last fling before she tied the knot with Grandpa?"

"So what?"

I chew the inside of my lip. Indeed, so what? So what because Mom harps on being "proper," doing everything by the proverbial good-girl book. *But that's Mom, not Grandma. Grandma didn't subscribe to the same philosophy.*

"Maybe you're right," I concede.

"Of course I'm right." Sam flashes a grin. "But what am I right about this time?"

"It doesn't really matter." But saying the words doesn't mean I actually believe them. But what is it that actually bothers me? That Grandma had an affair? That Grandpa isn't Mom's biological father? The lies? Would it bother me if this was my mom we were talking about instead of Grandma? But that's absurd because Mom would never have done that. They've been married for . . . I count back in my head.

"Oh my god," I startle Sam with my outburst. "Like mother, like daughter. Mom and Thomas. Holy crap."

"What are you talking about? What does Thomas have to do with this?"

"Mom used to tease that Thomas was big and busy and didn't have time to hang around for all nine months." I grin. "He wasn't early."

Sam hoots and rocks back on her butt, then slaps playfully at my crisscrossed legs. "You are certainly the black sheep, or is it white-sheep in this case? You're the only woman in your family who wasn't knocked up when you got married."

"How did neither of us ever question that?"

"Because you had no reason to. It was a secret your parents chose to keep."

"Think my grandmother knew?"

"Probably."

"Then there's me. And Uncle Joe."

"Where are you going with this?" Sam stops sorting socks and refocuses on me.

"Grandma had Mom, then Joe. Mom had Thomas, then me. Even Bree has two."

"Okay . . . ?"

"Then there's me." My fingers flutter by my stomach, playing a soundless lullaby on an invisible piano for a baby that doesn't exist.

"Oh, Maya." Sam grabs my hand, stilling the movement and crescendoing emotion.

Her thumb rubs a slow, soothing circle on my hand.

"Enough on me. You had news to share," I turn the focus away from me.

Sam swallows and picks at the cuticles on her left hand. "It can wait."

"No, it can't."

"Really, it's okay."

She's saved from further prodding by a gentle knock on the glass door of the boutique. Taylor holds up a large bag with a yellow owl on it. Both stare in through the glass. I turn to Sam.

She answers with a sheepish smirk. "Refreshments have arrived."

"The Yellow Owl delivers now?"

Her face flushes and she hops over a box to let him in.

"Sam?" I draw out her name, making it sound long and saucy. The red deepens and she turns away to open the door.

Moments later, another knock. This time it's Vale, holding up two four-packs of beer from the local microbrewery.

"Sam." No playful question to the way I say her name this time.

She waves me off and pulls Vale and the beer inside. "I figured we'd need reinforcements."

"Seriously," Taylor says, scanning the volume of boxes. "But first we eat."

"Four orders of spicy shrimp? Good thing there's more beer in the car." Vale laughs.

We settle on the floor, food containers

spread on a handful of boxes between us.

"So, Maya, how's the merry-go-round coming? Still on target for the Fourth of July reopening?" Taylor asks.

"I think so."

"You better be more sure than that," Sam teases.

"She'll be ready. She's been working round the clock on it."

I look at Vale, trying to decide if the comment has a hidden dig. He winks.

"Wait till you guys see it," he says. "Each animal is more beautiful than the previous. This carousel has never looked as good." His face beams with pride.

I have no words.

Taylor holds up a red crustacean by the tail and studies it. "Why doesn't that thing have a ride in the shape of a shrimp?"

His expression is so serious that both Sam and I dissolve into giggles.

"No wait, he's on to something," Vale steps in to defend his buddy. "Shrimp, crabs, a dolphin or two. Oh, and a couple of mermaids." Vale high-fives Taylor. "We're a beach town, why do we need horses and lions?"

"Don't forget the ostrich," I add.

Sam coughs a laugh. "Wait," she feigns shock. "The ostrich I saw jogging on the beach last week isn't a local?"

We all break into fits of laughter.

"People. . . ." Sam claps her hands five times, teacher style, and I giggle when Taylor and Vale chant "one, two, eyes on me" in time to her claps. She shoots them a look that falls three blinks short of menacing.

"Okay, okay, we have work to do." I try my hand at rallying the troops, only to end up with a balled-up napkin bouncing off my forehead. "Nice." I throw it back at Vale.

By midnight we're done with the food, drink, and rearranging the store. Sam yawns and surveys our work, nodding appreciatively. "You guys do decent work. Now shoo. I need my beauty rest before I open tomorrow." She smothers another yawn.

"We'll walk you to your car," Vale offers.

Sam and Taylor exchange a look. Taylor slaps Vale on the back and says, "I got it, man. You guys go ahead."

Vale puts his arm around my shoulder as we walk away, and squeezes gently. "I bet he's getting it."

I elbow him gently and lean into his side when he puts his arm around my shoulder. We walk and talk; about Sam and the store; about his day and mine; about the heartburn we'll have tomorrow from the spicy shrimp.

And for those blocks, for those minutes, we're the couple we used to be.

EIGHTEEN

I straighten and stretch my back. The clock blinks over another hour.

I have less than an hour before our dinner reservations. Vale texted earlier that we were going out to celebrate. He hadn't said what we were celebrating, and I'd exhausted all of my ideas.

Even the horse wasn't giving up any new secrets today. Each new layer of paint removed revealed another layer. I know the original paint is there, the pinstriping and special Hank details waiting to be released from captivity. But today, the merry-go-round magic is on strike.

Every carver has his signature details. I'd been reading about the old-school carvers. They were a fascinating breed. Most had started as carpenters. Like Hank. Some had fallen into carousel-making by accident. Like Hank. I'll have to ask him about his ancestors, and how he got involved.

I check the clock. I know there isn't time for a side trip to visit him now, but I can't fight the urge to go see him. It's been three days since I've been to Tower Oaks. Three days of mounting questions. But after the last time, I'm also a bit afraid to return.

I have to tell him I'm Meera's granddaughter. That I'm Claire's daughter.

But each time I've started to go, a ghost has held me back. She'd kept me away from Hank for three years. Maybe longer. She'd wanted the secret for herself.

Maybe she thought I'd tell Mom, explode her beliefs in who she was. Maybe I would have. I had the perfect chance and didn't though.

Are there secrets that belong to only one person? No. If it didn't have the potential to affect someone else, then it wouldn't be worth keeping it a secret.

As the keeper of a secret, how do you decide whose world you're going to shift? And when to nudge it off its axis?

How many times during that lunch had I tasted the words? And the times since when my fingers have twitched to call. And yet I didn't, couldn't, let the words loose. Why? Out of loyalty? Pity? Fear?

Whatever the reason, their secret is now mine as well.

Does knowing change how I feel about Grandpa? Grandma? Mom? No and yes. But maybe not the way she expected.

Then again, I have no idea what she expected or why she lied. There's really only one person who may have answers. Tomorrow I'll go see Hank.

Right now, though, I have another secret to sort out. What are we celebrating tonight?

I close up the studio and enter the house. The breakfast dishes are on the counter, clean and dry. Vale cleaned up before leaving for work. The bathroom remodeling will be delayed, he'd apologized over scrambled eggs. Paying work was getting in the way.

This is when having one full bathroom doesn't work. Luckily, we have the half-bath, but I want to soak in the tub or stand in the shower until the water turns cold. Washing my hair in the kitchen sink is getting old.

But it's all I have for now. I go upstairs to retrieve the shampoo and conditioner and a couple of towels. I still end up drenching myself and the floor. This is one skill I hope not to have to master.

The afternoon sun has dipped enough to send rays under the closed door of the spare room. It's not really a spare, but I haven't been able to think of it as anything else.

Except maybe the room that's never opened.

I've ignored it for a year, walked past as though there weren't a door there at all.

I stand at the top of the stairs and look at the sliver of light. We'd picked that room because of the afternoon light.

The sun had been brilliant that last day. It had heated the repolished floors and shone a spotlight on the mural I'd started painting. It had cooked the room far beyond cozy.

Everything about that day had been dazzling and wrong. How can a perfect late-spring day become your darkest nightmare?

I reach for the handle. My hand, suspended in midair, shakes. The light from under the door dims then brightens. My skin prickles.

It's nothing but a cloud, Maya. It's time. You can do this.

My fingers graze the handle. There's no electric jolt, no sparks, no fairy dust. I push down on the handle. There's a faint click as the latch springs back and the door becomes light in my hand. I give it a gentle nudge, and it swings open.

A sob pushes up from my diaphragm and lodges in my throat.

This was the last place I'd seen her alive. She'd brought lunch. We'd sat right there in the middle of the room on the yellow-and-blue carpet, eaten our sandwiches, and talked about the mural.

The idea for it, along with pregnancy heartburn, had woken me up at two A.M., and I'd rushed in here to rough it out. We'd already painted the walls — yellow on the bottom two-thirds and a summer-day blue with fluffy clouds on the top third. But this wall, the one across from the window, demanded something special.

The faint outline of my sketch is barely visible now. There's an ear, a muzzle, a front leg raised in anticipation, a tail whooshing behind. The dream had been so vivid. A merry-go-round, wooden horses going up and down. Music getting louder in time to the whirling of the platform. People laughing as the world around them blurred into fuzzy colors.

The outline on the wall is the perfect replica of the horse in my studio.

Something yellow on the bookshelf catches my attention. The stuffed dog Grandma had bought when I was born sits alone and forgotten. His colors are faded from years of love, but he'd once been bright yellow and blue, as bright as the colors in this room. He'd been the inspiration for the color scheme. Well, him and the rug. The rug that's no longer here.

I touch my flat stomach. No baby. No cramps.

I walk into the room and stop in the middle. The wood floor is polished, clean. I wonder if the blood had soaked through the rug into the floor.

I turn, a slow-motion 360. The rocking chair waits patiently in the corner, angled to see the entire room and catch the last soft caress of the setting sun. To the left of the rocker is the bookshelf, painted white to match the window frame above it.

To the right of the rocker is an empty blue-and-yellow wall. That's where the crib was going to be. Who canceled the order for the crib and matching dresser? How did I never think to question that before?

Across from the crib is the wall that should have been perfect.

I sink into the rocker, grabbing the dog on my way down. I pull him into my chest and bury my nose in his head. He smells of dust and neglect. A faint hint of paint lingers, but I can't be sure if it's on him, in the room, or in my mind.

I've wished, pleaded for a do-over of that day. I've rolled the details over and over in my mind until every last one is lodged deep, like a splinter you can't extract.

The floor of the merry-go-round mural is

outlined in black paint. So is the roof. The rooster at the tip of the roof shines a brilliant black. The ostrich's beak is black, and the chest strap is partially painted. Also black.

Black was the only color I'd had on hand that morning. I'd made a list of the colors I needed. Vale had told me to wait; he'd stop by the store on his way home then help me paint in the evening, when it was cooler. The forecast was calling for thunderstorms in the late afternoon, with cooler temperatures and rain the following day. Perfect for painting, he'd said.

But I'd been possessed by the dream that had given birth to the mural. I'd wanted to finish at least one merry-go-round before the baby was born. So when Grandma said she'd go to the store for me and buy the paint I needed, I didn't argue hard enough.

The doctors had said it could have happened anywhere, at any time.

She'd been feeling run down — not that she complained, and not that it slowed her down. But I heard the sighs when she sat, and the catch of breath that she dismissed as nothing. I noticed the deeper bags under her eyes and the paler tone of her skin.

I should have insisted she rest. I should have made her go to the doctor. I should have told Mom. But she'd made me pinky-promise not to.

I should have been more patient and waited for Vale. I should have left that stifling room. I should have listened to my body. But I'd been impatient, selfish.

When my dad called with the news, I should have let him come for me immediately. But I'd said no. There was nothing to do for her, and I couldn't face my mom. It was my fault Grandma was dead. I told dad I'd wait for Vale, we'd go to their house later. I had to stay here, in this room. I had to wait for the paint to finish the mural. So I'd gotten on the stepstool, in the heat, with the open paint can in my hand.

I outlined the ostrich. I outlined the carousel house. She'd said she would return within the hour. It was so much longer than an hour. But she'd said she would be back. Like a woman possessed, I kept outlining my mural with the one color of paint I had. And I waited.

But in the heat, on the stool, paint fumes and realization stealing what air there was, my magical merry-go-round blurred.

My body feels heavy as the memory of gravity slams into me. My brain clouds with the memory of the loss. And yet, I see myself capping the paint, pushing the stepstool back to the corner.

Did Vale know what really happened that day? If he did, he's been keeping the same secret.

The rocking chair moves under me with each muscle contraction; forward, back, forward.

I'd been against having one in here. Too old fashioned, I'd never use it, just one more place for clutter to collect. I'd had all the excuses. My mom bought it anyway. "You'll love it, Maya, you'll see."

Why hadn't they canceled the order for this as well?

I let my head drop back and clutch the stuffed dog to my chest. I close my eyes against the sting of tears and allow my legs to push harder against the floor. Forward, back, forward. I wait for the racking sobs, the ripping heartache. There's only deafening emptiness.

"Hey, what are you doing in here?" Vale's warm hand rests on my knee.

My eyes flutter open. They feel rough, like I've been staring into a wind tunnel. Or the sun.

"There was a light from under the door." Like that explains everything.

Vale's expression turns worried.

"The sun."

It doesn't ease the concern etched between his brows.

"The rug is gone."

He nods.

"You?"

He shakes his head.

"My dad?"

"Why does this matter, Maya?"

"It just does."

"It doesn't."

We both look at the spot where the rug should have been.

"This was supposed to be our future."

Vale sits at my feet, holding on to my calves. "Listen to me." He tightens the hold on my legs to make me focus on him. "It was an accident. A horrible, unfortunate accident."

I shake my head, triggering a waterfall.

"Dammit, Maya, enough. When will you stop punishing yourself?"

"What if I can't have any more babies?"

"Why would you think that?"

I shrug. The dog slips from my hands, landing on the floor between us with a gentle thud that echoes in my chest.

"What happened to the rug?" The rug would have muffled the thud.

Vale exhales and releases my legs. "Let it go."

I look from the shiny black-plastic eyes to my husband's sad brown eyes.

Vale sighs, resigned. "I asked your dad to throw it away. I couldn't get the blood out."

I wait for more tears. This time, they don't come. My body stays quiet, my mind still. Waiting. Still nothing.

Suddenly desperate to get out of the room, to feel something, I stand and pull Vale to his feet. Gripping his hand, I lead him to the bedroom. He stops at the door, but I walk to the bed. I turn and pull my T-shirt over my head, then let my shorts drop to the floor. Vale's eyes roam my body, his Adam's apple slides up and down.

The ceiling fan twirls overhead and the cool air makes my skin tingle. I reach for Vale's hand and pull him toward me. He snakes one hand around my waist, the other cups my breast. A moan breaks the silence. I undo his pants, push off his shirt.

We tumble to the bed, naked, fumbling with each other like two inexperienced teenagers. It's been too long. We've been too far apart.

I wrap my legs around his hips and pull him closer. He moans and I tense. Vale pulls back and, with hands on either side of my head, pushes up to look me in the eye. "Maya, look at me. Are you sure about his?"

I nod and tighten my grip around his hips, drawing him closer. His upper body closes the distance between us and his lips find mine.

"Let's make another baby. Now. Please, Vale. Now," I breathe the words between kisses, our bodies moving with an urgency of a year's denial.

With an abruptness that leaves me gasping, Vale rolls off. "No."

The fan taunts me from above, the cold making me feel even more exposed and vulnerable. All the months when Vale wanted to make love and I'd turned him away, unable to trust my body — now this. Heartache and humiliation take hold. I leap from the bed and bolt for the bathroom, but there's no floor, no sink, no door. No hiding.

Vale's arms close around me from behind. "Stop. Shhhh," he whispers into my neck.

My body vibrates from the tsunami building inside. I don't push him away though. I don't have anywhere to go. He turns me without releasing me.

"Look at me." He dips his head until we're eye-level. "This isn't the answer. We'll get the baby-making underway when the time is right. But not like this. Not now."

He leads me back to the bedroom. I stand

in the doorway, arms wrapped around my body as my husband pulls on boxers and shorts. He tugs a T-shirt out of the dresser. He takes a step closer, his hand barely grazing my waist. It scalds my oversensitive emotions. He leans to give me a kiss and I squeeze my eyes shut, unable to make eye contact. I wrap my hands around my waist in a protective hug, wanting to erase the memory of his touch.

"Put something on and come downstairs. Let's stay home tonight instead. I'll fix us something to eat."

I stay rooted to the spot, arms pretzeled tight around my naked body, and listen to his footfalls going down the stairs and into the kitchen. I stumble half a step back and dissolve into a puddle on the hardwood floor.

If we had that blue and yellow rug, I could have moved it into this room. Now I need to buy two rugs.

Nineteen

"Ouch." I jerk my foot away, slamming my knee into the wood picnic table in the process. Dov is teething on the rubber toe of my Converse sneakers.

Bree looks under the table. "Oh good grief. Come here, you mutt." She tugs at his collar. The puppy performs a reverse army crawl, but not without one final chomp on my toe. Denied my shoe, he proceeds to gnaw on the wood bench.

Vale leans into me and whispers, "Still think we should get a dog?"

"Yes. And new shoes."

It's been three days since my failed seduction, which wasn't much of a seduction at all. We've been tiptoeing around the subject and each other ever since. More so than usual. And in true Maya fashion, I dealt with it by sequestering myself in my studio.

I haven't been to see Hank or gone for a run on the beach. I've dodged calls from my family and responded to Sam with the shortest of texts.

For all the attempts at hiding, I'm now sitting at my brother's house. "Mandatory fun night," is what Vale had said when he pushed me out the door. So far, it hasn't been much fun.

"Who wants well-done steak?" Thomas is fanning flames from the grill.

Bree rolls her eyes and twists out of the picnic table. "Good thing I bought back-ups."

"You should help. I'm not sure she has backups for the backups," I say to Vale, nudging him.

"He's got it. And if not, there's always pizza delivery." Vale takes a draw from his beer. "Are you still mad at me for insisting we come?"

"No."

"Are you sure?"

"No."

He chuckles. "What can I do to redeem myself?"

I pretend to ponder the dilemma, then hand him my empty plate. "Refill on the guacamole and chips. Don't be stingy. And another beer." I call after him.

He flashes a grin over his shoulder and disappears into the house.

Thomas has finally gotten the flames under control and dinner is once again moving forward, this time more carefully supervised by Bree.

The kids and puppy are chasing each other at the other end of the fenced-in backyard. The squealing and barking drown out the lawn mower in a neighboring yard.

Eventually, the exhausted puppy throws himself at my feet, tongue hanging out the side of his mouth. Megan disappears into the house only to emerge a few minutes later with an assortment of nail polishes and paintbrushes. "Aunt Maymay, will you paint my nails?"

I flex my left hand and look at my fingers, short nails overrun by cuticles, and the only color is flecks of brown from the morning's work on the carousel horse. "Have you seen my hands? Do you really think I'm qualified?"

Megan scrunches her nose and squints at my hand. "But you're an artist so I bet you can do something pretty on me."

"No pressure there," Bree says, taking back her spot at the picnic table.

Megan hands me a bottle of hot pink nail polish. "And then I want white polka dots."

"So how was lunch with your mom?" Bree attempts a casual tone as I dab hot pink polish on her daughter's tiny fingernails.

I don't break my concentration from the delicate paint job. "The usual."

The corner of Bree's mouth pulls in. I can tell she's itchy to ask outright but doesn't want to open a can of family slime in front of her daughter.

"What kind of relationship do you have with your mom?" I ask. It's somewhat of a trick question. I know Bree isn't very close to her mom, although she claims otherwise. Then again, I suppose the interpretation for a "close relationship" is subjective.

"We're very close, you know that. We don't see much of each other since they moved to Arizona but we talk at least once a week." Bree's tone bristles.

"What do you talk about?"

There's an uncharacteristic furrow to Bree's brow. "The usual I suppose. What the kids are up to, their schedules, weather."

The usual. Those aren't my usual discussion topics.

Did Grandma and I talk about schedules and weather? I guess we did. But we talked about so much more, too. I'd confided in her about almost everything.

Mom and I rarely talk on the phone. When we do or we're together? Schedules and weather. Okay, so I guess those are usual topics. And that makes me sad.

I finish painting the last of Megan's fingers then watch as Bree takes Meg's small hands and blows on the hot pink polish to speed up the drying. Meg meanwhile is running a monologue that in the few minutes of drying time has spanned the gamut from her new swimsuit that matches her friend Amy's but now that they're not best friends anymore she won't wear it, to the flavor of cake she wants for her birthday party five-and-three-quarter months away.

Is their relationship predestined to become an emotional tug-of-war? Maybe. And maybe that's why I hoped for a boy when I found out I was pregnant.

Megan shoves her pudgy fingers in front me. "They're ready for their dots."

"Steaks are done." Thomas puts a tray of meat on the table. "What are you two talking about? Maya has that constipated look she gets when she doesn't care for the topic. Wait —" He pauses for effect. "You're talking about Mom."

I glare at him. "Not funny."

"But I'm right, aren't I?" he gloats.

"Can you two stop for a day? Set a better example for your kids." Bree swats at Thomas with a flyswatter.

"Yeah, Thomas." I taunt, then wink at

Alex and Meg, who are watching with anxious delight.

We settle into neutral conversation while we eat. The kids and puppy alternate bites with sprints. By the time we're done with dinner, I'm exhausted, and I haven't gotten off the bench once.

Bree talks Alex and Meg into popcorn and a movie. While she gets them settled, Thomas lights citronella candles and refreshes drinks.

"So, Vale," Thomas asks, his mouth so close to the lip of his beer bottle that his S's whistle. "What's the latest on Seattle?"

I can feel their eyes on me. I watch the flickering flame on the candle in the middle of the table. I release a long breath, and the flame performs a perfect limbo before straightening and sputtering in protest.

Yes, Vale, what's the latest on Seattle? Let's hear how you spin this. I still have a week, and he hasn't brought it up with me since setting the dreaded deadline.

"Not much to tell." He's still watching me.

The deepest discussions we've had the last few nights have revolved around what to have for dinner or who needs the car. Since I haven't left the studio except to eat or sleep, and food has consisted of whatever

Vale felt like fixing, we've exchanged only a few words.

Which is probably why he insisted we go out tonight. The where was a surprise, although he'd hinted that oysters would be involved when I was reluctant to leave my studio. Now, not only am I not getting oysters, I'm also spending the evening under my brother's microscope. Even the discussion pointed at my husband has a side spotlight on me.

"Don't you owe them an answer?"

My stomach knots.

"Yes, but they're not pushing. I'll get back to them soon, though."

A week soon. I can't make that decision in a week.

"But you're interested?"

"Of course. It's a hell of an opportunity. But it's not that easy."

"You guys are about as subtle as donkeys," I grumble.

"Did she just call us asses?" Thomas feigns shock.

"I think she did."

Sounds from Disney's *Aladdin* fill the night as Bree opens windows in the family room. "I don't know why she insists on doing that," Thomas complains. "It defeats the purpose of putting the kids to watch something so the adults can have quiet time."

"She's just being cautious," Vale says, looking at the windows and flickering shadows from the TV. "Most accidents happen in or around your own home."

From the dark of the house, Genie is explaining "wish fulfillment" to Aladdin. "Three wishes, to be exact. And ixnay on the wishing for more wishes. That's it. Three. *Uno, dos, tres.* No substitutions, exchanges, or refunds."

What would my wishes be? I can only think of two. A magic carpet to whisk me away from here and back to my studio; and a time-travel machine to take me back thirteen months, to undo the damage.

TWENTY

"You're a little overdressed for the studio." Vale takes in my yellow capris, white T-shirt, and the blue sweater wrapped around my waist.

"Going to visit Hank. Unless you need the car?" I stop mid-motion, one foot in a flip-flop, the other sandal still in my hand.

"No, I have bathroom duty. George is coming over to help."

On cue, George knocks on the back door and, with Vale waving him to enter, comes into the kitchen.

"You look lovely as always, Maya." George gives me a kiss on the cheek.

"Thank you, kind sir." I curtsy.

"Just don't get too close to the hair. I think there may be a squirrel nesting in there. It's time to get the shower fixed." Vale winks and dodges when I pretend to smack at him with my bag.

"At your service." George bows.

I roll my eyes. "I'm leaving the bathroom in your capable hands. Don't screw anything else up." I wag a finger at Vale. "George, you're in charge."

"Hey." Vale squeaks, and George laughs.

"Smart woman." George winks. "No worries, we've got this."

"That's what worries me," I say, sliding on my other shoe. I wave good-bye and jog to the car, happily escaping from the discussion of moving water lines, and measurements, and best brand of grout.

I ease the Audi into the parking lot of Tower Oaks, anxious to see Hank — whichever Hank will be there today. An ambulance, back doors open, stands in the no-parking zone directly in front of the entrance. From my parking spot, I can see the front doors of Tower Oaks and the open back of the ambulance. No gurney.

My knuckles turn white with the pressure on the steering wheel. There's no reason for the skipping in my chest. No reason to think this has anything to do with Hank. And yet I can't make my fingers work on the door handle.

Through the frosted glass of the facility doors, I catch movement. I push the car door open and stand, my right leg still in the car, my heart hammering louder than the sound of the TV drifting from the second-floor room with the open window.

The shadows inside Tower Oaks continue to move closer until the large glass doors slide open. A square man with a buzz cut is the first out; the puff of air released by the opening doors ruffles his dark-blue scrubs. His left arm trails behind, pulling the gurney. The white sheet bulges around a human figure. I catch my breath as the other end comes into view. The medic at the head is a slight woman, her hair pulled into a tight ponytail, her dark-blue scrubs book-ending the stark white of the wrapped figure. She tucks a corner of the blanket under the rounded shape where the head is.

Simon follows them out. He stands at the edge of the sidewalk, watching as the medics push the gurney into the waiting ambulance. The square man walks to Simon and pats his upper arm before continuing around and getting into the passenger side.

Simon watches as the ambulance pulls away. He turns and catches sight of me, his body shudders as breath escapes from his parted lips.

I take a few hesitant steps toward him. I can't read his expression. I used to be able to read him perfectly. When I'm arm's-distance away, I stop, turn, and together we watch the ambulance as it disappears out of sight.

"That's one part of the job that never gets easier. Come on, I need a drink. Coffee will have to do, though."

I skip a couple of steps to catch up to him. He orders a latte from the young man at the coffee kiosk. I decline. I don't need more caffeine to spike my overactive pulse.

"Where's Barbie?" I whisper, hoping the answer isn't in the ambulance.

"Hair salon. Then brunch with her grandkids. She has nine, and they come for her every Sunday."

"Who was it?" I nod in the direction the ambulance went.

Simon looks down at me then at the doors to the West Wing. "Jonah. Nice old man. It's been a hard year for him and his family though. This is a relief for them. Don't look so scandalized, Maya. I'm not a monster, and I'm not overly jaded. Jonah had advanced dementia. He wasn't the person his family knew. Most of the time, he wasn't much of a person at all."

I flinch.

"Sorry, that sounded harsh."

It did. But I also understand. Mostly.

"How's Hank?"

"He's okay. He'll be happy to see you."

"You think?" I can't contain the jump of anticipation in my voice.

"I think. I have some calls to make and paperwork to do. I'll catch you later." He stands a heartbeat longer, maybe wanting to say something else, maybe waiting for me to say something else. "Okay, later then." He turns and walks the opposite direction from the West Wing.

The entrance to Hank's room is blocked by a cleaning cart. I peer inside, but he's not in there. I know he's okay and yet a fresh wave of panic flushes through me. I make eye contact with a nurse at the desk. She points to the courtyard.

I find him sitting on a bench, leafing through a magazine.

"Hank?"

He looks up and blinks at me, once, twice, then a flicker of recognition. "Nice to see you." Doubt crowds his forehead with more wrinkles. "Who are you again?"

I collect my heart before I step on it and move forward to sit on the bench next to him.

"Maya Brice. I'm the restorer working on your carousel."

His face lights up. "How is the old girl?"

He closes the magazine and sets it between us.

"Still beautiful." I suppress the shudder of déjà vu. "What are you reading?" I twist around to look at the magazine and stifle a wince; we're both repeating ourselves, again. Will every conversation with Hank be a dance of two steps forward, one back?

"Trash," Hank chortles. "The only thing these nurses bring us to read is trash. Who cares about some self-absorbed teenage music star? Or what celebrities are getting divorced? No respect for marriage or commitment these days."

I turn the magazine over and laugh at the cover. *Star News* winks at me in bright gold letters. It's one of those tabloids I'm tempted to pick up in the grocery-store aisle, but I always chicken out.

Hank assesses me for a quiet minute then says, "So Miss . . . um . . ." He waves the lapse away. "Tell me about yourself."

"There's not much to tell." I shrug, uncomfortable at being in his crosshairs.

He lets out a hearty laugh and leans back. "That's nonsense. A young lady who restores carousels and comes to sit with an old geezer. You, my dear, are fascinating."

I smile, can't help myself. He's utterly charming, and I picture my grandma as a young woman taken by a younger version of him.

"What?" He leans forward. "You're smirking."

My smile widens. "I was just thinking that you remind me of someone."

The twinkle in his eye from a moment ago clouds over and, just as quickly, the shadow is gone and a slow smile takes over his face. "I was thinking the same about you when you first walked in."

"When I walked in?" My eyes dart to the front door.

"Yes, when you walked in. There's a reason I sit on this bench. When the light cooperates, I can see everything in the lobby." He winks, and we both look through the wall of windows. He's right.

I feel a slight prickle on the back of my neck at the realization that he'd seen me, watched me. "Who do I remind you of?"

Another hearty laugh. "Someone from a long, long time ago. She was a beauty. Like you." He pats my hand and winks again. He's flirting. I feel the heat of a blush.

"But I want to hear about you. Miss . . . what did you say your name was?"

I deflate into the hot bench, the smug face of the self-absorbed teenage music star on the cover of the magazine beaming at me.

"Maya Brice."

"Yes, yes. Miss Brice." He waves his hand as though slapping away an annoying fly. "What would make a beautiful young woman choose to restore a decrepit old relic?"

I resort to my standard answer. "I got tired of being cooped up in the basement of a museum, restoring artifacts."

There's a slight narrowing of his right eye as he studies me. "And?"

"And I've always loved carousels, especially this one."

"Well lucky me that you're rescuing mine."

"Maybe it's rescuing me." The words take flight. I suspect that my face looks as surprised as his.

He recovers first. "It is a well-known fact that carousels are magic."

"My grandmother used to say the same thing."

"Your grandmother was a wise woman." He's looking through the windows, through the lobby, and by the low timbre of his voice, I'd guess through several decades as well. Does he know?

"You're married, Miss . . . ?" Hank indicates my left hand.

I roll my ring back and forth with my thumb. "Please call me Maya. Yes, I am."

"And you love him?"

"Yes, of course." The words fly from my mouth, more defensive than I'd intended.

"So why are you sad?"

"I'm not."

He smiles, his eyes glued to a shadow in the lobby. Simon is there talking to a couple, the woman leaning into the man for comfort. Could they be Jonah's family?

Hank turns to me. "But you are."

I don't know why, but the words I haven't wanted to say out loud suddenly have to be spoken. "It's been a hard year. My grandmother died and I lost my baby the same day. Nothing has been the same since." I tell him everything.

He pats my arm, a distracted attempt at comfort. I chew the inside of my lip, wishing I could walk through the door again and start over. *He doesn't know you, Maya. You shouldn't have dumped that on him.* I scoot to the edge of the bench, ready to push myself up, ready to apologize for that lapse in social graces. Hank rests his hand on my arm, anchoring me to the hot bench.

"You blame yourself?" His voice is low, his eyes seeing far more than I'm comfortable sharing.

I nod.

"Does he blame you?"

I shake my head. Vale never blamed me. At least not openly.

"You shouldn't carry so much guilt, Meera." His voice melts in the heat of the morning.

My skin prickles. *Meera.* No hesitation with that name.

I swallow the lump in my throat. "It's not that easy."

"You have to allow it to be."

"How?"

"By trusting." He smiles at the look on my face. "My wife, Annabelle, went through a similar episode. We lost our first baby. And our second. I almost lost her. When she got pregnant the third time, we were both too afraid to hope. Annabelle was so scared and depressed, and it was all I could do to hang on for both of us. Somehow we were blessed with Diane. Annabelle was so sure she'd be a terrible mother. But I knew better. I knew we were given Diane as a third chance. Because we both deserved another chance.

"I wanted to be a good father, but I wasn't ready the first time. I wasn't ready for Claire. We weren't ready, Meera. Annabelle's miscarriages were my punishment." He squeezes my hand, Meera's hand.

He inhales, exhales. "I'm an old man, Maya. I remembered that time." He winks and gives me a crooked, saggy smile. "I'm far less moony and romantic these days. Losing the baby is not punishment. It happened. Trust in your relationship. Trust me."

Before I have a chance to comment, he scoots a quarter inch away and tucks his hands into his lap. "Oh boy, here comes the warden."

The nurse I'd seen earlier walks toward us.

Hank pushes himself from the bench with a groan.

"Trust, my dear, trust." He taps his heart twice with his index finger then points at me with the same finger. An invisible current tying our hearts together.

"Hank." I want to tell him, I need to tell him.

He shakes his head without turning to look at me. "Enough for today. Good-bye for now, Meera."

Twenty-One

"Ah, shit," I mumble as I ease the car into the driveway.

The vanity is sitting outside, by the door to the kitchen. "Guess the measurements didn't work." Vale and I had measured and remeasured, argued and compromised. I argued, he compromised. The measurements were tight, but it fit. At least on paper it had fit. Guess I better get in there and figure out which one of us had been wrong.

I drop the bag with sandwiches onto the kitchen table and head upstairs, painfully aware of the deafening silence in the house. No hammering. No clang of tiles. No discussion.

I gasp in surprise as I make the turn into the bathroom. Vale and George are sitting on the floor by the door, surveying the room. They look up, perfectly synchronized. They heard me coming.

"What are you guys doing?" I push my

right fist against my chest, trying to slow the pounding. "You scared the crap out of me."

"We're taking a break. Admiring our progress," George drawls, and Vale nods in agreement.

"You're a little jumpy," Vale adds helpfully.

"Progress? The sink is outside." I stab a finger in the direction of the door.

Another finger points into the bathroom, and I follow the line of Vale's hand. My mouth drops as I take in the *progress.* The rectangular tiles I thought we were buying as accents cover two walls. The gentle ripples of the blue-green glass run at an angle, and I have the immediate sensation of standing in a waterfall. A showerhead pokes out of the wall in the far corner, while my claw-foot tub hunkers down in the adjacent corner. With the angle of the tiles, it looks like the waterfall is pooling directly into the tub.

"Wow. This is beautiful. This isn't what we agreed on though. These tiles were supposed to only be accents."

"I know. But this is more you. Us," he corrects himself.

There's more to his comment, more to his decision on what to do with the tiles. I want to ask, but it's not a discussion I want to have with George sitting at my feet. I look for any sign in Vale's face.

He turns back to his handiwork. "I'm glad you like it."

"How did you get it done so fast?" I step into the bathroom to get a better look. Two walls still stand naked; there's a hole where the toilet once was and an open space that obviously won't fit the vanity from the driveway; the shower needs walls and the tub needs a faucet, but the tiles on the finished walls shimmer, beckoning me into a soon-to-be calming oasis.

"The angle was his idea." George hitches a thumb at Vale. "Pain in my ass. Would have taken half the time if we'd just put them up the way they were intended. We'll finish the rest after lunch. You did bring lunch, right?"

"What?" I force my eyes from the tiles to George, who's looking at me like a puppy begging for food. "Oh yes, sandwiches are downstairs."

They're up and past me before I can sidestep out of the way. I give the bathroom another once-over before following.

"You guys do good work. When you work." I smile at them.

"Be nice, if you have any desire to shower

before the end of this year." Vale waves a chip at me.

Does that mean we'll still be here at the end of the year? I bite my lip to keep the words trapped.

"So, Maya," George says around a mouthful of meatball sub. "Vale was telling me you've been talking to the carver of that carousel you're fixing up. He must be ancient."

I picture the old Hank, with the paper-thin skin on his hands that accentuates every vein and the eyes that water slightly when he's thinking about something. The Hank who talks to me about the colors he used on the carousel and how he decided where to place each animal. The Hank who asks who I am every couple of sentences. The Hank who squeezes my hand when he knows I need comfort.

I picture the young Hank, with the strong, wide hands and ready grin, and the eyes that sparkle mischievously, like my brother's. The Hank who talks to Meera about dancing and running in the waves. The Hank who squeezes my hand searching for comfort.

I feel the electric pulse of anticipation and focus on the two men sitting at the table with me. "He's amazing," I answer, biting into my sandwich. The fragmented conversation with both Hanks tumbles in my brain.

Before either of them can ask for more on Hank, I wrap the rest of my sandwich and stand. "Time to get busy." I need to be with the horse, to sort through what I learned or didn't learn, to decide what to do with the secrets spinning in my head. Do I give them free rein to gallop into the open? Am I ready to let go?

I walk across the yard and unlock the door to my studio. It jolts awake under the lights. I pick up the tools I'll need to scrape off the rest of the old paint and stand face-to-face with the wooden carousel horse.

"No talking today. We have work to do."

The paper to my left ruffles then settles back into place. I glance up, surprised that the light has shifted from noon to evening.

"Hey." My brother's deep voice rattles the quiet of the studio.

"Hey back." I wait for him to come in. "What brings you here?"

"Peace offering." He hands me a cold bottle of beer, and I notice the one in his other hand is half empty. He catches my look. "I started with your hubby."

"Is he coming?" I look behind my brother to the still-open door.

"No. He said something about brother-sister time."

I give him a get-real gaze.

"Yeah, well, yesterday didn't go as planned, and Vale said you seemed even more agitated after your visit with the old man this morning."

"Oh he did, did he?" I'm not angry and yet I'm something, something I can't name. A feeling that's taken root so deep inside me, I wonder if I'll ever be able to extract it.

Thomas settled into the chair by my worktable and studies the horse over the lip of the bottle. "So, what's the deal?"

"What deal?"

"The horse. The old man. Your obsession."

"I'm not obsessed. I'm focused."

"That you are."

"What's that supposed to mean?"

Thomas holds up his hands. "I didn't come to fight. Really. I'm worried about you. We all are."

I deflate into the chair next to my brother. I've become *that* person, the one person in every family who people tiptoe around, whisper about, watch with concern.

"I'm fine." The belligerent pout in my voice proves I'm not.

"Wanna talk? I'm a good listener."

Thomas was never a good listener. The few times I tried to confide in him as a kid were disastrous. He'd gotten me grounded twice, and Sarah Kline, my sixth-grade friend stopped talking to me after Thomas ratted us out about going to the Dollar Store with a bunch of friends instead of staying at the school for the lame Valentine's Day Dance. That's when I stopped confiding in my brother. I look into his eyes, Hank's eyes, and calculate my options.

"What if I tell you Hank is Mom's biological father?" I level a how-about-that challenge.

He doesn't take the bait. "Have you been inhaling too many fumes?" He scans the room for evidence.

"I'm serious."

"You're nuts."

"I should have known you'd take her side."

Thomas sighs dramatically and plunks the beer bottle onto the worktable. "I'm not taking *her* side. I just think you're barking up the wrong infidelity tree."

"I'm not."

"Based on what, the inscription? A letter? Neither of those are proof of anything. And seriously, Maya, those were different times. That didn't happen back then." The pleat at the corner of his right eye counters the confidence in his tone.

"You mean getting pregnant out of wedlock? Like Mom did?"

A matching pleat gathers at the corner of his other eye, but he doesn't jump to correct me.

"Doesn't matter." I wave the jab away. "Hank told me."

Thomas stares, mouth slack. "I was wrong. You're not nuts. You're off your freaking rocking horse."

"That's not fair." Thirty-some years of being dismissed by my brother takes over.

"You're pouting." He does his big-brother eye roll.

"He's our grandfather, Thomas. I know it. I feel it. Here." I dig my fist into my stomach.

"That's heartburn."

"You're just like Mom," I snap, resorting to my childhood comeback.

"Lame."

We stare at each other in silent sibling stubbornness.

"Maya, you can't bring her back. And making Hank your new grandfather doesn't solve any of this. It's time to let go."

"I'm not trying to bring her back." I swallow and ignore the pursed all-knowing look on my brother's face.

Unlike during those childhood squabbles, Thomas doesn't charge into the arena for a fight. This time he allows a slow, thoughtful nod.

"Come visit him with me. Please? You'll see. He's amazing."

Thomas shakes his head. "I'm sure he is. But I'm not going to visit some old man you're fixated on. I'm glad you found your carousel builder and that he's helping you finish your restoration. You and Grandma always loved this thing, and I can only guess how special it is to talk to him. Especially since he obviously knew Grandma as well. I guess it's almost like having her back in some way."

I open my mouth to protest, but Thomas raises his hand to stop me.

"He has Alzheimer's, Maya. His memory isn't reliable. I'm not saying you shouldn't believe everything he says, but please don't upturn our whole world because of something you want to believe."

Want to believe? I don't *want* to believe. I do believe. Because it's true. I push down the bubble of doubt.

"It's the truth."

"Maybe. Maybe not. Why does it matter?"

All the reasons it matter, the reasons I've

been burning to find out more, fizzle.

"Because it's the truth," I say with far less conviction.

Thomas's eyes are on the horse when he answers. "The truth isn't always what you're looking for. Sometimes secrets are secrets for a reason. Unraveling them can destroy more than it solves."

He stands, kisses me on the cheek, and leaves. Whatever smart comeback and argument I could have unleashed are left rattling their cages inside my brain. And the most frustrating part is that I'm not sure he's wrong.

Twenty-Two

Secrets. For three years, I've been unraveling the secrets of the merry-go-round. For a year, I've been stewing over the secrets that led to the deaths of my grandmother and my baby. And for the last month, I've been torturing myself with the secrets of my family. All released by this one horse. The one horse who held so many great memories.

He's stripped to the original paint layer, and most of his dings and breaks have been repaired. Standing in the middle of my studio, he's nothing more than a wood creation. The magic, the memories, no longer transform him into the fantastical beast he was.

Yesterday, I finished rebuilding his tail. Today, I start painting. New layers of the old designs. A fresh start for new secrets.

The old ones will stay with me. And Hank.

There's a knock on the door behind me.

"I brought food."

My stomach grumbles a loud thank-you. "I wasn't expecting you home until late. Didn't you say you had a late meeting?"

"Yeah, but I snuck out for lunch." Vale sets the paper bag on the table and pulls out two burritos wrapped in aluminum foil. I'd gotten addicted to Jose's when I was pregnant. A wave of nausea rolls through my stomach. The fact that Vale picked this after over a year of not going there seems like a sign. A blinking red warning sign. *It's a burrito, Maya.*

He pulls the chairs to the table then sits in one. He unwraps his burrito and takes a big bite, his eyes on the carousel horse. "How long do you think it'll take to repaint him?"

I sit but don't reach for my food. "A week. Maybe two."

Vale's eyes dart to the calendar on the wall. Five weeks to the grand reopening ceremony. A big red square marks the three-week deadline for this guy to be reinstalled on the merry-go-round. I'd given myself more time with him than with the other animals. I'd wanted as much time with my memories as I could squeeze in.

What the calendar doesn't show is the looming deadline to decide on Vale's job offer. While I'd hoped the bathroom was a sign he'd made up his mind not to go, it's a conversation I've avoided like prune juice.

"Can you take a couple of days off?"

My eyes instinctively go to the calendar, but I know the answer. "I can't."

"Please, Maya. It's important." He inhales, and I can almost hear him count out the stress before continuing. "I have to answer Ed."

My insides liquefy. He's moving up the deadline. "It hasn't been two weeks yet."

"I know." He puts the burrito down and swipes at a glob of sour cream and guacamole that's oozing over the edge. "I want you to come to Seattle with me."

"Seattle? Me?"

"Yes you. You're the only wife I have." His attempt at levity falls with the glob of guacamole.

"I'm not going."

He blinks, fast, as though recovering from a slap. A verbal slap can hurt far more than a physical one.

"I'm not talking about a move. Yet. A visit to check out the city. See what you — we — think of it."

"Why now? You know I'm on a hard deadline. This project is important."

"We're important, too."

We are. But . . .

But I can't leave. If I'm not here, how can I keep their memories alive?

"Just a visit, Maya."

I want to scream at him to leave me alone, to not push me. And I want to fling myself at him and tell him I'll follow him anywhere.

I shake the voices out of my head. "I can't go."

Our eyes meet, and for the first time, I see a hardness in Vale. The sadness, hope, and love that tempered my guilt this last year are gone. I broke the final piece holding us together.

He stiffens, stands. "I'm leaving on Sunday."

"Vale," my voice cracks.

"It's one week. I have to decide what's best for me. And you need to decide what's best for you." The door shuts behind him. I wince at the gentle click of the latch. A slammed door would have meant passion. A quiet click screams finality.

My burrito remains untouched. Another glob of sour cream oozes from his. I grab the trash can in time to throw up in it.

Twelve. Twelve people have walked out of Tower Oaks in the twenty-two minutes I've been sitting here. Twenty-three minutes. Thirteen people.

I wasn't able to refocus on work after Vale left. I tried. I put in my favorite Chris Botti CD. But neither Chris nor the carousel horse was holding my attention.

I should have gone after him. I didn't. Guilt kept me away. How has that become my standard excuse?

Twenty-four minutes. Fifteen people.

I wipe a drop of sweat from my cheek before it can dive-bomb my leg. If I'd kept the car running, I wouldn't have been marinating in this heat.

Vale had gone back into the house. Obviously, because his work clothes were on the bed. I assumed he went for a run. He hadn't left a note. I sent a text asking if he needed the car and almost jumped out of my shorts when his phone buzzed from under the pile of clothes on the bed. He never goes anywhere without his phone.

I left a note. Two actually. Seeing Hank had felt urgent, but now that I'm here, I can't get out of the car.

A man in a blue suit gets out of a blue SUV. He looks at me, steps onto the sidewalk, and looks down at the front of my car. Probably memorizing the license plate in case there's an incident and he's called as a witness.

An incident? Witness? Really, Maya? Vale's

right, you do need to get out more.

I make a show of gathering my belongings and get out of the car. I follow him in, aware that he's not the only one who paid attention to my loitering.

Barbie waves a paper cup in my direction as I enter. I wave back. The receptionist waves cheerfully as I march past. I wave, less enthusiastically. Even Nurse Julie smiles at me as we pass in the hall. I force a smile. I've stepped into the twilight zone.

I hear Simon's laugh, strong and sure, then Hank's wobbly laugh joins in, along with a flirty female giggle. There's a collection of people standing around the nurse's station, and a half-eaten cake on the counter.

Hank looks up and motions me over. My heartbeat picks up in anticipation while my feet slow. Which one of me will he welcome to their party?

Hank waves me forward. "Come, come. We're celebrating the doc's birthday. Have some cake." He holds out a paper plate with a square hunk of cake precariously tilting on it.

I overrule my feet and shuffle forward. Hank beams at the nurse perched on the Formica desk on the other side of the counter. As I come closer, I see Simon. He's leaning back in a chair, feet propped on the edge of the desk, inches away from the nurse's knee. There isn't much distance separating them.

"Here," Hank says, thrusting the plate at me. "Miss, umm . . . ?"

"Maya," Simon's tenor fills in before I have a chance.

Hank blinks three times in quick succession, as if trying to trap the word into memory.

"Maya Brice, I'm restoring your carousel," I add, taking the plate dancing in front of my face. I glance at the odd shape left on the counter, the cake cut and eaten so that all that's left is *Hap Bir Do S.*

How could I have forgotten it was his birthday?

"Happy birthday." Does he know I forgot? Would he have expected me to remember? Of course I should have remembered.

Since his birthday fell during the summer, we were always together at the beach. For his fifteenth birthday, his parents had planned a bonfire on the beach. We'd roasted hot dogs, made s'mores, and ran into the cold night waves.

I flush with the memory of his eighteenth birthday. Our eyes meet, and I wonder if he's remembering the same. His parents had taken us for a nice dinner, then Simon and I had gone for a drive in his brand-new black Jeep, a gift from his parents. My gift to him had been hesitantly unwrapped then devoured on a secluded beach. It had been the first time for both of us.

"Eat," Hank commands. "And I don't want to hear about you being on a diet. Girls these days are always on a diet. It's silly. Men appreciate women with curves. Don't they, Doc?"

The nurse pfuts and waves the comment away, then nudges Simon's thigh with the toe of her sneaker. He winks, and I fumble to keep my cake from plummeting to the shiny tile floor.

"So, Miss, umm, what did you say your name was?"

"Maya."

"Brice."

Simon and I answer at the same time. A shiver rattles up my spine.

Hank looks at me with concern. "You're cold? Come, my room is warmer." He grasps my upper arm and pulls me gently across the hall.

The back of my neck prickles as we walk into Hank's room. I know Simon is watching.

"So, Miss, umm . . ."

"Brice."

We settle into the chairs and I silently curse that I'm once again in the chair with my back to the door. Is Simon still watching us?

"Yes. Miss Brice. What brings you to me today? More questions about the carousel? You're obviously not here just for the cake." He chuckles, and with a pleased smirk, commands, "Eat."

I take two minibites, then set the plate on the table next to me.

Hank shakes his head. "Ahh, girls these days. When I was your age we appreciated women with substance." He looks to the dresser on the other side of the room and the cluster of framed photos.

"You must have had quite a few girls trying to catch your attention."

"Not that many." He looks at me, and I'm pulled into a sudden memory that trembles behind his rheumy eyes.

I stand and walk to the dresser. I pick up a picture of a young Hank with his wife. "Tell me about her."

"My Annabelle. She was my everything. She came into my life at a time when I needed positivity. And there she was. It started as a summer infatuation. She was here with her sister and brother-in-law. At the end of their vacation, I couldn't bear the idea of losing her. She had such a fresh outlook and a spirit that made everything feel possible. I had nothing left here. The carousel was done and running, and I was back to floundering as a carpenter. I couldn't get another carousel gig. There were too many of us and not enough need for the hand-carved ones. The modern amusement parks wanted fiberglass animals or mass-produced ones.

"So I followed Annabelle to Kansas City where her family was from."

I spin to look at him. "You lived in Kansas City."

"Yes," he answers, taken aback at the abrupt interruption of his story.

"When?" Did Grandma know he'd moved to Kansas City? Did she know when he moved back, or did she think he was still there when she came to visit me?

"From August 1954 until March 2007."

I stare. I'm not sure if I'm more astonished at the additional link between us or the fact that this man, who can barely remember who I am from visit to visit, can remember dates so clearly. Then again, by now I've come to expect the unexpected with Hank's memories.

He mistakes the look of surprise. "Not the

place you'd expect a beach boy to end up, is it?"

"No." I collect my thoughts. "I lived there, too. Not at the same time obviously, but I lived there, too." My voice fades like the echo of my thought.

"What about her?" I pick up a recent picture of Hank and my grandmother. They're at the beach, sitting side-by-side in the chairs Grandma schlepped every time we went to the beach. A red-and-blue-striped umbrella casts a dark circle. They're both looking at whoever took the photo, smiling, relaxed.

He looks from me to the photo and back to me. *Now would be the time to tell him, Maya.*

Voices in the hallway chase away the words threatening to explode from my mouth.

"There was cake and we weren't invited?"

"You don't need cake. You need rice cakes."

"Oh, stuff your rice cakes. Might as well eat cardboard."

"Wouldn't hurt your waistline to gnaw on that either."

"Stop nagging me, woman. You're not my wife."

"And thank god for that."

"Hank, you old goat, get out of your

room. We need a fourth player for Rummikub."

Hank looks up, and I swivel to see three bodies trying to cram through the door at the same time.

"Ouch. What was that for?" An old man with wild, bushy gray hair frowns and rubs his side.

"You're standing on my foot." The pixie grandma standing next to him pushes his shoulder.

"Will you two stop fighting for one minute? Geez," says a voice from behind them. I recognize the voice as the rice-cake hater. "Let me through." Hands part the two bickering bodies and a bald head pokes through, followed by a surprisingly square body.

As though busted by parents, Hank straightens his sweater then runs a hand over his thinning hair.

"Hi, Joe," Hank says to the square holding up the bald orb.

"Well, well. And who do we have here?" Joe grins at me. "Shame on you, Hank, for hogging the beautiful ladies. At least sit in the lobby so we can all enjoy, instead of having to just look at the prunes." He shoots a look at the door where the pixie is still slapping at the significantly taller man next to her.

"You could use a few more prunes in your life. Might help that problem you have," she says, gesturing wildly at Joe.

Hank stands and shuffles to where I'm standing. I replace the picture frame, suddenly shy under the scrutiny of the three musketeers.

"Miss, umm . . ." Hank blinks three times quickly, then shakes his head and takes a different approach. "This is Joe, and those two are Dottie and Nick."

Joe sweeps his right hand to his middle and bends in a grand bow. "A pleasure to meet you."

"I'm Maya Brice." I rub my lower lip to hide the smile. "Nice to meet you, too."

Dottie pushes past Nick and shuffles over to stand in front of us. She slaps Joe on the back. "Quit posturing, you old fart. No one is impressed. Hi." She flashes a smile at me and sticks out a child-sized hand that has a surprisingly strong grip.

"Hi." I can't take my eyes off her smile. Are those her real teeth?

"We didn't know you had company, Hank. Sorry for interrupting," she says through the perfectly formed teeth. Though she's speaking to Hank, her eyes are trained on my face. She doesn't look sorry at all. "Hold the prune juice — I know you."

I feel my mouth stretching, the easy smile from earlier becoming tight. Was she one of Grandma's friends?

"Yes, yes." She slaps at my arm playfully. "You used to come into my shop with your mom. Tall, elegant woman. She was one of my best customers." Dottie beams at me then turns to each man in turn with an I-knew-it nod. "Your mom had a nose for the quality jewelry and impeccable taste picking gifts for people. Then again, I had impeccable taste for ordering those things in the first place."

Her store? I slap a few brain cells into motion trying to find the hidden memory of a feisty pixie in a store.

"Dee's." My voice is a mixture of question, surprise, and pleasure. "Dee's was your shop?"

Dottie grows a full quarter inch taller at being recognized. "Ah, if only my memory was as sound as yours. I stink at names." She taps her temple with an elegantly manicured finger.

"That's not the only thing you stink at," mumbles Nick.

Dottie ignores him. "How is your mom? Remind me of her name?"

"Claire," I mumble, chancing a look at Hank for a flash of recognition. He's busying himself with the pocket of his slacks. "She's fine. Good."

Dottie continues to beam at me. "I remember you had a fascination with an antique rocking horse I kept in the store. Your mom would get so upset when you insisted on riding it."

I remember that rocking horse. It had a leather saddle and bridle and real horsehair mane and tail. The first time I saw it, the real hair freaked me out. Then it fascinated me, and I couldn't stop brushing it with my little kid fingers. "Mom and I got into a huge fight once over that rocking horse."

"Oh, I remember. You made such a scene that two customers came to ask what was happening."

"I was grounded for a week after that. To a seven-year-old, a week is a lifetime."

"I remember you stayed far away from that horse on subsequent visits."

"Yeah, Mom wasn't one to cross." I shift my weight and my gaze. She still isn't.

"Way to go, Dot, you made the girl uncomfortable," Joe says, shaking his head at her.

"I certainly didn't mean to. My goodness." She looks offended and worried.

"It's not a big deal. It was a long time ago." I attempt to defuse the bickering.

Dottie's expression softens at being released from her mistake. She must be about the same age as my grandmother. As Grandma would have been, I correct myself. But while Grandma had embraced her grandma-ishness, as she called aging, Dottie is clearly clinging to youth. Her auburn hair is cut in a tight bob, the edges skimming the ridge of her jaw. There's not one gray hair on her head. A silk scarf, expertly knotted and positioned on her right collarbone, matches her cashmere sweater. No wonder my mom was so devoted to Dee's all these years; the owner is a poster girl for fashion.

"Okay, okay, come on, leave the kids alone," Nick says with a wink. "We'll find another fourth."

Hank shuffles uncomfortably next to me.

"I really should be going," I offer, although the idea of going home is not appealing and, for once, neither is going back to the studio.

"Are you sure?" Hank asks.

"Of course she's sure." Dottie pats my arm. "Pretty young girl has other evening plans than hanging with geezers."

Hank looks from me to her. My heart squeezes at the confusion on his face.

"It's fine, Hank. I'll be back in a couple of

days. I need to get more work done on our carousel horse, anyway." I kiss his cheek, say my good-byes, and head out of the room.

Behind, I hear Dottie's less-than-discreet whisper, "What does she mean 'our carousel horse'?"

Two male voices drown out the third. The only thing I can make out is the escalating argument over who's more constipated. It's not just kids who bicker over everything.

Twenty-Three

I'd already been asleep last night when Vale came to bed. He'd crawled under the blankets, the movement so gentle I'd barely registered it. I woke around three A.M. and felt him next to me, but the gap between us felt too wide to cross. And he'd left for work before I woke up this morning. At least he'd left a note. *Need more sticky notes.*

Sam kicks me under the table. "Are you going to order or just keep reading the menu for the zillionth time?"

I glare at her then order two eggs, scrambled like my life, with whole-wheat toast and a side of bacon. Because every emotional crisis needs bacon. "And an Oreo milkshake," I call after the waitress, who gives me a thumbs-up.

"Milkshake? For breakfast?" Bree looks scandalized.

"It has milk in it."

"And a lot of sugar." She purses her lips

in disapproval.

I make a mental note to take her kids out for breakfast one morning and let them order milkshakes.

Sam assesses me. "You look like crap."

"So glad you're my best friend."

"She's not wrong," Bree adds. "Although I wouldn't have said it quite like that."

"Did you two kidnap me from my studio to insult me?" I'd tried putting them off but they wouldn't take no as my final answer.

"Nope." They answer in tandem.

This will not be good.

I ask about Bree's kids, about Sam's store, hoping to deflect whatever they have planned. I don't believe for a minute that this will work in the long run, but they play along, asking about Hank and the carousel horse. We talk around our food and, just as I'm relaxing into the discussion, Bree and Sam exchange a look.

"What?" My skin tingles with the shift of tension.

Bree takes control. "Vale came by last night. He was pretty upset."

I wish the booth would swallow me and spit me out in the middle of the ocean. It doesn't, of course. I'm not that lucky. I'm not lucky enough to sidetrack either of the two terriers sitting across from me, either.

I'm actually surprised Sam didn't sit next to me to block me in. As though sensing my itch to flee, she puts her foot on the vinyl seat next to me, creating a barrier.

"You need to go with him," Bree continues, undeterred.

"I can't. I have a deadline."

"He said you told him you won't go. That's different."

"That's not what I meant."

"But it's what you said?"

"I guess. I don't remember the exact words. But it's not what I meant. I was upset and surprised and upset."

"That's a lot of upset," Sam quips. Bree and I both stare at her.

"I can't just pick up and go. The horse isn't done, and a lot of people are counting on me. Why is my career less important? Would you guys be having this conversation with him if the situation were reversed?"

"But it's not, and we're worried about you, so we're asking."

I should feel relief that I have friends who care, and I do, but the care is overwhelming and, at the moment, unwelcome.

"It's been a year, Maya. Vale has been patient and supportive. You need to pull yourself together or you will lose him. This job offer and trip to Seattle couldn't be any easier to interpret." Bree folds her napkin into a perfect triangle, her two-carat solitaire and diamond-wedding band glisten under the bright overhead lights. She got the ring and her law degree the same day. She's put the ring to good use while the law degree hasn't left the box in their basement.

Bree is black-and-white. And marriage is white. Anything to keep your marriage is right. She fusses with her egg-white omelet and sips her low-fat latte.

Would she be giving me the same lecture if she'd lost a baby? If she'd killed that baby? If she'd betrayed the faith her husband put in her to protect their unborn child?

I have nothing to say. Anything I bring up will expose me, and that's not something I can do.

Sam squeezes my forearms. Maybe she knows. Maybe they all know. Maybe that's why they all tiptoe around me. But whatever anyone thinks they know, they can't be sure unless I let it out. And I won't.

"He doesn't want to go, not really," Bree pushes. "But you keep forcing him away."

And pushes.

"You have to do something before it's too late."

And pushes.

"You shut him out. You shut us out. You can't keep doing this, Maya." Her mouth moves. I feel like I'm underwater. *Whawhawha.* She keeps talking or moving her mouth. Breathe, Bree.

No, I'm the one who needs to breathe.

"Hey." Sam's sitting next to me, her arm around my shoulders. "Okay, Bree, she's got the point."

"I'm not going to Seattle and you're not going to browbeat me into it." I pull away from Sam.

"But Maya —" Bree starts.

"Enough." Sam growls.

"No, Bree." I cut her off at the same time. "You don't get to lecture me about moving or putting my marriage first or anything else. I don't live your charmed life. Every day I wake up hoping this is just some nightmare."

I pull a twenty-dollar bill from my wallet and let it fall to the table. Without looking at either one of them, I slip out of the booth and leave the restaurant. I'm sure everyone in my path hears the pounding of my heart, the roaring of my pulse. I bump into a man entering the restaurant but don't stop to apologize.

I walk. I don't know where I'm going. I just walk. Past stores with "open" signs, most still empty except for the workers prepping for the day. Past restaurants, most still closed.

The beach is already crowded. For once, though, I don't step down to the sand, the pull of the waves not strong enough to overpower the emotional tug of the carousel.

The sounds of hammering, talking, and clanging of metal hang over the still merry-go-round like a cloud. It's a reminder that my portion of the restoration work is just that — a portion.

I open the gate and enter. The chaos inside the fence welcomes me, soothes me.

"Look busy, boys, the boss is here." Jerome's baritone cuts through the shriek of power tools.

"Funny." I let him pull me into a hug and allow the tension to be squeezed out of my body.

Jerome has been a family friend for more years than I have fingers and toes to count. His father and my grandfather were poker buddies, even though neither actually played poker. They met once a week and decided "poker buddies" sounded more manly than "shell-finding buddies." We'd gotten rid of jars and jars of shells after Grandpa died.

Jerome had taken over his father's contractor business and had done numerous jobs for Vale and his company. When I was putting together the carousel-restoration proposal, having Jerome on the team was the easiest of choices.

I break away from the hug and survey the merry-go-round. All of the floorboards have been replaced or repaired, buffed and polished to a shiny old-world look. The animals have been reunited and all have gleaming metal poles anchoring them to their spot. The drum panels surrounding the machinery and gears are in place.

I'd repainted the landscape images on the drum panels early in the restoration process. One panel, however, remains dulled with age and elements, a decision I'd fought for in the proposal. One drum panel, one ceiling pane, and one animal would be kept as close to original as we could. I'd felt it was important to maintain a glimpse into the historic charm and romance that these merry-go-rounds once embodied.

"Glad you stopped by." He transforms into professional Jerome. "I wanted to talk to you about a problem with one of the ceiling panels."

I follow him to where a panel rests against a wood-construction horse. "This thing has been giving me fits. When we went to reinstall it, this happened." He points at a decorative swirl running down the panel, about five inches from the edge.

I kneel to get a better look. There's a hairline crack that to the naked eye is part of the design. Then again, considering this will be above everyone's head, it won't even be visible to the naked eye.

But Jerome is a perfectionist, which is why I wanted him on my team.

I run my finger the length of the crack. "We should be able to fix it with cellulose filler. If we're careful with the application, we can get away with touching up a couple of places instead of redoing the entire panel. There isn't enough time for that."

"I want to show off the rest of the work." He takes me on a tour of machinery and gears, the heart of the carousel. Without them, the fancy outside panels and the carefully carved animals are nothing more than landscape ornaments.

But when the merry-go-round begins to spin and the music plays, the magic takes over.

I picture a young Hank and my grandmother riding on the same animals I rode with Simon and then Vale. I wonder what it was like for Hank to share the carousel with Annabelle, for Grandma to ride with Grandpa. Did it hold the same magic?

No — at least not for me. With Simon, the merry-go-round sprinkled our dreams with the hope of young love, and it listened to our secrets. With Vale, the carousel slowed from the frenzied excitement of wishes to the steady circling of possibilities. With Vale by my side, the carousel didn't feel like it spun as fast and the music didn't sound as loud. It felt steadier and more secure.

I turn, wide-eyed, startling Jerome with the sudden movement. "Jerome, I need to go. Thank you for everything." I reach up on my tiptoes and kiss his cheek. "You're brilliant, by the way."

"Of course I'm brilliant. But what did I do? Tell me so I can do it again for another kiss." He grins.

I give him another kiss, wave at the rest of the team, and tap on my phone as I leave the bubble of my magic carousel.

"Hey," Vale answers on the third ring. "Good timing. In ten minutes you would have gotten my voicemail."

"I think my luck is, indeed, changing. Can you be home by seven tonight?"

"Sure." He sounds skeptical but intrigued.

"Perfect. I'll see you then."

"Wanna clue a guy in?"

"Nope. You'll find out at seven."

"Okay," he draws the word out, but I can hear the smile.

The magic of the merry-go-round. Each animal has its own beauty, its own secrets. But it's when they're all together that the magic happens.

I've been off-balance because I separated myself from others. Like my carousel animals, I really do need my tribe.

Twenty-Four

I close my eyes and listen for the sounds of the house. The sighing of the air-conditioning as it clicks on. The grinding of ice cubes releasing into the tray in the freezer. The jackhammering of a woodpecker on the woodshed adjacent to the laundry room.

I set the grocery bags on the counter. Under the fluorescent flicker from above, the old kitchen looks sad. Last year we replaced the appliances, but the rest of the kitchen is hopelessly out of date. The grayish linoleum tiles are bubbling in a couple of spots. The once-shiny white cabinets are a dull, bleached, sandy color. And the greenish-gray Formica counter is begging to be ripped to shreds.

I grab my phone and type, *"Kitchen redo next?,"* then hold my breath waiting for an answer. He's leaving in a couple of days for his "visit" to Seattle.

There's no guarantee he'll be back. And if he doesn't return, will I stay here?

Before I can lower the phone, Vale responds. *"Back away from the hammer! We still need the sink to 'shower' in,"* comes Vale's response.

Staying or not, he has a point. Maybe I can nudge the decision toward staying. *"Hurry home. Fixing dinner."*

"Don't burn the house down. Bathroom is almost done."

Tonight will be the fresh start we need. Tonight I'm sprinkling carousel magic on us and giving myself permission to face forward.

I organize the ingredients on the counter and check the recipe. Restoring ancient artifacts I can do. Matching paint for historic carousel animals, I'm on it. Fixing beef stroganoff, however . . . I'm out of my element.

When it looks like the food is safely simmering, I pour a glass of wine and move to the front porch. A breeze kicked in while I had my head stuffed in a cookbook. The salty wind teases my curls, and I relax into a rocking chair.

I'm halfway through my glass when Vale climbs the steps to the front porch.

"Hi." He eases the screen door closed

behind him but stays by the door. He takes a deep breath. "Is that beef stroganoff?"

"Yup." I grin. "And no appliances were harmed in the process."

"I'm impressed." He covers the few strides across the porch and sits in the chair next to me.

"It smells wonderful. I'm starving."

"Sit tight. I'll get you a drink first." I stand and put a hand on his shoulder to keep him from moving.

He covers my hand with his and pulls it gently to his lips. "Can dinner wait?"

"Yes." I extract my hand then lean down and kiss him on the lips. "But first we need to talk."

Vale groans in mock exasperation. "Withholding dinner and sex? Wicked woman. If this is about the bathroom, I swear it's almost done." He traces an *X* over his heart.

"It's not about the bathroom."

"Oh phew. So?"

"Wine first." A few minutes later, I'm back with the bottle and a second glass.

We clink glasses then sip from our wine. The neighbor across the street pulls into his driveway. The car idles while the song finishes.

Vale laughs. "At least he has okay taste in music."

We default to small talk. The neighbor's music, the other neighbor's yappy dog, how much longer the construction on the house at the end of the street will mostly take. Vale tells me about his day and asks about mine. Normal couple talk. The kind of couple talk we haven't engaged in lately.

Come on, Maya, it's time to bring up the complicated stuff. Magic carousel dust. Magic carousel dust.

"I've been thinking about Seattle." Vale turns to look at me with a hopeful lift of his eyebrows. "But," I push forward before the hopefulness spreads and I lose my nerve. "I can't go right now. The reopening is only a few weeks away, and I'm committed to this job. For many reasons."

He nods.

This isn't so hard. I can do this. "I can't promise that I'll want to move later, but I am willing to discuss it. After the carousel is done."

Another nod, and I can almost hear him flipping through the mental index cards of appropriate responses. "I'm good with that. I wasn't asking you to abandon the project. You know that, right?"

"I do. But a trip right now doesn't fit with the schedule."

"I respect that."

I wait for him to offer to postpone his trip.

"I'm still going." He swirls the wine, watching the red liquid wave up then down the sides of the glass.

The answer knocks the wind from my lungs. "Why?" I manage.

"Because I still believe it's the right thing to do. The time apart will be good for sorting through what we want. I want that job to be a new beginning for us."

"You don't think we can have a new beginning here?" My heart pounds louder than the neighbor's music.

He takes a long swallow. "I don't know."

I close my eyes and picture the merry-go-round. "I stopped by the carousel site this morning. I've been so intent on the individual pieces that I haven't thought about how it all fits together. In my mind, each animal, each component was its own unique entity. When I saw the rest of the carousel today, almost complete except for one ceiling panel and one horse, it suddenly hit me — the magic is in the whole."

I wipe at tears traversing the outline of my cheeks. "I don't know how we . . . I . . . let this get so far out of hand. I didn't mean it to. I just . . . I don't know."

The words, the emotion, pool at my feet, and I feel drained and relieved.

Vale's voice is low with emotion when he finally speaks. "It's been a challenging year."

I wait for him to continue, to tell me we'll be okay, that we'll get through this. He doesn't. He pours himself another glass of wine and sips, eyes on the shadows passing on the street.

When did it get dark? I look at my watch. When did it become so late?

"I didn't realize how late it is. The food is probably ruined." I wipe away the last of the tears and stand.

Vale grabs my hand as I walk past, jolting me to a stop. "Maya . . ."

He's interrupted by a phone ringing inside the house.

"That's mine." I tense. A call at this hour can't be good news. He releases my hand and a frustrated sigh.

The phone is on the kitchen table, next to my keys and the cookbook I'd followed so carefully. I pick up the phone and frown at the unfamiliar number. Then scowl at the brown blob in the pot on the stove. *Way to fix a romantic dinner, Maya.*

"Hello?" I steel myself for whatever is coming.

"It's Simon. Hank had a stroke." No hello. No I'm sorry to call so late. No warning.

My knees shimmy and I flop onto the

nearest chair. “Is he . . . ?”

“He’s alive. It appears to have been a mild one, but we won’t know the full extent until we run more tests. I should have a better idea tomorrow. His daughter is making arrangements to come. She said it was okay to call you. He’ll need the support until she can get here.”

Breathe, Maya.

“Will I be able to see him tomorrow?” I can feel Vale standing in the door, watching. I squeeze my eyes, shutting him out.

“He’s in the hospital.” Not exactly a yes, but it’s not a no.

It’s my turn to say something.

“Okay. Simon?” My brain races with what else to say. “Thanks for letting me know.” The phone goes dark as Simon hangs up. No good-bye, no I’ll see you tomorrow.

“Simon?” Vale’s voice is rough, sandpapered by hurt.

“Hank had a stroke. He was calling to tell me.”

“Why is he calling you?”

“Because Hank doesn’t have family here.” Except he does. Me.

Vale’s mouth tightens, eyes narrow, his expression warring between understanding and anger. “Why was he calling you, though? And why does he have your cell phone number?"

"Why is this an issue?" A warning bell in the back of my mind screams for me to shut up, back up, stop.

"If my ex was suddenly an integral part of my days, wouldn't it be an issue for you? And if she was calling me at all hours, you'd be upset." He crosses his arms, his presence filling the doorway, sturdier than any solid structure.

"I wouldn't be upset. I trust you." I try for self-assured, but neither of us is impressed. Trust, once shaken, is harder to grasp. And without it for stability, every slight shift feels like it could be the end.

He shifts his weight, his eyes blasting through the layers of guilt and secrets I've built around myself.

"No, you don't. If you did, you wouldn't have shut me out. You wouldn't be hiding behind whatever wall you've erected around yourself. Because, yes, I know there's something. But you know what's worse than you not trusting me? You don't trust yourself anymore. And that is impossible to recover from."

TWENTY-FIVE

Neither of us slept much last night. The stroganoff had ended up in the trash, untouched. The romantic evening was shattered.

My phone rattles on the breakfast table, the unread text jittery for attention.

"Aren't you going to respond?"

For the last thirty minutes, Vale and I have been in a silent truce over coffee. Rehashing last night or discussing plans for the day are equally precarious topics.

My fingers graze the edge of my phone. We both know who's texting. He's sent five messages already this morning.

I'd looked at the first, but at the glare from Vale, set the phone down without answering. Now every incoming message is a silent standoff.

"Can we talk about last night?" I turn the phone upside down so the temptation is less. The phone responds by vibrating again with another incoming text.

"No. Not now."

"Yes now."

"No, Maya. Not when there's a strong probability one or both of us will say something we can't take back."

He gulps the last of his coffee, sets the mug in the sink, and turns the faucet on. The water gushes into the metal sink, loud and intrusive but he's made his point.

Finally, he turns the water off, leaving only the annoying clock to torture my nerves.

"George will be here soon. He's helping me finish the bathroom today. I'm leaving for Seattle in the morning and want it done before I go."

Last night was supposed to have been the first step to bridging the divide between us. I didn't want him going to Seattle with a giant cloud hanging over our marriage. Not that one night would wipe it away, but at least it could turn it from dark gray to a lighter gray. Instead, he'll be leaving holding the tail end of a tornado.

"Round trip or one way?" The question is barely audible.

He leans against the counter, arms bent and ready to push off.

"Still round trip."

I bite my lip to balance the sting behind

my eyes.

Another text rattles my phone.

"Just answer it already. It's about Hank, right?"

It feels like a test, one I'm doomed to fail.

It only takes nineteen minutes to drive to the hospital. Another twenty to get out of the car. There's an ambulance backed into the emergency area, the back doors closed, occupant already deposited inside. Is it the same ambulance that brought my grandma here? The one that brought Hank?

The paramedics get into the cab, and I squint into the awkward lighting to get a better look. Are they the ones who brought me here? I remember crazy details about that day — the smell of the paint, the way the paintbrush felt in my hand, the rough feel of the stepstool under my bare feet, the smell of coffee on the doctor's breath, the sting of the IV. There are so many details I've pushed into the darkest part of my subconscious — had I still been in the nursery when Vale came home, was it him who called the ambulance, who told me about the emergency C-section and losing the baby?

"Stop it." I force my body out of the car, across the parking lot, and through the main doors. A volunteer at the information desk directs me to the third floor. A nurse on the third floor points me to room 325.

He looks so small in the hospital bed. I watch from the hallway as a nurse checks his temperature and blood pressure, adjusts his oxygen line and IV drip. She places another blanket on his feet and straightens the blanket across his chest. Her lips move, and I wonder what she's saying to him. I wonder if he's able to speak. But I still can't bring myself to move those last few feet into his room.

Instead, I take a half step back and allow the wall to hold me upright.

There's talking, beeping, an occasional groan, more talking, more beeping, now someone is crying, someone else is laughing. How can there be so much noise in an ICU unit? I look around for the culprits, wanting to tell everyone to just shut the hell up and leave these poor souls to rest. They need their rest.

That's when I see him. He's standing by the door to Hank's room, hands in pockets, eyes on me.

"Did you sleep at all last night? You look tired."

A silent laugh rocks my body. "Says the man who looks like he could dive headfirst into the deep end of a coffeepot."

"He's my patient." Simon answers. "What's your excuse?"

"I was worried about Hank." *And I'm worried about my marriage.*

He shifts to look into the room. The vein at the base of his neck pulses.

"How is he?" I break the silence between us, my voice barely carrying over the sounds of the ICU unit.

Simon back steps until he's leaning against the wall next to me, our shoulders almost touching.

"Okay. All things considered. It was mild. His right eye and the right corner of his mouth are drooping, and it's affected his right hand, but otherwise he seems to be mostly okay."

Simon shifts to look at me. "He'll be happy to see you. He was asking for you this morning."

My head jerks to look at Simon. "Me?"

He rubs at a black spot on the white tile with his left foot. "Meera, actually."

My eyes drop to the black mark on the floor. Tears turn it into a muddy puddle.

"Maya." It's little more than a breath, but it's enough to disarm my resolve. Simon's arms wrap around me, pulling me in, and I bury my head in his chest. After all these years and everything that's happened, I still fit in that very same spot.

I breathe him in. If I squeeze my eyes shut, squeeze out the sounds, the years, it could almost be the young us. His body hums against mine, the same intense current I drew from when we were kids.

"Um . . . hum . . . excuse me? Dr. Riley?" A voice from the door breaks into our private circle.

Simon loosens the hold but doesn't let me go. "He'll be okay, Maya. He should be back at Tower Oaks in a few days."

He leans back enough to make eye contact. I nod, straightening away from him. Only then does he acknowledge the nurse standing in the door to Hank's room. "Yes?" He turns to the nurse, who is openly sizing me for fit with either or both men.

"He's restless. Keeps asking where Meera is?" She must have heard Simon call me Maya, because she shifts her body to block the door as I step forward.

Simon turns to me. "Are you okay to go in?"

I study the black splotch on the floor. It's no longer a puddle, there are no more tears. I know what I need to do.

"Yes." I pull myself taller.

He may be asking for Meera, but somehow

I have to tell him who I really am. Before it's too late.

Simon places his hand on my lower back and nudges me forward. Together we cross the hall. The nurse turns sideways to let us pass but makes no effort to conceal her curiosity.

"Hank?" I ease into the chair by the bed and reach for his hand.

He rolls his head to the left. The hard hospital pillow barely changes its starchy shape. With the left side of his face smushed into the pillow, the droop on his right side becomes more pronounced. I force my smile wider.

"I. Thought. I. Heard. Your. Voice." The words are slow and slightly slurred. He shifts, winces. I look frantically around for the nurse or Simon.

"How are you feeling?"

"Hard," he exhales the word.

A steadying hand pushes on my shoulder. "Does something hurt, Hank?" Simon asks.

The pillow creases under the slight movement as Hank shifts to look at the speaker behind me.

"Can you show me where?" Simon gives my shoulder a comforting squeeze before stepping forward.

The blanket twitches.

"Your stomach?"
The pillow creases again.
"Okay, let's take a quick look then."
Simon walks around the foot of the bed and lifts the blanket just enough to get a look. Hank winces as Simon's hands explore his midsection.
"I'll have the nurse give you something to make you more comfortable." Simon tucks the blanket around Hank. "And I'll give you two a few minutes to talk. Not long." He waits for me to acknowledge his words then walks to the door. Behind me, I hear whispers as he gives the nurse instructions.
The nurse returns and injects something into Hank's IV. "This should ease the pain."
She checks his IV one last time then walks to the foot of the bed, stops, and looks up the bed to where Hank seems to have dozed off. She turns to leave and whispers, "Not long, he needs to rest," as she walks past me.
Not long. I need a long time though. I need time to get to know him. For him to get to know me. I need time to finish the horse and bring Hank to see the restored merry-go-round.
I look up. He's watching me. "You. Look. Tired."
"I'm fine. Don't worry about me."

He coughs a half laugh. "I always worry. About. You." He winces.

"I'm fine." I repeat, trying for more authority over my emotions. Hank's good eye blinks at me. "Really."

"You should rest." His eyes flutter.

"*You* need to rest." I start to pull my hand away but he tightens his hold.

Even in the hospital bed after a stroke, he has a firm grip. What those hands must have been able to do when he was young. A mental snapshot of the carousel horse in my studio flashes past. What those hands did when they were young, I correct myself.

He squeezes my hand, more gently this time, and seems to deflate into the bed.

His breathing gets deeper and the grip on my hand releases. I blink in time to the machine pulsing the jagged line of his heartbeat. *Keep beating. Please.*

"Why so sad, Maya?"

I look up, the world moving in slow motion. It's the first time he's called me by my first name without me prompting him. And the first time he hasn't asked what *my* name is.

"I'm not." I fake a smile.

"It's me you're talking to. You were never able. To hide emotions from me. Please. Meera. Talk to me."

The fake smile fizzles into a grimace. Who do I answer for? How do I navigate this?

"I'm just worried about you." It's true even if it's not the full truth.

"Bull." His chuckle turns into a wheeze.

I smile at the stubborn glare he's attempting. "It's true."

"It's. Not. All." He doesn't give up.

"It's not," I concede.

"So. Why. Sad? And don't. Say. Me." He blinks, or winks. It's hard to tell.

You wanted the opening to tell him, so tell him.

"I had a fight with my husband last night." I hear the words, the wrong words.

"About?"

"The past." What had the fight been about? My emotionally exhausted brain juggles the options. Me shutting down. Me not being willing to move forward. Me not being willing to move, period. Me and Simon. "Me, actually. Doing all the wrong things."

"He's upset. That you. Came. To me." It's not a question and he's not talking to me. "Oh, Meera." He labors to catch his breath or maybe he's catching his thoughts. "We knew it was a mistake, that we couldn't work. What we had was brilliant. Explosive. I've never forgotten. That night. But we both knew. And we were right. He was the better man. For you. The better man. To be your. Husband. To be the father. Of your child. It wasn't me. Not then."

The wrinkles on his cheeks appear to slide down, leaving smooth, papery skin behind. His eyes disappear behind folds of skin, his eyelids thin and brittle. His jaw moves as if he's chewing on something.

"Hank?" I whisper.

Wrinkles slowly crawl back up the boulders of his cheekbones and he opens his eyes. There's a film across his gaze, and I'm suddenly not sure if he's even aware I'm here.

"Tell me. About. The carousel."

"The carousel?" I paddle fast against the rapids of my emotions. Which one of us is he asking?

"What. Animal. Are you. Working on?"

I relax into the hard chair. This conversation I can do. "The big stander. The one in front of the ostrich."

Hank's mouth contorts into a lopsided smile.

"My grandma and I used to play rock, paper, scissors when I was little over who got to ride him. Now that I think about it, I have the feeling she let me win most of the time. She was quick, no hesitation usually, but now I can see that she was always half a blink behind when we played. She was good." I smile at the memory.

"That game. Always amused me. My daughter. Loved it. Over. And over. Best three out of five. Five out of seven. Seventeen out of nineteen. Annabelle didn't have the patience after the fourth or fifth game." He takes a few shallow breaths, machines beep and gurgle around us. "Is he almost complete?"

"He is. I'm mostly done with the body. The saddle will take a bit more time. I want to get the details almost like they were. And then the head. I always leave the head for last."

"It's. The portal. To their magic. It was the last. Thing. I finished, too." His breathing is shallow, labored. I move to get up; I should let him rest. He reaches for my hand again, keeping me in place. "I hope to see the work you've done, Maya. I want to see the love you've restored into the old girl."

"The grand reopening is on the fourth of July. I'd love to take you." *Now, Maya, tell him now.*

He squeezes my hand. "You're a good girl, Meera. Always." He releases my hand as his eyes flutter shut.

Twenty-Six

I watch Hank sleep, the beeping and hissing and clacking of machines playing a bizarre symphony.

Despite the "not long" warnings, neither the nurse nor Simon had returned to shoo me away. After an hour, though, the hospital sounds get the best of my anxiety. I leave a note with the nurse for Hank. My number and a promise that I'll be back. Soon.

I pull up to the house and turn the ignition off. I should go talk to Vale. I should get to work on the horse. I ease myself from the car, unsure which should to follow.

The back door opens and George steps out. "Hey, Maya. Vale took my truck to the store. We're almost done with the bathroom; you'll be showering in there tonight."

"Good news. Thanks." I duck into the studio. Good news? The bathroom being almost finished, or that my husband isn't home? A question I prefer not to explore.

Not now at least.

For the next few hours, I lose myself in painting. The scrolls on the saddle pad require a steady, slow hand. There's an ornate pattern, but all I can see is the thin tip of the paintbrush as it glides along the pencil marks. Coloring inside the lines. Ever since I grabbed that first fat crayon and Winnie the Pooh coloring page, I'd painted perfectly inside the lines.

I like my crisp edges. I like knowing where I'm going and what to expect. I like clear pictures. So ironic, then, that my life has turned into an abstract painting with jagged lines jutting out in unexpected places, colors overlapping haphazardly, and lines running off the page.

I dip the brush into the black paint and trace the outer edges of a swirl. Another dip and I fill in the narrow strip, careful not to bump out of bounds.

I lean back and look at the faint pencil marks I've drawn on the wooden carousel horse. Guidelines. Dip, paint, and the guidelines transform into a bold statement of color. If only my world was this precise. But no, someone erased the guidelines for my life.

■ ■ ■ ■

"Hey."

I jolt upright, almost knocking over the small can of paint next to me. "You scared me."

"I knocked, but you obviously didn't hear me. You've made great progress." Vale motions at the horse.

I stretch my back, arching, and then bending left and right. "He's coming along. This part will take longer than I anticipated, though."

"Why?" Vale steps closer and peers over my shoulder. "Wow, that's some detailed work you have ahead of you."

"Right? Hank had his signature details on all of the animals, but this guy got extra love. And that love now translates into extra-sensitive restoration work. The previous renovations painted over most of the intricate work. I was surprised how much more I found once I stripped those layers."

Vale walks around the horse, surveying with an architect's eye for detail. "You've done a beautiful job. It's clear how much he means to you."

"Thanks," I mutter, feeling suddenly shy.

"It's time to get ready for the party," He

shows his watch.

"Do we have to?" I groan. I'd forgotten about it. No, not exactly. I'd chosen to ignore it.

Every year, my mom throws a First-Saturday-of June pool party. The irony is that the pool doesn't get any of the party. No one swims. No one wears swimsuits. They don't even come in casual pool-party attire.

The parties, however, are always a hit. For everyone but me.

"Please can we skip it? I have work to do, you have work on the bathroom, and you're leaving tomorrow." I'm grasping at curly straws.

"Nope, we're going." Straight answer from my straight-straw husband. "Bathroom is done. You can't use that as an excuse." He reaches a hand to help me up.

"Maya, you look beautiful." Dad leans in for a hug and kiss.

Thomas slaps Dad playfully on the arm and shoos him away. "You clean up okay, Sis." He pulls me into a bear hug then whispers, "She's been looking at the door and her watch every thirty seconds waiting for you. Be prepared."

I feel my whole body constrict.

"And no, you're not making a break for it." He releases the hug but grasps my right hand and pulls me in the direction of the patio. My head whips around searching for Vale, who's already deep in conversation with a man in pink Bermuda shorts and a white T-shirt.

"Don't leave me," I mouth. Vale waves. Either he didn't pick up what I said or he's issuing a challenge. Fine.

Thomas leads me to one of the bars strategically placed around the pool. As usual, the only things in the pool are large floating candles. I order a gin and tonic from a bartender wearing a Hawaiian shirt. Tiki lights flank each bar and create a perimeter around the pool and patio. I notice a handful of tables on the grass beyond, each with a hurricane lamp in the middle. Waiters, also clad in Hawaiian shirts and khaki shorts, wander around with trays of hors d'oeuvres. No hubby manning the grill over burgers and hot dogs for my mom.

"Bree said you had breakfast together yesterday." He sips at a beer in a frosty mug. Mom doesn't miss a detail.

"Then you already know what we talked about, and thanks for the chat because there's nothing more for me to add." I kiss his cheek and search for someone whom I desperately need to talk to.

"Not so fast." He puts a hand on my arm. "I also talked to Vale this morning."

I take a long, slow drink, enjoying the sting of the gin. I motion the bartender for another. One G&T won't get me through this interrogation.

"Why aren't you going with him?"

"If you've talked to everyone, then you know the answer. Don't be Mom."

"Don't be nasty."

"I'm not."

"You are."

"Will you two stop? Nothing's changed."

I whip around at the sound of his voice.

"Simon?"

He laughs and nudges Thomas. "She always was sharp, wasn't she?"

"You mean sharp tongued." My brother smirks.

Simon pretends to size me up. "Nah, she's harmless." His grin widens in response to the rising color on my cheeks.

"Why are you here?" I ask, wanting to regain some power, although I'm clearly outnumbered.

"I came with a date."

"A date?"

"It's what single people do when they want to spend time with someone." He winks at me, and my face flushes hotter.

"Or what married couples do to reconnect with each other," my brother adds.

"You two suck. Enjoy each other's company." I gulp the last of my drink and motion the bartender again. This will cost me tomorrow, but tonight, I don't care.

"Oh, relax." Thomas steps closer. "More tonic than gin," he directs the bartender before strutting off to play the perfect son next to the perfect hostess.

"Huh."

"What's that supposed to mean?" I turn to Simon but miscalculate the distance between us and bump into him.

He puts a hand around my waist to steady me. His touch ignites the spark I'd felt this morning when he'd hugged me at the hospital. Where is this coming from? And why now?

"I thought your relationship with Thomas would have mellowed."

"Why?"

"You're not kids anymore and not vying for Mommy's attention like you used to. Although what do I know? I don't have anyone to compete against."

"I was not competing with Thomas. And I was *not* vying for my mom's attention." Even to my slightly tipsy ears, I sound shrewish.

"Okay, Maya, whatever you say." He winks, his fingers tapping a beat on my hip, sending shivers of excitement to parts that shouldn't be reacting.

I sidestep. "So who's this date?"

"Her name is Manda. I met her when she came to visit her grandfather at Tower Oaks. We've been out a few times."

"How did you and Panda end up at your ex's party then?" I scan the yard for anyone who could be connected to that name.

"Her name is Manda and she's friends with Bree."

"Where is Bree?" I twirl, hoping for a rescue.

"Sick kid."

"Oh. Where's Panda?"

"Manda," he says pointedly, although he doesn't hide his amusement. "She was talking to one of her clients."

"Won't she be looking for you?"

"I'll go find her in a minute. But I wanted to talk to you." His tone loses the playful smirk from a minute ago.

"What about?"

"Us."

"Us? There is no us."

"There was. And suddenly there wasn't. I

don't think we're as through as you pretend."

"Didn't we already have this discussion? And you're wrong." I take a gulp of my drink, the clear liquid scalding my throat. "But I do have a question: What letters?"

"Letters?"

"The other day you mentioned sending letters. It's been bugging me, but we haven't had the opportunity to talk since."

He lifts his glass and studies the contents. I stare at his hand, the index finger separated from the other three, its tip almost at the lip of the glass. *Stop it, Maya.*

"Forget I said anything. It's ancient history," he responds to the ice cubes, swirling the drink. Mint and lime infuse the air.

"You don't bring something like that up if it's not important."

He lowers his drink and his eyes settle on me.

Suddenly self-conscious under his scrutiny, I take a long drink of my gin and tonic even though it's more melted ice than gin, and I've lost all taste for it.

"You really never got any of my letters?"

I shake my head, not trusting my voice. I'd thought he was so angry and hurt that he never wanted to hear from me again after I left so abruptly. But if he'd written, why hadn't I gotten those letters? "Did you send the letters to England?"

"It doesn't matter," he says. "We can't undo the past."

Would I want to if we could? Some. But maybe not all the right parts.

"Simon," I take a half step closer.

"Don't." He sets his glass down on the tray of a passing waiter, his eyes on something in the distance. "You should get back to him. And I have to find my date."

As Simon walks away, I notice Vale standing across the pool with a cluster of people. Our eyes meet, and he turns back to his companions. My parents are not far from Vale, talking to another couple I recognize but can't place. The woman says something, and Mom laughs, touching her arm. Dad says something to the man, and they clink glasses in solidarity.

I check my watch. Somehow in the all the fun I wasn't having, an hour and a half has passed. I set my glass next to Simon's and join my parents.

"There you are, darling." Mom kisses my cheek. "You remember Kathleen and Edward Moore, right?"

"Of course." I smile and extend my hand, the perfect daughter of the perfect hostess.

I contribute the minimum to the discussions on gardeners and the photography exhibit at Gallery Michele. I zone out when the discussion turns to tennis. I'd never gotten the hang of the sport, much to my mom's disappointment.

"Maya, we're so excited for the carousel reopening. I've been hearing wonderful things about your restoration work."

I thank Kathleen for the kind words and shoot a questioning look at my mom. Her face gives nothing away.

"There you are." Vale fills the space my father had occupied next to me moments before. He doesn't put his arm around my waist like he normally would have. Like Simon had just done. I shiver.

"Are you cold?" I can't tell if his question is tinted with concern or sarcasm.

"No. Yes. I don't know. Just a sudden chill."

I scan the dimly lit backyard until I glimpse Simon with a tall, leggy redhead.

Vale puts his arm around my waist. "We should get going. I have an early car tomorrow." He'd turned me down when I offered to drive him to the airport. I'd been equal parts disappointed and relieved.

We say good-bye to my mom, find my dad and Thomas, then walk down the long driveway, lined with solar lights.

We get to our car and Vale reaches around me to unlock the passenger door. I turn into him, our bodies connecting. His eyes bulge in surprise.

I tip up until our lips meet. He steps forward, pushing me half a step into the car. My back arches over the contour of the car. A moan bounces between us. Me or him?

He breaks the kiss, his tongue flicking my ear, trailing down my neck. My knees buckle and I grab a fist of his shirt.

He pulls away, and I'm left blinking into the night, my parents' over-the-top house lit in all its glory behind him, the muffled mingling of music and laughter carrying in the dark of the night.

"Let's get home." His voice is thick and low.

I slide into the car and squeeze my eyes shut, trying to focus on the passion that burned inside me moments ago. I won't think about what ignited it. Or who.

TWENTY-SEVEN

I listen as the town car crawls out of the driveway then down the street. Vale tried to convince me to stay in bed this morning, but that didn't seem right, especially after last night.

The annoying clock ticks 5:23 A.M. A bit early to start on anything. I unfold from the kitchen table and take my coffee to the front porch. Birds are tweeting their morning hellos, no doubt comparing good worm-hunting stories. A man wearing shorts and a sweatshirt, his hood pulled up over his head, walks by with a bulldog dragging at the end of the leash. The dog seems as thrilled about being awake as I am. His head rolls in the direction of the porch and he makes a grunting noise but doesn't have a chance to build it into a bark before his owner tugs at the leash and hisses a "move it already."

Vale was reluctant to move this morning as well. He'd apologized for the trip, even offered to cancel, although we both knew it was a halfhearted offer. Maybe last night was the beginning of a fresh start after all. Or maybe it was a desperate attempt at salvaging the unsalvageable.

I breathe in the warmth of the coffee. I want that "it's going to be okay" feeling Vale promised. I really do want to believe last night was a new beginning.

The wind kicks up and I pull the throw blanket tighter around my shoulders with one hand, the other cradling the coffee mug close to my chest.

I listen to the thump-thump of tennis shoes on concrete as a lone jogger passes by, to the scraping of rubber wheels as the neighbor moves his trash bin. The morning noises get louder, more urgent. The easy quiet of the night pushed aside for the frenzy of another summer Sunday.

I want to reclaim those hours not long ago, when my mind had given way to my body. For the first time in over a year, I didn't think and I didn't second-guess. I let my body need the contact, the release.

And this morning? I'm pretending not to hear the whining of the guilt.

Through the open door, I hear my phone ping with an incoming text, and then another. Reluctantly I untangle from the blanket and walk to the kitchen. The phone glows on the kitchen table.

I'll see you in a week. I love you, Maya.

It can be the beginning of our next chapter. I just have to make it so.

There's still four hours before visiting hours at the hospital. Hopefully work will keep my mind occupied until then.

In the bedroom, I pull on a pair of sweats and a sweatshirt Vale left on the bed. The bed. I see two bodies, arms and legs entwined. Did Simon make love to Panda last night?

"Stop it." I turn from the bed and stomp away from the swirling emotions. Where did that come from?

The studio feels cold this morning. I tuck my hands inside the sweatshirt sleeves and survey the carousel horse. There's still a lot of work to be done, and my deadline is getting close. The black swirls on the saddle pad are done, but I want to give them a bit longer to dry before I start on the rest of the saddle pad details. I can start on the girth this morning though.

I mix the paint but can't bring myself to go closer to the horse. Even the lyrical notes of Chris Botti aren't soothing my jitters. I punch the "off" button on the CD player.

"Get a grip, Maya," I scold myself. I dip

the brush into the paint then lay the first strokes onto the raised-wood girth.

It takes a few strokes before I settle in, but I'm soon lost in the repetition and detail. The chime of an incoming text doesn't register immediately. It's only when the reminder chimes for the third time, that I finally connect with the sound.

"Hank is asking for you. And we should talk."

Hank. I glance at the clock and suck in air. How did it become one o'clock in the afternoon already?

I clean my brushes and cap the paint container. The rest of the girth will have to wait. And I still need to decide if the inscription stays or gets filled in.

I jog across the space between the studio and house, a silent argument running in my head over whether to change or just go. I smell of paint and my hands and clothes have splotches everywhere, but I don't want to lose more time. A nagging anxiety pulses through my decision-making. I grab my keys and bag and dart for the car.

Absently I glance in the rearview mirror and groan. I have a big black splotch on my cheek. Oh well, maybe it'll nudge the conversation directly to the merry-go-round. Maybe Hank can tell me what he'd like done with the inscription.

■ ■ ■ ■

The hallway seems to stretch forever, an eerie quiet that makes the hair on my arms stand.

Hank is propped up in bed, the TV flashing pictures with no sound. I knock. He turns to look then rolls his head back and blinks at the TV. Maybe he doesn't recognize me? Maybe he's upset that I didn't come earlier?

"Hi, Hank. What are you watching?" Another step forward, and now I can see the flashing pictures of *Wheel of Fortune.* We stare at the screen as Vanna turns glowing letters to display an incomplete phrase. "Do you know this one?"

There's a rustle from the bed. Hank shakes his head, but he still doesn't say anything.

I ease into the chair and we continue to watch the soundless flashing of images. When the show is over, Hank flicks the remote control at the TV then levels his attention on me.

"You have paint on your cheek." No hi, hello. No pleasantries whatsoever.

I rub at the spot again and wince at how raw my cheek feels from all the rubbing. At this rate, I won't have to worry about removing the paint because there won't be any skin left.

"I was working this morning." Duh. There's something in his demeanor that's setting me on edge. It's not the Hank I've come to know over the last few weeks.

"Rubbing it won't help." He continues to stare.

I nod and shove my hand under my thigh. Maybe a change of topic will help. "How are you feeling?"

"I'm here." He turns away and stares at the dark TV.

"Do you need anything?" I squirm in the chair, the vinyl creaking under my shifting weight. Hank is watching me again.

"What were you painting?"

He hasn't given any indication who he thinks I am today, and I'm momentarily at a loss for how to respond. "The girth of the big stander horse." I opt for the present.

His eyes narrow a fraction. For the first time since I entered, I notice the slight droop of the right side.

The fingers of my right hand develop a mind of their own, pulling and twisting the fingers of the left hand.

Hank winces at the sound of a cracking knuckle. "You shouldn't do that." The puffing of the blood pressure cuff punctuates his comment with a huff and sigh.

"My grandmother used to say that." *Tell him.* The gruffness of this Hank steals my words.

His mouth tightens, the right side drooping even further. "She's right."

I push my hands under my thighs again and search for something to say. He's never been difficult to talk to. Both Hanks have been chatty and warm. I scooch forward in the uncomfortable chair. I could leave and come back. Maybe he doesn't even want me here.

"I can come back later if that would be better."

He turns from the lifeless TV, his droopy eye releasing a tear. One tear. "Laters are not a guarantee."

"No, I guess they're not."

We're silent, listening to the sounds of machines trying to guarantee more laters.

"Why the carousel?"

I squint past the noise in my brain, hoping to catch the thread that led to that question.

Hank harrumphs, or at least tries. "The carousel. Why are you restoring it?"

"Because it's an important part of the history of this town. I didn't want that to get lost."

His stare elicits more babbling about the importance of history. I stop to catch my breath and my thoughts.

"Okay. What's the real reason?" His tone doesn't leave much interpretation to his mood, and once again, I find myself cursing Simon for the earlier texts calling me here.

"Because of the dreams the carousel inspires and the memories I didn't want to lose."

"That's a big project for such personal reasons." I can't tell if he's impressed or irritated.

"I didn't do it for me personally." My irritation duals his.

"Then for whom?"

"Why does that matter? Isn't it enough that the carousel, your carousel, is getting another chance?"

"Ahhh." It's an annoying nonanswer, and in Hank's case, could just as easily have been a sigh of relief at the release of his blood pressure cuff, except for the smug look on his face.

"What's wrong with second chances?" I want to hear him say it. I want him to move this conversation, not just poke at me.

He closes his eyes and sinks into the

whiteness of the sheets. I've lost him to sleep.

I stand and tiptoe to the door.

Behind me, his voice is soft, almost apologetic. "Second chances can be good. But some dreams are better left to fly away."

I stay in the hallway, reluctant to leave but unable to stay.

"You look upset." Simon stops next to me, and together we watch a sleeping Hank.

"Why did you text me that he was asking for me? He was borderline hostile."

Simon looks surprised, either by the question or the sharpness of my tone. "Because he was asking for you."

"Me or Meera?"

"You, actually."

I turn abruptly and walk to the ICU waiting room. Simon follows, waiting patiently as I first fidget with the water cooler then poke buttons on the coffee machine.

"I'm not offering coffee, you look wound up as it is, but I can help with the water before you break the handle."

I take my mostly empty paper cup and retreat to the other side of the room. Simon fills another cup and comes to sit next to me.

"Listen . . . ," he says at the same time I start talking. He defers to me. "Ladies first."

"No, that's fine. You go." Because while I'm bursting, blurting what's on my mind won't get us far.

"I'm sorry if I made you uncomfortable last night." He lowers his voice when a family walks into the lounge. They settle into a tight huddle at the opposite corner.

"You didn't." He did.

"It was wrong to go to the party. When Manda suggested it, she didn't know about us. I should have told her. But I wanted to see you."

"You see me when I come visit Hank."

"I wanted to see you outside of your visits with Hank. I wanted to see you with *him.*"

I twist to look at Simon. "Why?"

He keeps his eyes on the growing group. "I wanted to see if you were happy with him."

"And you thought you'd get that from a few sightings at a party that my parents were throwing? You know I hate those events to begin with."

"I remember." His smile takes me back more years than I want to travel.

"Did you get what you were hoping for?" I'm angry, but I'm also flattered.

"Yes and no. I wanted a reason to pursue you but, in a way, I was hoping to see you were in a good place."

"That makes no sense."

"I didn't come here to screw with your life, Maya. I returned here for a job. But yes, part of me was hoping you and I would have a second chance."

"I don't think that's possible."

Simon reaches for my hand. "Thomas said your husband was going out of town. Have dinner with me tonight. Just catching up. Please?"

I'm going to kill my brother. My stomach somersaults and I feel the word yes forming. Luckily a few brain cells are still on duty, and I manage to squeak out a no instead.

"What are you afraid of? Two old friends having dinner. That's it."

"I'm not afraid, Simon. And we're not old friends."

"Your grandma and Hank managed to rekindle a friendship." His eyebrows challenge me. His aim, as usual, is pinpoint perfect.

"Then maybe when we're eighty we can have dinner."

I leave the ICU waiting room, focusing on my footsteps, my breathing. This would not be the time to hyperventilate. Although there could be worse places to faint than in a hospital.

Twenty-Eight

For at least the thirtieth time in the last half hour I check my phone for messages. Still no missed calls or texts. I check the coverage bars, which are, of course, full. And who exactly am I waiting to hear from? Vale? Simon? My traitor brother? No one. I'm not waiting for anyone.

Restlessness takes over and I start to pace. Kitchen, family room, back to kitchen.

I'm drained from the emotional upheaval of the day, but every corner of the house acts like a gate in a pinball game. Bing, change direction. Bing, change direction.

Hank said some dreams are better left to fly away. Flying . . . why haven't I heard from Vale yet? I text a "hi" and get an immediate smiley face and "hi" in return. Okay, at least I know he's alive.

The house echoes my neurotic ramblings. I should have gone for dinner with Simon after all. At least then I wouldn't be stuck here arguing with myself. Two old friends, right? *No, not two old friends.* Is this the dream Hank was referring to? But he and Grandma were still friends, despite their past. Or because of their past.

I pull open the fridge then give the doors a hard push shut. There's nothing appealing in there. I should have agreed to dinner. I could call him and tell him I changed my mind.

No, bad idea. How dare he make assumptions about my happiness anyway? And how dare he still know me well enough to be right?

Maybe a bath will mellow the brain cells.

Every time I walk into the finished bathroom, I find myself standing for a jumping heartbeat, taking in the transformation. It looks like something out of a remodeling magazine. And it reminds me how long we've waited to make this house "ours." Did we wait too long?

I never really pushed though. Deep down — or, if I'm honest, not so deep — I think I was still holding out for that dream house on the beach.

Since the first time I saw it, I'd fantasized about living there. Simon and I had been boogie boarding, moving farther and farther from the overcrowded part of the beach.

The house had been under construction during the winter and spring. That summer day, it stood in its glory, ready to welcome its family.

And I'd wanted to be the family it welcomed. Simon and I had jokingly said "one day it'll be ours." We'd spun dreams of sharing morning coffee on the upstairs balcony as the sun tickled the sea awake. Watching our kids play in the sand then sprint over the dune and fall laughing onto our lush lawn. Throwing parties on the patio in the summer and by the fireplace in the winter.

I'd shown Vale the house when we first moved back. But for some reason, I couldn't picture the two of us in that house, the dreams we shared belonged elsewhere.

Some dreams are better left to fly away.

I turn on the faucets and pour a capful of bubble bath into the tub. When it's almost full, I sink in and close my eyes, waiting for the eucalyptus oils to work their magic.

Stop thinking, I scold myself. *Relax. No thinking.*

And no banging. Who the hell is banging on my door?

Water and foam splash onto the floor. "Shit." I slide across the wet tiles.

I toss sweats and a T-shirt on and jog down the stairs in time to the incessant banging. I yank open the front door, ready to yell at someone. Anyone but him.

"You didn't answer the phone." Simon feigns innocence. His right arm lifts to half-mast, until a brown bag creates a barrier between us.

"Simon?"

"Yes."

"What are you doing here?"

"I texted and left a message. I didn't want to eat alone."

"Simon?"

"Yes."

We're not making much progress.

"I said not tonight." I'm suddenly aware he's no longer looking at my face. I glance down, following his gaze. "Oh shit." I clamp my arms around my chest and back away from the door. I'd yanked the clothes on while still wet, and the T-shirt is soaked and clinging in all the wrong spots. Or right spots, judging by the expression on Simon's face.

"The food can wait if you'd like to finish your bath. Ummm, eucalyptus." He inhales and mischievousness sparkles in his eyes.

"I'm fine. I just need to change." I squeeze my arms tighter.

"May I?" He waves the bag and points at the kitchen.

My stomach gives a lurch. Just hungry, I justify. I tick off something that can double as a nod. Simon walks past me and into the kitchen. My stomach gives another lurch. Can't justify that one.

I two-time the steps and slide into the bedroom, then return to the kitchen in dry clothes. He smirks at my choice of a sweatshirt this time.

"Simon, why are you here?"

"Told you already, I didn't feel like eating alone."

"Except that I told you it wasn't a good idea." I stand, arms crossed.

Simon takes several containers out of the bag and points at a couple of cabinets. I point at the one next to the fridge, where the plates are. He removes two plates then points at the drawers. I point at the one next to the dishwasher. He plucks out two forks and two knives and places everything on the table.

He moves through my kitchen, unsure of where things are but sure in where he is. I'm intrigued and annoyed. Seeing him at Tower Oaks and the hospital is weird, but weirdly normal. He was always going to be a doctor. He's one of those people who decided what he'd be in kindergarten and never wavered. Me? I changed my mind every other week and switched majors three times in my first year of college.

But here, he's just Simon, and the feelings that were stirred up in me last night are now in full boil.

"Relax, Maya. It's just dinner." He gestures for me to sit then opens a bottle of beer and places it in front of me.

"Eat. It's your favorite." He pauses, serving spoon hanging in midair. "Well, was your favorite. Hopefully you still like it."

I inhale. Cumin, coriander, garam masala. Still my favorite. I hate-love that he remembered.

"My wife divorced me because of Indian food."

"What?" I swallow hard. I can't tell if he's serious or not.

"I'm serious. Every time we went out, which was often because she couldn't even fix her own coffee, I wanted Indian. And I kept ordering that for her." He points at my plate with his fork. "She's a vegetarian."

I spear a piece of chicken. "Oops."

"Yup."

"Why did you really divorce?" I skate the hunk of chicken through the masala sauce then shove it into my mouth.

"We should never have gotten married in the first place. I don't really know why or how we lasted almost five years. Not true. We lasted that long because I was never home. She loved the idea of being married to a surgeon, and she tolerated my crazy hours through med school because her friends thought it was so romantic. When I switched my specialty, she switched the locks. A week after our divorce was final, she married a hotshot gynecologist ten years older than her." He forks in a mouthful of lamb curry and shrugs.

"And you never remarried?"

"Obviously." He smirks and I feel the flush through my cheeks that has nothing to do with the spicy food. "Too complicated," he adds, and takes a drink from his beer.

"What made you switch to internal medicine?" He'd always talked about being an orthopedic surgeon.

He's quiet for a minute. There's sadness in the droop of his mouth. "When my grandfather was moved to a nursing home. I was doing my residency in orthopedics at the time and spending every waking, and a lot of sleeping, moments at the hospital. When Grandpa fell and broke his hip, we agreed the assisted-care facility was the right place for him. But whenever I was there visiting and tried talking to his doctor, I got the uncomfortable feeling the guy just didn't care. He didn't know anything personal about his patients, didn't hang around talking to them or inquiring about how they were feeling or what they were doing — or what they weren't doing, which is often more telling."

Simon stops talking, but the bitterness in his voice floats around us. I sneak a look at him, wondering if I should say something, but he's staring straight ahead, sorting through the past.

"It made me sick to see how he would blow in, do a cursory exam, and blow back out. Sometimes he'd only say hi and bye to the patients, beyond the necessary open your mouth, lift your arm."

His words pick up speed as he talks.

"And then Grandpa had a heart attack. It's not something I can prove, but in my gut I know the doctors didn't react fast enough. Maybe it wouldn't have mattered. But when he sat in Grandpa's empty room and told us what happened, it felt like he resented us taking up his time with pointless questions. That's when I decided to switch."

Simon shrugs, as though it was just that obvious and that simple.

"No regrets for giving up orthopedic surgery?"

He looks at me, an expression I can't identify on his face. "That's one of the few things in my life I don't regret. If I can make a difference to someone who's at the end of their life, then I've done my job. As a doctor and a human being."

We finish eating, discussion shifting to neutral topics. When we're done, I put the dishes in the sink, grab two more beers, and lead the way to the front porch.

The evening is warm but doesn't yet have the fullness of full-blown summer. Between the heavy meal and the still air on the screened porch, I catch myself sinking into a comfortable ease. Two friends spending an evening together.

I finally break the silence. "Do you like being back here?"

"Yes and no. It's a nice place, but I still feel like I'm visiting."

"Did you buy a place?" Such a normal question yet it feels loaded.

He swallows, and I can almost feel the lump in my own throat. "No. Almost though. I made an offer on a house, but thankfully someone outbid me."

"Thankfully?" I try to read his expression. It shouldn't surprise me that I can't, but I'm still caught off guard.

"It was the beach house we used to fantasize about." He doesn't look at me.

I don't remember the house being up for sale. "It was for sale?"

"It was about to be put on the market. The owners were Manda's clients, and in a moment of insanity, I told her to put an offer on it for me."

"Manda." I shudder, the vision of them in bed in the house we were supposed to share rolls through my stomach like a rotten fish.

"We're not involved, if that's what you're gagging about." I hear the smirk in his voice. "I told you I met her when she came to Tower Oaks. We got to talking, went out a couple of times, and she decided to make me her pet project."

"I wasn't gagging."

He laughs. "You were. I know you. Now tell me why you carry the guilt of the world around."

"Wow, Simon, way to cut to the heart of things. You should have been a cardiologist."

"Or maybe I'll start moonlighting as a therapist. I have a way with people, you know." His smirk deepens and my stomach somersaults.

"Yeah, well, don't give up your day job."

He feigns a shot to the chest. "Way to hurt a man."

We exchange smiles and a look that lasts

longer than one between friends.

I stand, and the sudden movement sends the rocking chair banging into the siding of the house. "I need another drink. You?" I take a few steps toward the screen door into the house, but before I reach for the handle, Simon grabs my wrist.

"Don't." He stands, still holding my hand. His fingers open my fist and wind through mine.

"Don't," he whispers, the word brushing my cheek.

"Don't . . ." he breathes the word onto my lips.

"Please." My voice is raspy and unsure. Please what? Please Simon don't do this; or please me, don't feel this? I squeeze my eyes shut. I can't look at him, can't feel the feelings that are shifting inside me.

He touches my cheek, lifts my chin. "Thirteen years. I've waited thirteen years. I wanted to hate you, but I can't. I convinced myself I should leave you alone, but I can't do that either."

"You have to." My voice quivers, and I pull my hand from his, put a step between us.

He touches a rogue curl, then my chin, tilting my head so I'm forced to look at him again. "I will when I'm convinced you're better off without me."

My phone pings from somewhere in the house. A text. Probably Vale. A flash of guilt pushes me two steps away from Simon.

"Thank you for dinner, but you should go now."

He takes a step toward the door. "We don't always get a second chance. There's never a third chance."

The old wood screen door slaps shut behind him, and I listen to his footfalls crunch over the pebbled sand that covers much of the sidewalks around here.

The phone buzzes again. Second chances. Are we all hoping for one? And what do you do when the second chance you thought you wanted shows up on your doorstep?

Twenty-Nine

The text from Vale checking in from the other side of the United States had been followed by a text from Simon, checking in from the other side of town.

I tossed in bed for longer than was sane before giving in and coming to the studio. At least the carousel horse's second chance is under control.

The light shifts as the sun muscles out the night. I stand, stretch. My head throbs from lack of sleep and paint fumes.

I send Sam a text. Maybe she can meet for coffee on her way to the store. I haven't talked to her since the disastrous breakfast Friday morning.

Before I've had the chance to set the phone back down, it vibrates with an incoming message. *"Couldn't sleep either. Already at the store. Come over. Sock Sorting Therapy is the next big thing."*

"On my way." I don't bother to change,

just grab my keys and some money. Thankfully there's a coffee shop between my house and Sam's boutique.

Forty minutes later, I tap on the glass door of Socks-A-Lot, a paper cup in each hand.

Sam unlocks the door and ushers me in. She wrinkles her nose as I walk by with the cups.

"What's with the face?" I hand her the cup with the vanilla latte I ordered for her.

She takes it but then shoves it back at me and backpedals, almost falling over a couple of boxes. "Throw it away. Out there." She waves me out of the store.

"It's your favorite," I say in defense of the offending cup.

"Get it out. Get it out." She flails her arms.

"Okay, okay, don't rip your arms out of the socket. Geez." I drop the untouched latte into the trash can on the sidewalk and return to the store, keeping my drink close to my chest so she doesn't evict us as well. "What was that about?"

She grabs an assortment of headbands out of a box with so much force that I worry for their safety. I take a green-and-blue one from her and shove it onto my head then duck to see my reflection in the tiny mirror on a nearby display rack.

Sam pulls it off. "Not your color."

I reach for a purple headband with white and teal polka dots. Sam snatches it back. "Not your style."

She slides the not-my-color and a fistful of not-my-style accessories onto a display.

"What has you so crabby this morning? I'd offer to get you coffee but, oh yeah, I did and you threw it and me out. What gives?"

"Nothing," she sulks. "I'm just not feeling well, and the smell of the coffee made me want to hurl."

"Lovely." Sam definitely has a way with words sometimes. "Flu?"

"Maybe. I don't know."

"So, what's the story with Taylor? Is it serious?" Maybe she'll talk boys if she won't talk health.

She twists away so I can't see her face. "He's pretty great, isn't he?" She sways and grabs the counter. "Crap. Third time that's happened this morning."

I take her by the elbow and lead her to a cluster of boxes. She sits without argument.

"Shouldn't you be in bed? Have you seen a doctor?"

She shakes her head. "Darcy will be in at noon. I'll go home then. I'll be fine until then. It's pretty slow in the mornings. And yes, I've been to a doctor."

"I can stay and help out if needed."

"That would be great, thanks." She closes her eyes and draws in a slow, deep breath.

"Okay, Sam, you're scaring me. What's going on?"

She takes my hand and squeezes it. An un-Sam-like gesture that seizes my gut. Something is wrong.

"This isn't how I imagined telling you. Oh hell, I have no idea what I imagined."

I fight the urge to grab her, shake the news from her, run from the store not to hear.

"I tried to tell you a couple of times but, I don't know, it was never the right time." Her eyes turn watery, and she wipes the unshed tears.

"You're scaring me. Just spill."

She gives my hand another squeeze. "I'm sorry. Taylor thought we should talk about it together but I don't know, I thought it should be just the two of us. Not like this though. This wasn't how we were supposed to talk." She gestures at the store and the boxes we're sitting on.

The borderline panicked part of my brain wants to crack a joke about the status of her relationship with Taylor since he's clearly in the know when her best friend isn't, or about the box that's caving under her weight. But the look on Sam's face tugs at the terrified part of my brain.

"Just tell me. We'll get a second opinion. Or third if you've already gotten a second. Whatever it is, Sam, I'm here, I'll be here." I take her other hand. I won't lose my best friend. I can't lose her as well.

Sam blinks me into focus. She takes a deep breath that feels like it's being sucked right out of my lungs.

"I'm . . . oh god, Maya." She exhales and I catch myself inhaling. Her chest expands and mine collapses.

"Okay," she starts again. "Oh god, okay, Maya, I'm pregnant."

I realize she's looking at my stomach. My hands become clammy and I pull them away, wipe them on my pants. I'm supposed to hug her and say congratulations. I'm supposed to gush about how wonderful this is and ask how she's feeling.

"I was afraid to tell you, but I had to tell you. I'm sorry I didn't tell you sooner, but I didn't know how." She stops, out of breath.

I pull her in for a hug. "Oh, Sam, I'm sorry."

She tenses and tries to pull away. I tighten my hold. "I mean I'm sorry you didn't think you could share this with me."

She relaxes into my hold, but there's still an awkwardness in the embrace, and we both break contact.

"How far along are you?" The questions I'd been asked by friends and strangers race through my mind.

"Fourteen weeks."

"Three months?" My voice is too loud in the too-quiet store.

Sam nods, still avoiding eye contact.

"And Taylor . . . ?" I allow the question to hang.

She nods again, this time adding a slight smile.

"Wow." I exhale, waiting for my brain to stop spinning.

"Yeah, I wanted to tell you right away, but I was afraid to upset you. And then I was afraid you'd be upset that I kept this from you. But obviously I can't keep it secret forever."

I want to be excited for her. I am excited for her. But sadness and anxiety whirl through my brain.

Sam looks at me and I watch, helpless, as she swallows a lump of emotion.

"How are you feeling?" I wince at the banality of my question. She's my best friend, this is not how this moment should be.

"I'm okay. Queasy one minute, starving the next. Exhausted, excited, terrified. You know." She gives me a hint of a Sam smile that promptly dissolves into tears. "And weepy. I'm so sorry, Maya, that was a stupid thing to say."

Sam was with me when I found out I was pregnant. We'd gone out to lunch at the Taco Hut because she was having cravings. The moment we sat down and unwrapped our food, I'd turned greener than the guacamole. When I returned from the bathroom, Sam was grinning like the cat who ate the stork.

We'd stopped at the drugstore on the way home, and she sat with me on the cold bathroom tiles, staring at the pregnancy test stick, and waiting for the timer to go off. And then she'd sat by my side on that same cold tile while I alternated throwing up and crying my lungs out after coming home from the hospital without a baby.

I wasn't quite sure if my family didn't trust me to be alone those first few weeks or just didn't want me to feel alone. It didn't matter, though. There could have been a pod of well-meaning people and I still would have felt alone. And empty.

But it was Sam who held my hand and helped me change out of clothes I'd worn for days. She got me out of bed and into the studio. And she dragged me out of the house that first time then rushed me home when our quiet moment on the beach was disturbed by a small herd of squealing, giggling toddlers.

"It wasn't a stupid thing to say, and you're right, I do know. It's okay, Sam. Really. I'm happy for you. You're happy, right?"

She nods. Tears drop from her eyelashes, and she sniffles.

"No crying. This is wonderful."

"You mean it?" One hand wipes at her cheeks, the other covers her still-flat stomach.

I force the corners of my mouth to stay up and swallow the grapefruit-sized lump in my throat. "I mean it."

I want to hug her, but all I can convince my arms to do is squeeze her upper arms. I want to be okay with this, but this is Sam. Sam who doesn't even like kids and had no interest in settling down. She wasn't supposed to have a baby before me.

"Still want to help with the merchandise sorting?" Her discomfort radiates from her. Or maybe that's my discomfort being deflected.

"I should get back. Deadlines . . . the horse . . ." My brain hiccups through excuses.

"Maya." Sam laces her fingers through

mine, trapping me. "I know you hate hearing this, and I'm probably not the person to be saying it, but I think you should get pregnant again. I know the first time wasn't really planned, but you wanted that baby, and you would have been such a great mom."

I force a smile and pull away. "I'm really happy for you, Sam. You and Taylor will be great parents." I give her a kiss on the cheek and turn for the door.

"You're upset." She sounds like a little girl who's just been brushed off by an angry parent. My usually fiery friend stands next to me like a scared child.

The hurt and guilt and hopelessness that have become my constant companions dissolve into a pool of tenderness. I hug my best friend tight — tighter than I did when she was my lifeline.

"I'm not upset. I'm happy for you. A little sad, but that's not because of you. I love you, and I'm happy for you. Really."

"Really?" She sniffles into my shoulder.

"Really, really."

There's a knock on the glass door behind us. I pull back, and Sam ducks her head to wipe at her glistening face. "You have customers to attend to, and I have a wood horse to attend to. I'll come by tomorrow."

Sam sniffles. "I'm glad, you know. About the baby."

"Me too," I say and mostly mean it.

I smile at the customer who darts past me the moment the door is unlocked.

The walk home is a confused mess of emotions. Every family I pass is a reminder of what Sam is gaining and I've lost. Every couple is a reminder of what Sam has nurtured and I've broken.

One block, I'm shattered, the next I'm hopeful. A child's trike — shattered. Mom and toddler waddling hand-in-hand — hopeful. Guy getting into his car and blowing a kiss to his wife — shattered. Dad carrying beach paraphernalia — hopeful.

I *am* happy for Sam and Taylor. Now I have to stop being sad for me and Vale.

Thirty

"Look how handsome you are with your shiny new bridle." I step back to admire the still wet paint.

I stretch my back and glance at the window. It's becoming light out and birds are chirping their good mornings to each other. I should venture out today. Or at least return a few calls before the national guard shows up on my doorstep. Although I guess my guardsman would be Taylor, coming on the orders of his commanding officer, Sam.

I responded to one of her texts Monday evening and told her — again — that I wasn't upset, and I *was* happy, and I *was* okay. But since then, I've ignored seven texts and three calls.

I won't be lucky enough to hide much longer. And I don't want to hide any longer.

I cup the horse's muzzle with my hand and whisper into his ear, "I'll tell him today."

■ ■ ■ ■

"Hank?" I tap gently on the door. He's propped up in bed watching TV again. This time it's a talk show.

He turns to the door, momentary annoyance at the disruption wrinkling his one good eye. He stares, and then, like a light bulb that takes a minute to reach maximum brightness, the sag of suspicion turns into sunshine.

"Meera, you came." He reaches a fragile, bony hand to me.

My heart slams into my ribs then free-falls.

The right eye droops with concern. "Meera? Is everything okay?"

I move forward, dropping my disappointment at the door.

"Of course. How are you feeling today?" I ease into the chair by the bed.

"Better, now that you're here." He grins at me.

"The nurse mentioned you'll probably be released tomorrow. That's good news."

The host of the TV program is standing between two guests on stage, her body and extended arms creating a barrier between them. He has, like last time, been watching without the volume.

I nod at the TV. "What's that about?"

"Ah, who knows? Pure trash these programs."

"So why do you watch?"

He considers me then the TV. "I don't. I just want the company."

Those simple words, said with a matter-of-fact shrug, tear a hole in my lungs, and I collapse into the back of the chair.

Hank clicks the remote and squirms higher onto the bed. "But you're here now."

Speak, Maya. Say something.

I wanted to tell him that I'm Meera's granddaughter. His granddaughter. I wanted to offer to take him to see our special horse when he's up to the trip.

I look to the dark TV for help. I wish the remote could change the scene reflected back at me.

"Will you go with me to visit the old merry-go-round, Meera?"

Our eyes meet in the blackness of the TV screen. "I'd love that, Hank."

He fusses with the blood pressure cuff and winces at the tug of the IV. "As soon as they spring me from this hellhole."

A nurse enters the room and bats his hands down. "Mr. Hauser, you and those busy hands of yours need some rest." Her tone is light, her smile genuine, and Hank relaxes into the pillow she repositions for him.

"I can go, let you get some rest," I offer but don't get up. My body refuses to move.

The nurse gives me a sympathetic look. "Nah, stay. Just make sure this character doesn't try to escape again." She winks at Hank.

I feel like a little kid given permission to stay up past my bedtime. And by the look on Hank's face, he feels the same.

After she leaves, he returns to the carousel. "It's been years since I was last there. Strange isn't it? I miss her. Well, I miss her the way she was in our day. I miss her magic. That's what brought us together." He flashes a mischievous grin.

He sobers, his droopy eye suddenly drooping further. "But the magic isn't always enough, is it?"

"No, it isn't." How many couples rode that carousel, any carousel, and believed that their happiness would circle forever? How many parents watched their young children squeal in delight and hoped that their happiness would never stop?

"Life, parents, timing were all stronger than the magic," Hank mumbles.

"Do you ever wonder what could have

been?" I ignore the groaning of the chair and push deeper into it, bringing my feet up. I rest my chin on my knees and hug my shins, waiting for Hank to tell me the rest of the story.

Hank's features disappear into exaggerated wrinkles, forced from the grin. "You used to sit like that and watch me paint the animals."

I straighten, self-conscious. "Really?" Although I shouldn't be surprised, I was Grandma's mini in almost every way.

"And no," he continues. "I don't think about what could have been. With or without your mother, it wouldn't have worked. Life works the way it's supposed to. I believe that. It's the only choice."

His words fade into the hissing and beeping of hospital machinery. In the length of an exhale, he's asleep.

What did he mean? I never met my great-grandmother, but from the stories, she was nothing like Grandma.

Grandma used to poke fun at Mom for being just like her grandmother. I was never sure if Mom bristled because she didn't want to be like her grandmother or because she was annoyed at being the outsider with her own daughter.

Life works the way it's supposed to. Did I

believe that? Would life have been better for Grandma if she'd married Hank back then? Would Mom have turned out differently? What if Simon hadn't proposed that night? What if I hadn't gone to England? What if he'd come after me? What if I'd gotten his letters?

I ease out of the chair, careful not to scrape the metal feet on the floor. I leave a message with the nurse to let Hank know I'll be back. Right now, I have a few questions for my mom.

"Maya, darling, what a surprise." Mom steps aside to let me pass, our air kisses needing passports to reach each other.

I'm expected to emit some pleasantry or another, but my brain is in a university dorm in England.

"Why did you let me think all those years that Simon never came looking for me?"

"What are you talking about? That was a lifetime ago. Come in, it's hot." She turns and strides to the kitchen. I follow, fighting the mounting annoyance of a child who's being unceremoniously dismissed.

"Why did you send me to England?" I'm that petulant child not willing to be dismissed. Poke, poke.

She sighs dramatically and indicates for

me to sit on one of the shiny black-leather counter chairs. She pours two glasses of iced tea and places a coaster and a glass in front of me. The glass is, of course, precisely centered on the coaster.

"England was the perfect next step for your education. Look at your career, darling. You wouldn't be here today if you hadn't spent that year studying abroad and making connections."

I can't stop staring at her. This is the first time she's ever used the word *career* to describe what I do. Okay, that's not exactly true. She'd been very supportive about my *career* working in a world-renowned museum. When my career took a turn to a converted garage — well, that word was left in the bowels of the museum.

"So, you sent me away for the good of my career?" I cringe inwardly at the tone of my voice, the petulant child suddenly aware she's tripped the fuse.

"I didn't *send you away* as you're implying. *You* wanted that opportunity, Maya. Don't twist memories to suit your need for a fight."

"I don't want a fight. I want the truth." I wince at the irony. I still haven't told her about Hank.

"What truth?" She takes a drink from her

iced tea. The glass remains sparkling clean around the rim, not a hint of her crimson lipstick. She's the only person I know who wears lipstick in her own home. "The truth that you needed to expand your education? The truth that you needed to experience life? The truth that you were too young to settle down?"

"Those weren't your decisions to make."

"They were. You didn't have the maturity."

"I had the maturity to know I wasn't ready to get married when Simon asked. I had the maturity to get on that plane for London."

"But you lacked the maturity to know why you said no to Simon. And you didn't have the strength to live with your decision," she says, cutting me off. "Maya, you were miserable those first months. Both of you were. But darling, you both needed to find your own way. If Simon had found you, you would never have stayed there. And then what?"

"We would have gotten back together." I want to sound sure, defiant. I don't. Not even to myself.

"You would have missed out on so many things."

"Like you did?" It's a low blow, and I regret the words before they've had the chance to hit their mark.

Her shoulders drop a centimeter, just barely enough for the visible eye but enough to register on the Richter scale. "Like me."

She takes a sip from her tea, fussing with the coaster before continuing. "I married my first love. Don't look so shocked. Your grandma tried to talk sense into me. She said her mom had forbidden her to marry her first love, and while she'd hated her for it at first, she came to realize it was the right thing. She loved your grandfather."

I chew the inside of my cheek. As much as I want to blurt out that she may not have married her first love but she did have his baby, my brain pulls rank over my temper.

Mom takes another minisip. "She had a good life with him. You have a good life with Vale. He may not have been your first love, but I think he's your forever, like Grandpa was for your grandma."

She holds up a hand to stop me from arguing, and my mouth snaps shut, back teeth grinding in protest.

"You have enough of my stubbornness. If Simon had found you, you would have shut your brain down and listened to your heart. You would have done it because it was the opposite of what I would have encouraged you to do. I didn't listen to my mom or my brain and here I am." She sweeps her hands, indicating the grand house around her. "I, my dear daughter, have everything but love, despite marrying my first love. I'm not saying it doesn't happen. There are plenty of people who marry young and live happily ever after. I wasn't one of them, and I wanted to protect you."

"If you're so unhappy, why didn't you leave?"

"Because I couldn't. I didn't know how. What would I be if I wasn't married to your father?"

"You'd become whatever you wanted. And maybe you'd finally be happy."

She moves the glass of tea half an inch to the left. "I may have been defiant, but I was never strong. And I still love your father."

The woman in front of me holds no resemblance to the perfectly pressed mother I barged in on. And the fire I brought in with me has shriveled to smoldering embers.

The overwhelming loss sputters deep inside, and a desire I haven't felt — haven't allowed — in years, stirs. "But you are. I wish I had a smidgen of your strength." I wait, hoping she'll step from behind the counter, walk to me, and give me a hug. A big, soothing, maternal hug.

"You are far stronger than you give yourself permission to be." She doesn't walk around, doesn't give me a hug, but she does open a door that's been all but sealed shut.

"I don't feel strong. I feel lost."

"You have been. And that's understandable. But it's time for you to accept support from the people around you. That doesn't make you weak."

"What if Vale and I can't get past this?"

"Do you want to get past it?"

I nod.

"Then do." She waves away the unacceptable alternative.

Then do. If only it were that easy.

THIRTY-ONE

Except to eat, sleep, and shower, I haven't left the studio since the discussion with my mom.

Yesterday I'd called the hospital and talked to the nurse. Hank was being moved out of ICU, and she expected him back at Tower Oaks by the end of the weekend.

I want the horse done when I bring Hank to see his merry-go-round. That's when I'll tell him. That's when I'll be able to open my own door

"Okay, you need to sit quietly now and let those dry," I say to the horse, nodding at his hooves. As if I've just completed a pedicure on him. As if he were going anywhere. "I need fresh air. I'm going for a run. You behave while I'm gone."

I change clothes and send Sam a text to meet at the Sugary Spoon. That should give me plenty of time.

Sam is already there, sitting at an outdoor

café table, a box at her feet.

"Hey, how are you feeling? Ohhh, did you bring me goodies from the boutique?" I kiss her cheek and paw at the box as I sit in the empty chair.

The box yelps, sending me backward, the iron chair screeching in response.

"Not exactly." Sam leans forward and flips the top of the box open. Inside is a blanket piled up on the sides and, curled among the folds, is a tiny mass of quivering puppy. "Someone left him like this in front of the boutique. Can you imagine? I'm pretty sure he's a basset." She looks up, a mixture of sadness and anger flashing in her sea-blue eyes.

I reach into the box and pull out the puppy. He lets out a little harrumph, then, apparently deciding I'm okay, curls up in my arms and buries his head in the crook of my elbow.

His paws and ears are the biggest things on him. His long back is a patchwork of black and brown with freckled white folds at his neck. A squiggly stream of white from his forehead to his nose gives him a perplexed look.

"Oh my god, Sam. He's so sweet." I stroke his soft puppy fur.

"I'm glad you think so," she says, eyeing

the two of us. "I can't keep him. I have my hands full these days between the boutique and Taylor and, pretty soon, the baby."

I look from the sleeping bundle in my arms to my friend. "Ahh, Sam . . . ?"

"Please, please, Maya? He's so darn cute. And you said you wanted a dog." She flashes a you-can't-deny-me grin.

The puppy squirms in my arms and snorts in what must be quite some doggie dream. "I don't know."

"You want a puppy?"

"Yes. No. Yes."

"Geez, Maya, wishy-washy much? I'm going to get us drinks while you two get to know each other better."

Before I can protest, she disappears into the café.

I rearrange the puppy on my lap. He grunts, opens his eyes, and blinks at me. A yawn takes over his scrunched little face, and with another grunt, he balls in my lap, asleep. His trust in my ability to protect him warms me at the same time it scares me cold.

Sam returns with our drinks. She sighs into her paper cup, takes a sip, and pulls a disgusted face. "How did you stand this stuff?" She sucks in a gasp, her hand flying to her mouth. "Oh, Maya, I'm sorry. That was stupid."

I wave away the apology. The burning acid at the mention of my pregnancy has eased into a gnawing ache. With Sam pregnant, I'm going to have to get over myself. Finally.

"Stop apologizing." I keep my eyes on the puppy. I don't want Sam to see that it's not okay. It will be, it just isn't yet. And I can't will it into being.

Except that sometimes it's almost okay. Sometimes I almost forget that there'd been a person inside me, that I'd almost been totally, completely responsible for a tiny human being. Other times the terror of having been responsible for the tiny human inside me and my utter failure at protecting that human takes hold and leaves me gutted.

"I can't, Sam." I try to maneuver my arms from under the bundle of fur and wrinkles.

"You can."

Tears burn my eyes. "What if I fail again?"

"You won't fail now. You didn't fail then."

I blink at her. "Then what would you call what happened?"

"An accident." She doesn't back down.

"I should have known better. I did know better. What if I don't do better with him?"

"What if you do?"

The mound in my lap repositions, and I realize I've cupped my hands around him protectively.

What if I do?

"What are you smirking at?" I mock glare at Sam.

Her grin spreads. "You."

I lean forward and give the velvety head a kiss.

"What are you going to name him?"

"I still haven't decided if I'm keeping him," I respond, defiant with little conviction.

What if I can take care of him? After all, I'd been the one lobbying Vale that we should have a puppy, that it would be the perfect way to ease me back into the right mind-set.

"Fred."

"Fred."

Fred harrumphs.

On the way home, I stop at the pet store and spend a small fortune in puppy provisions. I'm congratulated by the clerks who help me, and by a lady with a Chihuahua in her handbag. I take a picture of Fred and text it to Vale.

"It's a boy. Can we keep him?"

Although, technically, I really should have sent that text before spending all that money on doggie beds and toys and poop bags and a sampling of puppy food.

The reply comes surprisingly fast. *"He's cute. Looks like it's a done deal. Don't buy everything in the store."*

I look around, anxiety beating at my chest. How does he know I'm in a pet store? I fumble to type an answer and catch the bottom of the photo I sent. I mentally kick myself. I posed him on the child seat of the shopping cart. The words *Pet Hut* visible on the plastic seat back. "So Mommy isn't very smart sometimes," I confess to Fred, who barks and licks my nose.

Now that we've adopted a puppy, the future swirls in my vision. I want to ask Vale when he'll be home, if he's even coming home, if we're going to be okay. I want to tell him about the horse and Hank, that I want to be strong. I want to ask if we're staying or moving and is that why he said not to buy too much for the puppy? *"How's it going?"* I type instead.

"Good. I'll be back Friday."

Fred leaps up and barks at a Weimaraner, who wags his stumpy butt in return. I recognize Max and his owner. We wave and he points at Fred, then gives me a thumbs-up. They disappear down the aisle of dried dog food, and I wheel the cart of puppy supplies to the car.

THIRTY-TWO

Fred hears the car before I do and unleashes a high-pitched puppy alarm. His little butt quivers in an amusing contradiction to what he no doubt assumes are ferocious growls.

"Wow, Maya, you got yourself a guard dog. How cute." Thomas high steps over the puppy, who's yelping in excitement and jumping as high as his pudgy little legs can propel him.

"Isn't he adorable? Can you believe someone dumped him in front of Sam's boutique?" I scoop Fred up and cradle him like a baby in my arms. His little legs flop sideways, revealing a round baby belly.

I rub, and he grunts his approval.

"What?" I challenge Thomas, who's watching me with an odd expression.

"I like this side of you. And yes, he is cute. The kids will go nuts over him." Thomas scratches the puppy's belly, which makes Fred squirm and grunt in ecstasy.

"So, brother dear, what brings you here?" Thomas pulls a pretend pout. "Oh stop."

"I'm here to corral you for a family dinner. Since Vale is out of town, we thought it was the perfect opportunity."

"We?"

"Come on, Maya, We haven't had dinner, the four of us, in ages. We could use some family time." Thomas jiggles the keys in his right hand and shifts his weight from left to right.

"What about Bree and the kids?"

"Nope, just us. Mom said she wants to talk to us about something important."

Mom never calls for important family discussions. It was always Dad who blew the family-discussion bugle. Granted, Mom did most of the talking, but he was the ringmaster.

"Any idea what it's about?" Our eyes meet in a rare sibling something's-up moment. "Did Mom tell you I was there Wednesday?"

"She did."

"Did she tell you what we talked about?"

He gives a nod-shake. "Why dredge up the past?" He sits by the worktable, picks up a handful of brushes, and swirls them against his palm.

I set Fred down and fold to sit on the floor next to the dog bed, where my new puppy has dropped in exhaustion. Being loved is hard work.

"I'm not dredging anything. The past found me."

"Lame."

I shoot him a look that's about as fierce as Fred's bark. "Don't you ever wonder why things turned out the way they did?"

"No. We make our choices and we move on from there. Looking back won't change the outcome."

"But we can learn from the past."

"True," he concedes without budging. "But what do you expect to learn from Grandma's past? Mom's past? Even your own that will help you move forward?"

"How to be strong enough to let go of the past."

"It's in you, not in them. I don't know what the story is with Grandma and Hank, but I do know that it doesn't matter."

"How can you say that?" Fred lifts his head and lets out a half-hearted bark.

"Because it doesn't. Whatever was between them ended. Why and when is their story. Our story starts when she married Grandpa."

He's not wrong, except that our story and their story are connected. Their story started ours.

"Bree wasn't your first girlfriend, but was she your first real love?"

He gives me an incredulous look. "Like true-love's first kiss? With the woodland animals frolicking around us?"

"Don't be a jerk." Although I'm not surprised by his snark. Heart-to-hearts were never our thing.

He sighs. "No, she wasn't. I didn't even want to date her at first. My college roommate was seeing her roommate. They kept trying to set us up. She was dating some theater dweeb who I'm sure was gay. And I was having entirely too much fun. Plus, she had a massive stick up her ass."

I practically give myself whiplash looking up at him. "So how did you finally end up together?"

"Remember Thanksgiving my junior year, when Stu and I went skiing in Utah instead of coming home?" I nod. "The girls went with us. Stu and Amanda broke up two days into the trip and left. Guess without a reason to blow her off, I actually started enjoying Bree's company. At least until we were on the plane going back to campus and she announced that we'd be getting married. Talk about ruining a fun weekend."

I gawk.

"Snap it shut, Sis. It took until the month

before summer break before I agreed to go out with her again."

"Before you *agreed*?"

"Yup. She'd ask every couple of weeks."

"Oh my god, really?" The idea of prissy, perfect Bree pursuing my brother doesn't mesh my perception of the woman he's married to.

"Really."

"Why did you finally agree then?"

Thomas shrugs.

"How did I never know this?" I still can't wrap my head around this alternate Bree.

"It's not like this is a topic you and I talk about regularly. Touchy-feely isn't what we do."

"Why is that?"

"Because you're a girl." He breaks the last word into two syllables, sounding comically like Lumière from *Beauty and the Beast.*

"Be serious."

"Beeee yourself." He mimics Genie from *Aladdin.*

"You're impossible." But I can't help laughing.

"Come on, we should get going. I may be the favorite heir, but she scares me."

"Fine. But I'm bringing Fred." I rub the soft belly and the puppy lets out a happy wriggle.

Thomas laughs. "I just hope for your sake he doesn't piddle on Mom's Persian rugs."

"Good point. She'll disown me." I pretend to ponder this horror for a minute then pick Fred up so we're nose-to-nose. "Hear that little one? I suggest the rug in the family room. It's the largest and will be the hardest to send out for cleaning. It'll make her extra cranky."

"Maya," Thomas reprimands, but laughs anyway. It's a uniquely soft moment between us, and I don't want it to end.

"I'm kidding." I flash the most innocent grin in my arsenal. "Go ahead. I need to change and will be right behind you."

Thomas shakes his head. "Yeah, no. I'm driving you there. And home, assuming you behave." He waggles a finger at me in a playful scold.

I fix the meanest stare I can on my brother, one neither of us takes seriously.

By the time we've pulled out of my street, Fred is already snoring in my lap. Thomas looks down and laughs. "Wow, he's noisy."

"Yeah, he makes weird sounds when he sleeps. I may have to rethink putting his bed in my room."

Thomas opens his mouth then closes it quickly. His jawbone seesaws back and forth a couple of times. I wait. He doesn't verbalize whatever he was thinking, and for once, I don't poke.

My phone rings before I get too far into speculating. The name blazes at me, and for a crazy heartbeat, I'm paralyzed. Thomas gives me a questioning look, and Fred repositions himself on my lap.

I tap the screen to accept the call at the last second. "Hi." The word comes out as a weird squeak.

"Maya, it's Simon." I nod, not that he can see me. I have the momentary urge to crack a joke about caller ID, but the edge in his voice stops me. "It's Hank."

Thirty-Three

He was going back to Tower Oaks tomorrow. Sunday I was taking him to see the carousel — our carousel.

I suck in a shallow breath. "I can't do this. This isn't happening."

Thomas wraps his arm around my shoulder. It's comforting and claustrophobic. I squeeze my eyes shut and count to five. The beeping and hissing of life-controlling machines heightens my anxiety, and I fight the urge to flee.

"He needs you, Maya," Simon says from somewhere in the distance. I open my eyes and he's a couple of strides to my left. "His daughter won't be here until later tonight. He's asked for you."

"Which me?"

"Both."

Thomas tightens his hold on me. "I'll go in with you."

I allow myself to be maneuvered the few

steps from the hall into Hank's room.

"You. Came." His words are raspy whispers that fight with the machines to be heard.

"Of course I came." My face hurts with the effort to appear calm.

"Come." His left hand lifts from the bed, hovers for two beeps then drops. I wince.

Thomas squeezes my shoulders. I step out of his hold. I have to breathe. I have to breathe for both of us, and Thomas's grip is making it hard.

"Don't. Be. Afraid." Hank wheezes. I blink back the panic.

With Thomas and Simon watching, I walk to the chair next to the bed and perch on the edge. Hank's hand twitches in my direction. I put a hand on top. Partly for him, partly for myself. Every time he moves it, I think of a dying fish, like the ones Thomas and my father caught one summer. The only time we'd gone fishing. I'd thrown up over the side of the boat and refused to eat seafood for years after. I swallow, forcing down the sour taste of that memory.

"I won't get to see the carousel." A tear travels the crease in his cheek.

I wipe at my face. "Hank, I have to tell you something. I'm Claire's daughter. Meera's granddaughter."

I try to catch my breath. So few words, and yet I feel like I've delivered the longest speech of my life.

He stares at me. I can't tell if the tears are a reaction to my confession or a side effect of the stroke.

"You look like her."

"I'm sorry, Hank."

"Why?" His gaze is more focused than it's been.

"For keeping this from you."

"I knew."

"You knew?" I slump in the chair. Thomas's hand covers my shoulder.

Hank releases a sound that could have been a sigh or a "yes."

"How?"

"You look like her."

"But . . ."

He pulls his hand from under mine and puts it on top. I'm trapped under Thomas's hand and Hank's hand and the weight of the past.

"It's okay, Meera. Knowing the truth." He inhales, exhales, closes his eyes. I wait, breathless. His eyes open, and he pulls me into a secret, buried for fifty some years. "*She* couldn't know. *She* needed to be Jonathan's daughter."

"But . . ." I stammer, stopped by the

intrusion of my grandfather into this conversation. Did he know or was this secret kept from him as well? "But . . ."

"No buts."

"She should know, she should be here." I start to get up, but I'm anchored in place by both men.

"No," Hank growls. "No," he adds, losing energy.

"Hank, please. Let me call my mom."

"My beautiful Maya. So much more beautiful than in pictures."

Machines beep, voices mumble, and the world slows.

Thomas bends and whispers, "I'll give you some time."

"My beautiful Maya." Hank tightens his hold on my hand. "Let go of the past."

I let the tears flow, unable to dam the flood of misery from this past year. "I don't know how."

"You must. Meera wouldn't want you to lose yourself because of her." I open my mouth to protest, but he squeezes my hand and continues, "Or because of the baby. You cannot live if you're weighed down by guilt.

"Meera hadn't been well for several months. She didn't listen to me either." His eyes close and his lips part, releasing silent words that I assume are meant for Grandma's ears only.

"And the baby? I don't know what happened, but I know you would not have done anything intentional. Accidents happen. You cannot go back, my sweet Maya. You cannot live in what should have been."

His body caves into the bed, spent from too many words. His eyes close, his mouth parts, small puffs of air joining the ensemble of sounds in the room.

I want to wake him, ask him questions. I want him to tell me stories and listen to mine. I want answers from him, from Grandma. I want to scream at all of them for keeping secrets. I want to crawl out from under all of our secrets and finally catch my breath.

Hank's hand tightens around mine. "I'm sorry, Meera. Annabelle needs me. You are with him. He'll take care of you. I will love you forever. But now, I need her." His hand goes slack, and a trickle of tears slides from his closed eyes.

Simon and Thomas each clasp an elbow and lift me from the chair. I pull away and lean to kiss Hank on the cheek.

His eyes flutter open. He smiles and his fingers graze my cheek. "The carousel. It holds our secrets. It's magic."

Thirty-Four

"Do you want to talk?"

I roll my head along the back of the chair to look at Thomas, and then roll it back. The pressure feels good, like a massage. Slow left, slow right.

We've been sitting on the front porch, mostly in silence. I'm empty.

Thomas takes the puppy for a quick pee then makes tea. "You're going to have to talk at some point," he tries again, handing me a mug.

I roll my head to the side and blink my brother into focus. "Why? Why do I have to talk? What will talking help? Will it bring any of them back? No. So what's the point?"

Thomas waits out my tirade. He was always good at waiting me out. Even as a child — especially as a child — I had a short fuse. I never held anything back. Until I became an adult. Until Simon proposed. Until I let them die. And every day since.

Tears stroll down my cheeks, slow, steady. I didn't cry at the hospital when Simon confirmed that Hank was gone. I didn't cry on the way home. I haven't cried in the three-ish hours we've been sitting on my front porch.

I also haven't talked since we walked out of Hank's hospital room for the last time.

"What time is it?" I look at my watch but can't make out the numbers through the haze of exhaustion and emotion.

"3:07 A.M."

"It's Sunday."

"It's Sunday." Thomas agrees. No snarky big-brother comeback though.

"Hank was supposed to be back at Tower Oaks today. I was going to pick him up after lunch and bring him here to see the horse. I couldn't even get this right."

Thomas sits up, abruptly. "Stop it. Now. Enough, Maya. This has been a horrible year for all of us, most of all for you. But you have to pull yourself out of this spiral of self-flagellation. You are not responsible for all the bad that's happened. Listen to me: You have to pull yourself together. Now, before it's too late."

"Too late for what? It's already too late for Grandma and Hank. It's too late for my baby."

"But it's not too late for you and Vale, and it's not too late for you to have a family."

"What if it is?"

He pushes his fingers into his hair. "You make me crazy sometimes. If you weren't my sister and I didn't love you, I'd tell Vale to leave your sorry behind and move on. I know that's harsh, but the only person who would have dared say this to you is gone. She'd be busting you so hard for how you're behaving. She would have sat you down and told you to stop wallowing, that life is precious. None of us knows how much time we have. Hopefully we die of old age. But it's not a given. And even that isn't much consolation for the people left behind.

"Grandma knew how to be happy," he continues. "She knew how to find happiness in anything, any situation. You used to be like that, too. She'd hate this."

I can't respond, can't defend myself.

Thomas takes my silence as permission to continue. "Whether you want another child or to save your marriage is your business. But you cannot lose yourself. Do that for her, Maya."

From inside the house, a phone rings. Thomas's. He stands but doesn't go in.

A wind breezes through the screened porch, rattling the rocking chair next to me.

The rocking chair Grandma used to sit in.

I watch the chair move back and forth. I expect to see her, head back, eyes closed, legs slightly apart, hands on the armrests, and fingers tapping to imaginary music.

Thomas is right. She'd be spitting mad seeing me now.

I stand and hug my brother. "You're released from crazy watch. I'll be okay. I have a horse to finish."

I watch as Thomas pulls out of the driveway and crawls away in the slowest escape he's ever made. I can almost feel his eyes on me in the rearview mirror. When the taillights finally make the turn away from my street, I enter the studio, my tired puppy companion at my heels.

I turn on the lights in the studio and look around. The dancing dust fairies don't feel like coming out this morning. Even the carousel horse seems to be drooping.

The glint I painted in his black eyes two days ago looks dull now, and the unfinished portions of his neck and hindquarters catch at my throat.

"You know, don't you?" I run a hand along his yet-unfinished neck. "I wanted him to see you looking shiny and almost as good as new." The horse blurs as tears take possession of my sight.

Today there's no music, no chocolate-orange tea, no talking. Just painting. Except for letting Fred out to pee, I paint. The only accompanying sounds are puppy yelps and snores.

"Maya?" A voice from the door startles me. Fred's head pops up, and he lets out a sharp bark and a growl that fades into a grumble as his head flops back onto his bed.

"Some bloody watchdog you are," I hiss at him.

"I brought you something to eat," Mom says, walking in and setting a bag down on the worktable. She looks from Fred, to me, to the carousel horse. "You're almost done."

"I wanted Hank to see him finished."

Mom's mouth tightens. "I'm sorry."

There's nothing to say. "Thank you," is inadequate. "I'm sad," is obvious. "It's unfair," is trite.

"Have you eaten anything at all today?" Mom takes out a couple of containers followed by two bottles of Orangina.

"You brought Orangina?" I laugh, taking a bottle.

"Orangina and tuna melts." Mom pushes one of the containers toward me.

"Comfort food?" It wasn't meant to be a question, but there's no mistaking the surprised uptick in my voice. It was my favorite consolation meal when I was a little girl. I turn quickly and pull up a chair, hoping the movement will mask my discomfort.

I look at Mom, perched at the edge of her chair, only her eyes moving as she takes in the contents of my studio, and very conscious of the harrumphing blob on the plush doggy bed at the end of the table. It's hard to tell which of us is less at ease.

"When did that happen?" Mom's chin juts in the direction of Fred's bed.

"*That's* name is Fred. And I got him yesterday."

"Does Vale know?"

My sandwich hovers between the Styrofoam container and my mouth, my fingers pinching into the warm bread.

I ease the sandwich back into the container just as the tomato attempts an escape out the bottom. I stuff a clump of warm, cheesy tuna into my mouth. "Sam found him in a box outside her boutique. And yes, Vale knows."

Mom's left eyebrow moves almost imperceptibly, and I'm sure she's itching to tell me not to talk with my mouth full.

"Do you know how he's getting on in Seattle?"

"I haven't really talked to him. He seems to be pleased though."

"How do you feel about that?" She plucks a string of melted cheese from the sandwich and pops it into her mouth.

Normally I'd snipe something hostile, but Mom seems oddly non-confrontational, and I can't deny the tuna melts and Orangina are a peace offering. "I don't know. I don't want to move. But I don't want to lose Vale either."

I wish for maternal advice like I'd wished for the maternal hug a few days ago.

"He's due back soon right?"

I nod.

"Then I guess you need to make a decision."

Apparently comfort food delivery is as touchy-feely as we're going to get.

"Mom, when did this happen between us?" I wave my hand in a small circle, Mom and I both clearly outside the warm, gooey center.

She takes a long drink then gently places her Orangina on the table, her finger tracing the embossed letters on the old-fashioned bottle. And for the first time that I can remember, Mom slumps in her chair.

"You came out fiery." There's the slightest hint of a nostalgic smile. "And challenged me every step of the way. Your way was never my way, and I couldn't convince you otherwise. Thomas, on the other hand, was more than happy to take my lead and do what was asked. He never questioned. You always questioned."

She watches me for a minute. I don't know whether to respond or wait. For once, I don't question.

"You and Mom were like two gulls on a wave." No clichéd pea pods for my mom. "Always in motion, always looking to see what else was out there, always free and on your terms. I was closer to Dad. I understood him, related to him better than to Mom. She intimidated me to be honest."

My eyebrows crash into each other. "Grandma?"

Mom laughs. An honest-to-goodness, from-the-belly, uninhibited laugh. "Your grandma. My mother. Scared the shit out of me."

I pick up my drink but before taking a sip, take a quick, discreet sniff. What's in here?

"Don't look so shocked, Maya. Your kids will probably see me much differently than you do. That's nature's private joke. Our own parents are never as fantastic as our grandparents. You'll see." She wags a finger at me.

A gull screeches outside, sending Fred into convulsions of high-pitched barks. He runs in circles around the studio before settling back in his bed. He's asleep in one snort.

"How much more do you have to do?" Mom closes the Styrofoam container on her mostly untouched sandwich and indicates the horse.

"Just a bit more on the tail." I stand, walk to the horse, and cup his muzzle in my hands. "A few touch-ups, some shading, and you will be one handsome pony."

"Do you always talk to them?" Her voice surprises me — not that she's there, but that she sounds interested. Sarcasm I expect. Even ridicule. Interest, however, is new.

"Yeah."

"Do they talk back?" There's something else in her tone this time, but still not what I've come to expect from my mom.

"In a way." I watch for a reaction.

"Your grandma always insisted that they talk. Drove her batty that I couldn't hear them. I was convinced she was two waves from being sucked into the loony bin."

Another thing I inherited from Grandma.

"Did she ever tell you what they said?"

Mom lets out a deep, throaty laugh. "Do you really think I would have had that conversation with her?"

It's the first time I've ever heard my mom poke fun at herself. My brain cells scurry, trying to think of something to say. I'm at a total loss.

I watch as she studies the carousel horse. Maybe she's trying to figure out where the voices would come from. Or perhaps what secrets he might be hiding from her. "He's beautiful."

I'm staring. I can't help myself.

"What?" She asks, surprised more than annoyed at my open mouth and unblinking stare.

"I thought you hated the carousel."

This time it's Mom who's left in open-mouthed surprise. "Why in the world would you think I hated it?"

"Maybe because you never wanted to go with me. Or because you always said it was a waste of time. You call it 'that thing.' Want me to keep going?" I hadn't meant to sound harsh. Old habits.

She shakes her head. "You and your grandma were nuts about this carousel. When I was little she was forever planning outings to the 'merry-go-round.' " She air quotes, but her tone holds a nostalgic fuzziness. "She even planned my fourth birthday party there. And every attempt she made, I battled — until I was, oh, maybe seven, and she just stopped. We'd pass the carousel and Mom would stop to look at it, then grab my hand and pull me on. You could tell it was killing her, but she wasn't going to fight with me about it.

"Once when I was in middle school, I was hanging out on the boardwalk with a bunch of friends and I saw her. She was sitting on the bench watching all the kids ride around on the carousel. She looked far away, lost almost, lonely, and sad. I didn't go to her and never mentioned it. I don't know if she saw me or not. She never said anything."

Her words fade into the past, and for a few minutes, we both look at the wooden horse in my studio, lost in our own thoughts. My heart twists for my grandma. I wonder if Mom is thinking about the cause of Grandma's sadness or remembering her own teenage unhappiness.

"And then you arrived." Mom's voice softens even more. "From the first time you saw that carousel, you were in love. Mom finally had a kindred soul. The two of you used to make up stories about the animals and talked about them like they were actual friends. Every drawing or art project you came home with had a carousel in it. And any time we drove somewhere and you spotted a merry-go-round, you made our life miserable until we stopped and you got to ride it. Over and over and over. Thankfully Thomas was old enough to ride with you."

"Why didn't you ever ride with me?"

This time when she turns back to me she's not surprised or taken aback. Her mouth pulls up at the corner, but her eyes don't follow. "The easy answer is motion sickness. We didn't have that many long car vacations did we?" I shake my head. "But I think it was also a fear of the magic that Mom used to weave into stories. Magic wasn't *real,* and if it wasn't real I couldn't analyze it and understand it, and that scared me."

I turn to the horse, thinking about what she just said. Magic. Believing. Getting carried away. That was the world I couldn't wait to get lost in. Still can't, for that matter. It was where I didn't have to pretend. And now? It's my escape from expectations and disappointments.

"And you, Maya — why do you love carousels so much?"

"Their magic." The words pop out before I can censor them. "The stories they keep. And this one because of the stories he was willing to share."

Mom looks from me to the horse.

Air swirls in my lungs and I feel lightheaded. The carousel horse wants her to know. He wants her to see his secret. He wants to share his magic with her.

"Come see." I hear the words, but the voice doesn't sound like my own. It has a raspy edge with a twinge of mischief skimming below the surface, waiting to bubble out. Grandma's voice.

Mom hears it too.

"His secret is on his girth. Take a look." I point as if she doesn't know what I'm referring to.

Mom walks over, one eye narrowing in on me, as though she's expecting me to pull a prank on her. I hold up my hands in a "see, nothing here" declaration of innocence. She squats down and peers at the horse's belly. "What am I looking for?"

"Close your eyes and feel along the girth."

The other eye narrows. On the exhale, Mom lifts her hand and runs it down the raised wood of the girth. Suspicion turns into a question as her fingers, no doubt, find the ridges of the inscription.

"Why didn't you finish this part?"

"It is finished. It's how Hank wanted him."

"Hank." She exhales his name.

"Look at it." I nod at the horse, and if I didn't know better, I'd swear he nodded back.

Mom bends down, twisting to get a better view.

I'm holding my breath.

She straightens, tugs her shirt back into position, not that it was anything but perfectly behaved already, and walks slowly back to the table.

I can't release the breath.

"It's getting late. I need to go and you need to sleep." She collects her bag from the floor and throws her uneaten sandwich into the trash.

I watch, unable to call her back. The words etched into the horse float in the air of the studio, a secret released into the world.

Now that it's out, I wish it were still mine. Still theirs.

Thirty-Five

Fred whimpers and paws at my shin, his nails leaving scratch marks. "Okay, okay." So much for a quiet cup of coffee first thing in the morning. He spins in circles, spiraling his way from me to the door, sitting — or more precisely collapsing — then popping back up on his short legs and running into my shins.

I put the mug on the counter and grab the leash and my credit card. I'll get a latte at the Sugary Spoon. Maybe Sam will be at the store already. I could use her take on the conversation with my mom.

I push the door open and Fred tumbles down the back steps in a crazed ball of gotta-pee. For as small as he is, I'm impressed he hasn't had any accidents in the house. That had always been one of Vale's arguments against puppies. Apparently, this one really wants to make the right impression.

The walk to the Sugary Spoon takes longer than usual. Fred runs forward, runs back, stops to smell something, runs forward, runs back, pees on the spot he was just smelling. And everyone we pass wants to pet him. Not that he minds, but after the seventh person who's stopped us, I'm less enamored with celebrity status.

The door to Socks-A-Lot is propped open, even though the sign still says "closed." The sun aims a ray at the window, and I have to squint to see inside. Sam and Taylor are in the middle of the store. I take a step forward then hesitate. Taylor says something, Sam laughs and looks at him. He turns to her, and I melt at the softness in his expression, the openness of hers.

Even through the window I can see the happiness radiating from her. They say pregnant women have a certain glow about them. I don't think I did. But Sam could teach the sun a lesson.

A couple walks by, the woman eyeballing me suspiciously while the man coos at Fred. Before they decide to call the police or out me for spying, I squat and say, loud enough for them to hear but hopefully quiet enough not to be heard in the store, "Hang tight, bud, I need to tie my shoe." Fred is happy to play along, grabbing my shoelace in his mouth. He growls and shakes his head, subduing his catch. His whole body shimmies, ears flopping. Less-than-menacing growls cause a small cluster of admirers to stop and comment.

Once he's convinced the shoelace is good and dead, Fred flops over, ears spread on the sidewalk, belly positioned for a rub.

"God, you're a goofball." I scratch the pink mound then do a double knot on my shoelaces.

I straighten and look through the window again. A cloud plays peek-a-boo with the sun, and this time I don't have to squint. Taylor steps toward Sam and envelops her in his arms. I smile, thinking of Sam's praise for his pecs. He takes a half step back and places his hand on her belly. An innocent, instinctual gesture that breaks my heart and crushes the pieces.

I'm struck by the contentment on their faces, their eager anticipation for the future. No past to shadow their joy. We had those moments. Vale made sure we would. He never doubted, and though I never voiced my fears, he knew and he soothed.

My throat tightens. He would have been a great father.

Sam sees me and waves, motioning for me to come in, and I hear Taylor's booming voice call, "Get in here, will you?"

I smile and wave, but I'm not going in. That's their happy cocoon.

I tug Fred forward the couple of blocks to the coffee shop. I loop the leash to the bronze ring by the door, under the sign for "Puppy Valet Spot," and instruct him to wait. He dissolves into a brown-and-white puddle, left front paw pinning his left ear to the ground.

"You really are a goof." I rub his head then allow the aroma of fresh-ground coffee beans to lure me away.

By the time I return, Fred is curled up in the lap of a little girl who's sitting cross-legged in the middle of the sidewalk. Next to her is a stroller with a sleeping toddler and a tired-looking woman giving the handle an occasional push-pull.

"Well, I see Fred has made a new friend." I smile at the girl, then at her mom.

"She loves puppies." The mom stretches the word loves a bit longer than necessary and punctuates it with an eye roll. This kid won't be getting a puppy any time soon.

"How old is he?" asks the girl, who I'm guessing is about Alex's age. She doesn't take her eyes or hands off the puppy. There may not be a puppy in the kid's near future, but there's a tantrum coming for her mom to deal with.

"You know, I'm not sure. I've only had him two days. Someone abandoned him. Can you believe that? A friend found him, and now he's mine." Fred wiggles happily in the girl's lap. I have the sudden urge to grab him and cradle him in my own arms. This baby, I can protect. This baby, I have to protect. He's my opportunity to prove that I can do this, that I'm worthy of being given a second chance.

The baby stirs in the stroller and the mom jiggles the handle. She reties her ponytail and inhales a lung-full of coffee-scented air.

"That smells amazing. I've been fielding 'Mommy-can-we' since before five A.M."

"Guess I can't complain about this one then." I scratch at Fred's back with my toe. "It was after six, and only a couple of yelps because he had to pee."

The mom hands a sippy cup to the baby, who promptly tosses it onto the sidewalk; then grabs at a ziplock bag of goldfish crackers from the little girl, who's about to feed one to Fred. I wonder if she takes turns with her husband doing the sleepless shifts. Would Vale have given me mornings to sleep in?

"But they're worth it. Most of the time. Maybe a little less at five A.M. and on almost no coffee." She grins. "Hey, don't you live at 12 Clairemont? The cute white cottage?"

I'm not sure what I'm more taken aback by — that she recognizes me and I don't have a clue who she is, or that she thinks my house is cute. "Yes." I eyeball the kids, trying to connect this family to one of the houses near me.

"We're a couple of blocks away. Number 37. We walk by your place every time we go to the beach. Can I confess something?" She blushes, or maybe we've been standing outside too long. "I always hope for a sale sign in your yard. I just love your cottage."

"Oh, thanks. It's cute. Not as cute on the inside, I'm afraid. We haven't had much time to update it." *Except for the bathroom. And just in time to sell?*

She sticks her hand out. "I'm Amy."

"Maya." I switch my hold on the coffee cup and shake her hand.

"Nice to meet you, Maya. Although now I'm going to feel a bit guilty wishing you'll move and sell the house." She grins sheepishly.

You may get your wish, lady.

"Would you like me to stay with the kids while you go get a drink?" I nod at the stroller.

A flash of longing and uncertainly crosses her face. "You don't mind?" Longing, or maybe that's desperation, wins out, and she disappears inside while she has the opportunity.

"I'm six," the little girl on the sidewalk says. "My daddy said I could have a puppy when I'm old enough to take care of it. I'm old enough." She announces with the sass of six going on sixteen. "I already help with him." She points at the stroller.

On cue, the toddler lets out a wail that startles both Fred and me. Fred jumps from his comfortable spot and, using the footrest on the stroller, lifts up to see what the noise is about.

"You just have to move the stroller," my know-it-all companion instructs. "Like Mommy was doing." When it becomes clear I'm not living up to her expectations, she huffs, stands, and takes the stroller handle.

While the bossy six-year-old bounces the stroller with her baby brother inside, I readjust the visor to keep the morning sun from his eyes and rescue his stuffed bunny before Fred gets to it.

"Thank you." Amy returns, slightly out of breath. "I really needed this. He barely sleeps, and when he does finally doze off, she wakes up. And this kid has two speeds, fast-forward and dead asleep. She even moves in her sleep. See this." She pulls up her shorts and shows off a perfectly sculpted thigh with a huge bruise. "She did that two nights ago, while sleeping in my bed." Amy ruffles her daughter's hair, the love in her eyes and voice send a warm vibration up my throat.

But for the first time in over a year, I don't feel like I'm about to crumble. I don't have the need to flee, hide, fall apart.

I catch a glimpse of Taylor, up the street, leaving the store. He closes the door behind him, hesitates, then puts his palm on the glass before walking away. I picture Sam on the other side, locking the door behind him, putting her hand to the glass in a good-bye.

I say good-bye to our new friends, promise Amy she'll be the first to know if we decide to sell, and coax Fred to follow.

We have four hours before Vale is due home.

We turn the corner onto our street just as the black town car pulls away from the house. I jog the half-ish block to the house, Fred keeping pace and barking with excitement.

The screen door to the front porch opens. "There you are."

For a few heartbeats, I'm rooted to the

sidewalk, torn between the man whose arms I want to throw myself into and the man I haven't allowed myself to need. Fred, however, has no emotional baggage and barrels up the stairs, past Vale, and straight to his food bowl.

"Wow." Vale chuckles. "He's made himself right at home, hasn't he?"

"Do you mind?" I thread the leash through my fingers.

"No. We talked about it. Kind of." He grins. "Come in." He pushes the door wider and steps to the side, leaving a space for me to pass.

I hesitate as my shoulder brushes his chest, that moment when I should stop and kiss my husband, whom I haven't seen in a week.

He puts a hand on the small of my back and kisses my cheek. I flush. At the awkwardness and the tenderness.

He follows me into the house, straight to the kitchen. I turn on the coffee machine, more as habit and the need to do something than actual interest in caffeine. The double-shot latte from the Sugary Spoon is making my nerve endings bounce like the giant inflatable outside the used car dealership.

"I wasn't expecting you until later." I take two mugs from the cabinet, return one, take it back out.

"I caught an earlier flight."

"Did you get any sleep?" Vale hates night flights. According to him, he can't sleep in public places. I've been on enough planes with him to know he falls asleep almost immediately.

"Nah, you know me." He rakes his fingers through his hair and gives me a sheepish, just-woke-up grin.

I pour coffee in both mugs and take them to the breakfast table. Vale follows and takes his usual seat. Fred is two steps behind and throws himself on Vale's feet.

"How did the meetings go?" I'm dying to know but, at the same, time I don't really want to know.

He drinks from the mug, wincing as the hot liquid goes down.

"Should I have warned you that contents are hot?"

"Ha, ha. I took a larger swig than I'd intended."

I nod, but he's not looking at me.

"So?" I prompt.

"So . . ." He hesitates. "So, it was interesting. It was an amazing ego boost. And it was eye opening."

I nod. This time he is looking at me.

"Maya, I talked to Thomas yesterday. He

told me. I'm sorry. I really am."

I suck air into my lungs. "Did Thomas tell you everything?"

"I'm not sure what 'everything' is. He told me you were headed to your parents for dinner when you got the news, and that you made it to the hospital in time to say goodbye."

"Did he tell you that Hank is — was — our biological grandfather?"

Vale's eyes widen in surprise.

"Guess I'm not surprised he didn't. That's a messy secret that doesn't float well in high-society circles."

"You know that's not it," Vale reprimands gently.

I let it go; there's no sense in getting into an argument over this. In the past few months, Vale has been much faster to stand behind Thomas during family bickers.

"Hank knew who I was. Maybe not every time I was there, but he knew. And he didn't say anything."

"Neither did you."

"Neither did I."

We're silent; the only sounds are the drops from the coffee machine and the snores from the puppy.

"So, listen . . ."

"So, I've been thinking . . ."

We revert to the semiquiet.

"You first," I finally concede. Anything is better than the loaded quiet.

"So, I had a long time to think. A week away and a miserable flight. I love you, Maya, and I want us back. I really think a fresh start may be just what we need."

A tear slithers down my cheek and plops into my coffee. I set the mug down and wipe my face with my palms. How can we be having this discussion again?

"Vale, I don't want to leave."

He holds a hand up. "Just listen. You'll be done with the carousel in a month. One month, Maya. Then we can take a sabbatical of sorts. We can rent a house and maybe even rent this place. It's gorgeous there. You'll love it. It's the perfect place for an artist."

You'll love it, he'd said. Not *you would* but *you will.* I bite back the urge to point that out.

"For how long would we be on this sabbatical of sorts?"

"One year? Two years? Who knows, maybe we'll fall in love with the place and want to stay. Maybe we'll fall in love with each other again." His voice drops, becoming suddenly shy, hesitant, hopeful.

"I don't know. This . . . I don't know." I

stumble over my thoughts. Deep down, I want to say yes. I want to fall in love with him again. I want to start breathing again. But I'm petrified of saying yes. Who will watch over them if I leave?

He stands, walks to the sink, and dumps what's left in his mug. "I get insecurity about making such a big step, but if we don't do something, we'll be taking a big step in the opposite direction. Is that what you want?"

"No."

"What do you want then?"

"I want what we had. I want a redo of the last year."

"That's not an option, is it? I don't have a time machine to go back. Or fast forward. All I can offer is my hand and a promise that I'll be with you. But it has to be moving forward. And you have to want to go. This, us, can no longer be one sided."

When I don't say anything, he shakes his head and continues. "I told Ed that I'll be there next month."

"You what?" I croak.

He shrugs a nonanswer answer.

"You accepted the job? Without talking to me?"

"I accepted *a* job. You knew my deadline for a decision was up. How long did you expect me to stay on hold?"

"You didn't even talk to me about it though. You decided by yourself. That's not about 'us' starting over. That's all you."

"Would your answer have been different if I'd waited?"

I hesitate a heartbeat too long.

"That's what I thought. I'm going to Seattle in a month, and I want you to come with me. It doesn't have to be a permanent move, but it has to be a step forward. We need distance from here if we're going to find our future together."

The ticking clock has just morphed into a lit fuse.

Thirty-Six

The trumpet tingles down my spine. It's my favorite of Chris Botti's songs, and I've almost worn out the back button listening to it over and over.

You can replay a song, a movie, a memory. But once a life is gone, it's gone.

Yesterday had turned upside down on me. Like so many days lately. Maybe I've forgotten how to be happy. Is that possible?

The music transitions to the next song on the album, and, this time, I let it.

After our discussion, Vale played the jet-lag card and went for a nap. I left a note that I was in the studio and for him to get me when he woke up. He hadn't. When I finally came up for air, it was almost midnight, the horse's hooves were done, the tail highlighted like an extravagant salon makeover, and Vale was still asleep. Again asleep. The dishes in the sink were proof he'd gotten up at least once.

He'd been asleep when I crawled out of bed this morning.

I know what Grandma would have told me. "Get your head out of your armpit, Mims. You can't smell the flowers if your nose is buried. And you can't see what's around if your eyes are closed."

A knock on the door is almost obscured by the final notes of the song. Fred snaps his head up and barks. If it wasn't for him wagging at the door, I would have assimilated the sound into a prank by Mother Nature, with an assist from my grandmother.

Then again, considering that it's my mom standing at the door, a prank by Grandma isn't a long shot.

"Can I come in?" She stands in the door, a purple bag in one hand and a yellow bag in the other.

"That's a lot of Orangina and tuna melts." I point at the bags.

She laughs. "No food this time." She comes in and sets the bags down by the worktable. Fred pads over, sniffs the yellow bag, shuffles to the purple bag and paws at it until he's collapsed the top enough to climb in.

"Fred." I grab for him, but Mom waves me away.

"That one is for him."

Fred backs out of the crumpled bag dragging a rubber chew toy that's at least half his size. Mom rubs his ears and whispers something to him that I can't quite make out. He responds with a wag and a lick to her nose. She laughs then laughs harder when she looks up and catches me staring. "Close your mouth, dear."

"Who are you?"

Her smile tightens but doesn't disappear. "I couldn't stop thinking about our discussion yesterday." She settles on the floor next to Fred, her eyes level with the horse's belly. She focuses on the girth, on a spot not visible from where we're sitting. "I knew. Not confirmed, of course, but I suspected. Your grandmother was a master at spinning stories. Your grandfather, not so much. And you always had questions. You wanted every detail on every part of everyone's lives."

Fred snuffles back into the purple bag and backs out with yet another gift.

"How many things did you buy him?" Between my shopping spree and my mother's, this puppy is one spoiled boy.

"That's the last of it. I promise. Except for these." She reaches into the bag and extracts a plastic container with paw prints painted on it. Inside are puppy treats. She takes one out and gives it to Fred, who thanks her with a slurpy kiss. She kisses him on the side of his muzzle. I force my mouth shut.

"I thought you didn't like dogs."

"Who told you that?"

"You."

She lifts Fred's ears and lets them flop down. "I didn't want the mess or the heart-ache."

"Mess, okay. But I don't get the heartache part."

"Dogs have too short of a life span. Especially the large ones that I always preferred. I couldn't stand the idea of falling in love with a dog then losing him a few years later."

"People die, too. That didn't stop you from getting Dad or us."

She smiles at my "getting" comment. "Your dad was already house-trained and he has a longer life span than a Great Dane."

I raise my eyebrows at her. I cannot quite figure out this new version of my mother.

"Anyway," she continues, and I try to focus on what she's saying rather than the alien sitting next to me. "During one of your interrogations, Dad said something that struck me as odd. I don't remember what it was now, isn't that weird? You'd think something that monumental would have stayed with me. The brain is an odd organism."

"Mom, focus." For the first time since I pieced together the relationship between Hank and my grandmother, Hank's Alzheimer's lands on my heart. Is it possible that my mom, a force I never questioned, could have inherited the disease? Have there been signs I didn't know to look for? No. But how to explain the person sitting in front of me now?

"I asked Mom about it, and she waved if off. Even that seemed odd at the time. But I guess it's also true that we see what we want to see, accept what's within our comfort for knowing. I didn't ask again, didn't question. But when she started visiting him, I couldn't hide from it any longer. Little things she'd murmur, the look in her eye — nothing specific, but just enough."

"Why didn't you want the truth? That seems so out of character for you."

"Because it didn't matter. Dad was Dad. He was already gone. I didn't want to lose him a second time. Hank was her memory, not mine."

"But still."

"Still nothing. My identity came from the parents who raised me. My happiness came from the people I chose to surround myself with."

She leans to one side and stretches until she can grab the yellow bag. She pulls it into her lap and looks inside. Fred paws at the bag, growls, and bites at a curly ribbon.

"Loss is hard to get past, but it's impossible to live in. I've watched you take tentative steps out of the cave over the last few weeks, then run back in the moment the light hits your face. I can't tell you what to do, you won't listen anyway, but it's time to stop being afraid of the light.

"Your grandmother bought this for you, for the baby, but didn't want to give it to you until after the baby was born. I think you should have it. I think she'd want you to have it. You're ready." She pulls the ribbon from Fred's mouth, hands me the bag, and pushes up. She nods at the horse. "You've done a beautiful job restoring him. Hank and your grandmother would be very proud."

Before I can pull myself together, the door to the studio closes, a hushed finale to an emotionally conflicting day.

I stare at the bag. Inside is a square box, beautifully wrapped in yellow-and-blue paper, with an elaborate matching bow.

My fingers tremble, fumbling with the

bow then the Scotch tape. It was a typical wrapping job for my grandma — more tape on the box than left on the roll, no doubt.

I slide a nail under the tape keeping the box shut then reach into the white tissue paper and pull out a snow globe. The white flakes, disturbed while I was extracting it, swirl around a miniature merry-go-round.

The storm inside the globe settles. And with it, the turbulence that's been raging inside me.

I look at the carousel horse in my studio. "You are magic."

Thirty-Seven

Fred trots into the kitchen carrying a rolled pair of socks. "Dammit, dog, I need those, and I prefer them dry." Vale is half a step behind, but every time he reaches for the socks, Fred ducks out of the way. "Why did we need a dog?" He collapses onto the chair next to me.

Yesterday had been business as usual. Vale had gone to his office; I'd spent the day in the studio.

But in a twist from our usual, we'd had dinner together, wine on the front porch after, and connected as husband and wife. Unlike the night before his trip, this time was slow and sweet and reminded me why I'd fallen in love with him. And what I'd be losing if I let him leave without me.

Fred drops the socks at Vale's feet and plunks his butt down, head cocked, tongue stuck out the side of his mouth. His front paws have the slightest of ballerina turnouts and my heart swells.

Vale's shoulders slump and his grin widens. "Yeah, okay, that's why we need a dog. You're lucky you're so cute." He rubs the puppy's ears. Fred licks his hands and stares adoringly at his new dad.

"I'm taking him for a walk. Want to come?" Vale stands and Fred performs a clumsy spin at his feet.

"Yes, but I can't. I have to check on something at the installation site and last touch-ups on the horse. He's being picked up tomorrow."

"Already?"

"Already. Time flies. Reopening is in three weeks."

"Excited?" He's beaming.

I want to beam. I am. Sort of. "Yes and no. I wanted to bring Hank. He should be there." I blink away tears and wipe at my cheeks. "God, I have to stop doing this."

Vale pulls me into a hug. "No, you don't. There's only so much space inside any of us for grief. You've had more than your share lately. If you don't let it out, you can't make space for the happiness."

I nod into his chest. There's a tug on my pant leg followed by a low growl. Another growl, this time from Vale. His body tenses, and he pulls away. "What the hell is he doing here?"

Vale steps around me and strides to the back door. Even his steps sound angry. "What can we do for you?" I wince at the edge in his voice and the possessive accent on "we."

"I don't mean to intrude. I have something for Maya. From Hank. Well, from Hank's daughter." Simon couches the delivery in soothing tones, no doubt in response to a look from Vale that I'm not privy to.

I slip under Vale's arm where he's gripping the door, his knuckles at eye level to Simon. "Hi, Simon."

"Hi. So, Hank's daughter asked me to give this to you and said she hopes you'll come to the funeral." He hands me a package wrapped in brown shipping paper.

"Okay." I take the package, hyperaware of Vale's outstretched arm resting on my shoulder, and the distance between the tips of my fingers and Simon's fingers as the package changes ownership.

"Okay." Simon lets go and takes a step down, so he's now looking up at us. Another step and he pivots to walk away. He hesitates, turns back, and adds, "The funeral is at four."

He walks slowly, and I struggle with the urge to call him back or run after him.

"I'll go with you." Vale's arm closes around my shoulders but feels possessive, not protective.

I duck backward, back into the kitchen. "No need."

"I want to."

I exhale, slow and measured, then turn to my husband. "I'd rather you don't, actually."

He flinches as though I've slapped him. And as quickly, his features harden. "Well." He turns and takes Fred's leash from the hook by the door. Without another word to me, man and dog depart.

I clutch the package to my chest. It's a book of some sort, from the feel of it. I pour another cup of coffee and go to the front porch.

I peel the paper away, holding my breath as the last piece of tape breaks. Inside is a black leather-bound journal. Hank's journal. Written in angled script, are notes from the early days of the merry-go-round.

Notes about what inspired him, the colors he chose, the animals he included, the paintings on the engine housing.

"And he told me he didn't keep records," I mutter. Although technically, he wasn't keeping records. There's nothing technical about the construction or design. No details about the paint used. Just his thoughts and feelings, things he saw on the beach, discussions with friends, dreams.

I flip through the book, looking for anything on my horse. On my grandmother.

She was here today, in my studio. The blue of his saddle pad will match her dress. The brown of her hair will be his mane.

I turn pages with shaky fingers.

One more day and the installation should be complete. She came to see us, wearing my favorite dress. Standing on the carousel next to her horse, she looked like an angel. My angel. And for a fleeting minute I almost believe we have a future together.

What a glorious grand opening. A big band in the ballroom, a tremendous crowd, and the only person who matters. What a dream to ride the carousel with my Meera, to watch her laugh, her hair waving in the wind. And her lips! I could die a happy man tonight.

My fingers stroke the page, trying to extract the happiness and love out of the long-dried ink.

I leaf through a few more pages until I find it.

I have only one regret in my life. That I never held my own daughter. It is a secret I will forever hold close to my heart, where it belongs. Our secret. Until we're together again, Meera, this time forever.

The pages blur.

Tomorrow I leave Kent, my merry-go-round, my past. Annabelle and I will make a new life, one that's ours, one without baggage and regrets. The life my sweet Annabelle deserves.

Today I made my last touch-ups to the carousel, to my — our — horse. One last gift.

For Meera. Forever.

Thirty-Eight

I stay hidden, far enough that I could be mistaken as a visitor for anyone else.

The three musketeers huddle together. Joe has his arm around Dottie while Nick stands, head down, arms clasped tight behind his back. Barbie is there, her face drooping more than usual. I imagine her clipboard. No more ticks next to Hank's name. A handful of people stand at the other side of the casket, their backs to me.

Close to the head is Simon and a woman who looks to be somewhere in age between me and my mom.

Simon looks up, notices me. His eyes scan my surroundings, then with the tilt of his head, he encourages me forward. I shake my head. I don't want to go closer. I want to remember Hank alive, sitting in his chair, swaying to the sounds of a jazz trumpet. I want to remember him sitting on the bench in the warm afternoon sun, complaining about the magazines the nurses brought in, or the laps around the building they made him do. I want to remember the man who talked to me about mixing colors and smoothing out the hooves of wooden carousel animals. I want to remember the man who looked at me and saw his first love, and the man who looked at me and recognized his granddaughter.

The crowd begins to disperse. People walk to the casket then to Hank's daughter. After a hug or handshake, they step to the side where an easel stands. It's hard to see the details, but my heart tells me it's the photograph that hung in his room at Tower Oaks. One by one they write something on the photograph, some taking longer than others, almost all wiping tears when they finish.

"Why are you standing back here?" Thomas's voice reaches me a heartskip before he appears at my side.

"I wanted the distance."

My mom appears on my other side.

I exhale, torn between relief and anger that they're here. They didn't open their hearts to Hank. They didn't even acknowledge who he really was within our family.

"Are you okay?" Mom asks.

"I will be." I know I will be. "Would any

of us have been better off if these secrets hadn't been hanging over us?"

"Maybe," Mom answers. "But if not these, there would have been others. These secrets were spun out of love, out of wanting to do the right thing. Parents don't always know best. Sometimes we screw up. But everything we do starts from love."

I want her words to wrap around my jagged heart. I want the storm cloud of secrets to blow away.

Mom touches my arm and turns. I listen to the crunch of gravel, the car door. Thomas gives me a kiss on the cheek and follows my mom. Another car door closes.

Simon embraces Hank's daughter and steps away. She walks to the coffin and places her hands on the top, then kisses the lid. Her right hand lifts, and I realize she's just waved at me. She places the hand over her heart, her lips move, and she turns and walks away. A man holds open the back door of a town car that swallows her before I can react.

"Oh god, Hank." The air leaves my lungs as I look at the plain wood coffin resting on rollers above an open rectangle in the ground. I'd been too numb at Grandma's funeral and my baby's funeral to process what was happening. Vale and Thomas had kept me as isolated as they could.

But here, now, there's no one to protect me. Only me.

"Bye, Hank."

Simon is leaning against my car, the frame from the easel at his feet. I hadn't noticed him walking this way. I stop a few steps away and indicate the car behind him.

"Your bodyguard didn't come with you."

"I asked him not to."

"Because of me?" He cocks an eyebrow in a way that at one time would have melted my insides.

"Because of me." I'm surprised by the lack of melting butterflies.

"Ah. Diane asked me to forward her condolences and apologies. She wasn't up to meeting you today. Maybe before she returns to England." I nod, not sure what to say. "She also wanted you to have this." He picks up the frame. It is, indeed, the photograph of Hank at the ribbon-cutting ceremony. His friends have all signed their names, some have even written a few words about the carousel.

Fresh tears come from the well I'd thought was dry. "Please thank her for me."

His eyes bore into me. "So, Maya, what now?"

"We all move on."

"What are you moving on to?"

Indeed, what?

"First the reopening of the merry-go-round. It's time for a new generation to experience its magic."

"And second?"

"Second, make some of my own magic." I meet his eyes. I know how Grandma was able to love Hank and Jonathan. And how Hank was able to love her and Annabelle. Simon will forever have a place in my heart, but he's not my future.

He knows it, too. Simon's mouth pulls into a line, and he pushes off from my car. He opens the back door and places the photograph on the backseat. It takes three easy steps and he's in front of me. His right hand brushes away a curl. He leans close and gives me the gentlest of kisses on the cheek. From anyone else, it would have been a friendly hello, good-bye. From Simon, it's a heart-wrenching choice. But the right choice.

"Good-bye, Maya. I'll see you around."

"Good-bye, Simon." I slip past him and into my car. He stays in my rearview mirror until I take the left turn out of the cemetery.

I skirt the house and go directly to the studio. There's a lot of work to be done, and I'm not ready to talk to Vale about the funeral. Or about Simon.

"Hi." I stroke his neck. "You look very handsome. Are you ready to go home?"

I pull the packing material he came in from the back corner and start the slow, sad process of wrapping up my horse. Because he is *my* horse.

I squat to wrap his left front hoof. "I'm going to miss you. We've had quite a ride together haven't we?"

I shift my weight until I'm sitting on the concrete floor. A raspy breath pushes past my lips and sends dust fairies scurrying away.

"You have to go back to your friends now, start over. How do I let go? There have been too many good-byes. Grandma. The baby. Hank. Now you. Our stories are so tightly wound together."

I stretch my arms back and cringe as the two knots in my shoulders collide. I look up, the bubble wrap forgotten in my hands.

"You really are magic though. Look at everything you've done for me. You brought me Hank and Simon. And in a weird way, I think you've even helped me get closer to Mom. You helped me see past the grief. And thanks to you, I think I can finally put the last year behind me."

Fred barrels into my side at the same time as I hear someone clearing his throat behind me.

"So, he's the one you've been talking to. Should I be jealous?"

"Nah. But he is a good listener."

Vale chuckles. The picture, laying on the table, catches his eye. "This is nice."

"It was in Hank's room at Tower Oaks. His daughter thought I'd want it."

"Very generous. Where are you going to put it?"

The idea comes to me before he finishes the question. "It belongs with the merry-go-round. I'm going to have them hang it in the pavilion and showcase it at the reopening ceremony. I wanted Hank to be there. Now he will be. Forever."

Thirty-Nine

The air hangs close, like an overheated stranger with personal-space issues. There are a lot of strangers crowding the carousel pavilion this afternoon.

I lean against the railing where the moveable walls have been pushed open to allow the ocean breeze through. There are too many people here for even the breeze to move. I look to the ocean, wishing I could escape to the sand and the waves. After all the years of wishing to return to the Carousel Beach of my memories, I'm here. Almost.

I had my quiet time with the merry-go-round this morning, when we came for the final walk-through. She's as beautiful as I remember her from my childhood. The magic is missing, though. Or maybe just for me.

Magic or no magic, I now have to play my part alongside the board of the arts committee, and the mayor, and the other high-ups who've come out of their air-conditioned offices to celebrate the Fourth of July and the grand reopening.

A ruffle of air moves the silk of my camisole. I pull at the delicate fabric and attempt to flap a hint of air to my sticky middle.

In fifteen minutes, the mayor will cut the ribbon and the merry-go-round will come back to life. All the years of work and love have led to this moment. The smiles on faces as people take in the transformation swells me with pride. Not for myself, but for Hank. I wish he could have seen this.

"Why are you hiding over here?" Jerome leans on the railing next to me. "You should be in the middle of this circus."

"Nah, you know me. I prefer watching from the cheap seats. Hard to believe that she's no longer mine. Not that she was mine, mine, but you know what I mean." I flush at my rambling. "God, I hope they don't ask me to say anything. Can you imagine?"

Jerome chuckles. "Don't worry, I know where the switch is to turn the old girl on. If you make an ass of yourself up there, I'll just drown you out with the merry-go-round music."

"Great pep talk, thank you."

"Don't mention it." He puffs out his chest then exhales with laughter. "Seriously though, Maya, it's been a pleasure working with you. I'm going to miss you."

I twist to look at him. "I'm not going anywhere." Has he been talking to Vale?

"Good." He bumps my shoulder with his. "And before the craziness officially takes over, I wanted to tell you how proud I am to have been associated with this project. You're a remarkable woman, Maya Brice."

"Awww, geez, you're going to make me cry."

"You really want to get choked up? Go look at some of those new messages being posted on the Memory Wall. That, my dear, was a stroke of brilliance."

The one side of the pavilion that doesn't open became my canvas for the Memory Wall. I hung the photograph from Hank's room at Tower Oaks in the center. To the right are assorted photographs of the carousel — some from its early days and some during the restoration process.

To the left is a huge corkboard. I'd been so moved by the notes left in the comment boxes during the years of renovation that I convinced the arts committee to make them a permanent part of the carousel. Slips of memories dot the corkboard, each with another snippet of hope and happiness from a stranger who discovered the magic. We'd placed a table with blank paper and assorted pens under Hank's picture. The crowd swarmed to the paper scraps like seagulls to French fries.

Kaitlin, the mayor's communications director, catches my eye and holds up her hand. Five minutes to go.

"You got this." Jerome pulls me in for a hug then disappears into the crowd.

I work my way through the people, mumbling hellos and thank yous and welcomes. The faces are a blur, but I purposefully don't stop for a closer look. The people who should be in attendance won't be here.

"Ladies and gentlemen, if I can have your attention. I'll make this quick, I know you're all anxious to get a closer look and a ride," Mayor Fischer's voice booms over the loudspeaker. "Several years ago . . ." He looks from me to Kaitlin, who holds up three fingers. ". . . Three years ago, our historic carousel was gifted a second chance. Thanks to the loving attention of Maya Brice and her team of experts, summer days on the Kent boardwalk will again be filled with the music and laughter that only a merry-go-round can produce."

I scan the crowd. Vale is standing with

Thomas and Bree. Alex gives me a blue thumbs-up and a wide grin, his teeth a matching blue. Megan clutches Bree's hand — or rather Bree clutches Megan's, trying to keep her from bolting to the carousel. Mom and Dad are a few clusters over, talking with a group of their friends. Toward the back, I spot Sam and Taylor. She beams at me while he beams at her. The two faces I want to see more than anything, though, are on the back wall, in a photograph of a similar event sixty-five years ago.

"On the back wall," the mayor continues, "you can read more about the history of the carousel and its restoration, as well as what you can do to help support the future of this beautiful piece of our community. Without further ado, please help me welcome Ms. Brice as we cut the ribbon and open the Kent Carousel for business."

I bristle at the word *business.* The carousel isn't a business.

I stretch my face into a smile and take my place next to the mayor, who's holding a giant pair of scissors. The red ribbon goes slack in my hand, and the crowd cheers.

Loralee, the events director, corrals the group of people closest to the carousel into a line to wait their turn. The first ride is for VIPs. I've been deemed a VIP, as have my family members, much to the delight of the kids. Vale is at my side with Megan and a slightly less-blue Alex.

"Congratulations. It's beautiful," Vale says and gives me a kiss on the lips. Megan giggles, and Alex pretends to gag.

Thomas picks Alex up by the waist. "Let's leave these yucky adults and go find an animal to ride."

Alex calls dibs on the lion. Megan runs for the ostrich with Vale as her chaperone.

The mayor and Jerome step up on the platform and walk through the maze of animals until I can't see them anymore. A dozen more people who I don't know congratulate me and take their spots on one animal or another.

I don't run to my horse, not this time. Grandma would have teased me for missing my spot. I step onto the beautifully polished wood floor as the carousel inches forward. With the first notes of the music, I can almost hear her laugh and call to me, "You'd better mount that pony fast, Mims."

I weave through the menagerie until I see him. Here with his herd he's even more stunning than he'd been in my studio.

There's no one on him, though, and as I come closer, I see why. Mom is standing between him and the jumper to his left, arms stretched between the two. She smiles when she catches me gawking. She tilts her head for me to come, and grabs at the pole for support as the carousel picks up speed.

"Close your mouth, dear. The photographers are snapping as fast as this thing is moving. You don't want an unflattering tonsil shot on the front page of the newspaper." She smiles demurely at a couple of cameras.

"How? What?" I stammer, unable to formulate a coherent question.

I mount my horse while Mom climbs onto hers. She wraps an arm around the pole, leaning her chest into it. Her other hand grips the leather reins as if she would be able to yank the horse to a stop if he gets too fast.

"I don't know what to say, Mom."

"Nothing would be advisable. At least not until this thing has stopped and we've come off alive."

I laugh. A real laugh, a laugh like I haven't felt in entirely too long.

As the merry-go-round spins, I catch glimpses of Hank and my grandma grinning from their forever picture; the shimmers of the setting sun on the ocean; a dolphin leaping over the waves; people talking, smiling, waving. The breeze stirred up by the motion of the carousel carries the smells of my youth — caramel popcorn, suntan lotion, wood, sea.

By the time the carousel begins to slow, Mom has released her death grip on the reins but not the pole.

Alex comes running to us when the carousel stops and the music quiets. "Grandma, you rode the up-and-down horse. Wow. How was it? That looked so fun. Dad wouldn't let me ride one of the up-and-downs."

"It was fun." She says, giving me a tight smile and Alex a wider one. She wobbles the few steps to the edge of the platform and makes a show of having Alex help her off. Grandma used to do that when I was around Alex's age.

I slide off my horse and wrap my arms around his neck. "I was wrong," I whisper into his ear, "you are still full of magic."

Kaitlin takes my arm the moment I step off the carousel and leads me to a group of reporters.

"Why this project, Maya?" a girl who introduces herself as Melanie from the *Kent Daily* asks.

"I grew up riding this carousel. It was where magic became reality for me. That sounds silly, I know, but it's true. My grandmother used to tell me such amazing stories about these animals, as though they were real. For us they were. Coming here always made me happy, it didn't matter what else was happening in my life at the time. I wanted to make sure other kids, and adults, had that same opportunity."

Melanie turns off the recording app on her phone, jots something down in a notebook, and thanks me for my time. I catch a roll of her eyes as she turns and walks away with her photographer at her side. She's not one of the lucky ones who will be transformed by the merry-go-round.

I weave my way to the outside perimeter in search of air and a moment of calm.

Vale catches my eye from across the pavilion. We've settled into a not completely uncomfortable routine since his return from Seattle. In some ways, it's been better than it has in months. But the moment I release the stranglehold on my breath, the reality of his pending move crushes me all over again.

The carousel kicks into motion again, and Megan appears at my side. "Come on, Aunt Maymay, ride with me. Please?"

"Yes, Aunt Maymay," Thomas says. "You look entirely too serious standing here by yourself. You okay?" He mouths the last part to keep Megan from hearing.

I nod. Thomas I can put off with a nod. Megan won't be dismissed quite so easily. But after five rounds on the carousel, even I'm ready for solid ground, and I hand Megan off to Bree.

"Ready to go?" Vale asks. We're less than a week from his start date at the Seattle firm, and now that the reopening ceremony is over, my excuse jar is empty. He'll be expecting an answer. Soon. "A bunch of folks are going to The Yellow Owl for drinks. Want to go?"

I don't. I'd prefer to stay with my carousel horse, but that's no longer an option. But I also don't feel like going home yet. "Sure. Sounds like fun."

I whisper my good-bye to the animals who've been my closest confidants over the last year. I know they'll protect the secrets and dreams of others, like they did mine.

Hand-in-hand with Vale, I walk away. The music picks up speed then slows. The buzz of voices is muffled by the surf. Late-afternoon runners jog along the beach while shell seekers stroll, heads down, oblivious to the party on the boardwalk. I spot him next to a lifeguard stand, bent over to catch his breath. A woman I recognize as one of the doctors from the hospital jogs in place next to him. Our eyes meet and he smiles, that smile that made girls, including me, swoon. I return the smile as he and his friend pick up their run.

Vale and I follow the handful of our friends two blocks to The Yellow Owl, where Taylor has secured a section of the rooftop deck for us.

"To Maya and her carousel." Taylor raises a glass when we've joined the group.

Up on the roof in the waning light, with the distant sounds of the carousel and the waves, I finally feel the noose around my lungs release. The anticipation leading up to today drains from me, and I relax into the festive atmosphere.

With the last of the fireworks, the party begins to break up. Vale, Taylor, Sam, and I are the last on the roof.

"Oh my god, quiet." I lean back in the chair and tilt my head to the few stars hardy enough to get past the lights of Kent.

"It's been quite the day." Sam scoots closer to me. In the three weeks since she told me about the baby, the baby-signs have popped.

"Have I told you how adorable you are prego?" I lean into her shoulder.

"You say that now. I bet you won't in a few months."

"You'll be gorgeous even then."

"Have I told you what an awesome friend you are?" She laces her fingers through mine.

"You say that now. I bet you won't if we move across the country." I lower my voice so it doesn't carry.

"Does that mean you're thinking of going?"

"Of course I'm thinking. Hard not to. But I still don't know what to do. I really don't want to go, Sam."

"I know." She squeezes my mind.

"Hey you two," Vale's voice breaks our moment. "Whatever you're cooking up, put a cork in it. It's time to call it a night."

Vale and Taylor help a busboy put glasses into a plastic bin.

"We need to get out of here before they make us do the dishes as well," Taylor adds.

Outside of the restaurant, we say our good-byes, and Vale and I watch Taylor and Sam get into his car. We'd walked the few blocks from our house to the beach and now, after a long day and in the heat of the evening, I wish we'd driven.

"Come on, I'm tired." Vale takes my hand and we retrace the morning's walk. A walk we've done so many times. Will there be more?

After the excitement of the day and the

noise of the evening, I'm reluctant to break the quiet between us. "Vale," I finally say as we're about to turn onto our street.

He releases my hand and puts his arm around my shoulder. "Not tonight, May. Tonight, we're going to enjoy the high of your success and the magic of the carousel."

Forty

I stretch and inhale the smell of coffee. I blink at the light, roll over and bolt upright when I see the clock. How did I sleep until ten A.M.? Even when I want to sleep in, I usually end up wide awake at seven.

I pull on shorts and a shirt, then pad down the stairs. No husband, no dog. But there's a mug with a sticky note on the counter.

Took Fred for a walk. Made coffee. Look on the table. p.s. Need to buy more sticky notes.

I pour a cup of coffee and go to the table as instructed. Vale has been working on a drawing of the kitchen. I pick up the plans and walk the new layout, running my hands over the Formica counter, the drab yellowy-white maple cabinets, the old faucet that spits when you turn it to maximum. I clutch the papers to my chest.

Why would he be making plans to redo the kitchen if he's leaving? *He or we?* Could it mean he's changed his mind?

What would this house become if someone else bought it? Would they gut my studio and turn it back into a garage? Would they redo the beautiful new bathroom? What about the dining room that's too small for a normal-size table? Or the tiny extra bedroom upstairs?

I take the steps two at a time, breathless, my heart pounding with sudden anticipation. I fling the door open, slick anxiety making my hands slip from the knob. What if it's not there?

It is, of course. The unfinished mural of the merry-go-round waits for me to put it back in motion. Would new owners paint over my heart? I can't let that happen.

The snow globe sits idle on the bookshelf next to the stuffed dog. I shake the glass orb and the miniature carousel disappears in a blizzard. And then, like magic, reappears.

There's a scratching of nails on the hardwood and Fred barrels up the stairs, beating Vale in a final sprint into the room. The puppy flops on his side with a grunt, then rolls onto his back, his baby belly round and inviting.

Vale doubles over at the door, hands on his knees. "I'm not sure which one of us got the harder workout."

I rub Fred's belly while he squirms with happiness. "Did you wear Daddy out?"

"Yes, he did. I'm amazed at the speed he can whip up with those tiny legs." Fred's tongue hangs from the side of his mouth while his four paws stick straight up in the air.

Vale takes a couple of steps into the room. "What are you doing in here? Oh, wow, a snow globe. I used to love these as a kid. Where did you get it?" He reaches for the orb in my hands.

"Grandma bought it for the baby. Mom thought I was ready to have it."

He pauses in midshake and looks from the snow globe to me. "How do you feel about that?"

"Okay, I guess."

"Are you going to keep it in your studio? Or in here?" He gives it a shake and we watch as the fluffy white flakes dance around the miniature merry-go-round before settling into the base.

In your studio or in here?

"Vale, why the plans for the kitchen?"

"What?" He hands me the globe, his forehead seamed in thought.

"The plans on the table downstairs. Why were you drawing a new kitchen design?"

"You hate that kitchen."

"So do you. But in three days, you're due in Seattle."

"You said 'you're due,' Does that mean you've decided not to go?"

"I was going to ask you the same after seeing the kitchen design."

He takes a long breath before responding. "I have to go, Maya."

"I know." I shake the globe, and we both watch as the fake white flakes swirl and twirl and finally settle. And as the miniature merry-go-round emerges from the blizzard, so does my decision. "I need to go somewhere, Vale. I'd like you to come with me." I stand and reach a hand to my husband. "No questions though. Not yet. Okay?"

He nods and follows me out of the house, to our car. I get into the driver's seat and tuck the snow globe in my lap.

Neither of us speaks during the short drive. I ease the car through the large gates of the cemetery and stop at the first fork. Vale covers my hand on the stick shift with his hand and together we shift from first to second. With a deep breath to steady my nerves, I turn the car left.

I park and together we walk the short distance. It's a large headstone for such a small occupant. There's a name etched into the stone and painted in black: Jonathan

William Brice. Jonathan William. Too long for someone that tiny. Would we have called him John? Johnny? Maybe Will or Willy. My heart catches at the date.

"What are we doing?" Vale folds to sit on the ground next to me.

"This belongs to him." I give the globe a shake and set it on the base. And as before, the emergence of the miniature merry-go-round through the white flakes settles the unsettled emotions that have been swirling inside me.

"I can't move to Seattle, Vale. I can't leave him and Grandma. Or Hank and the carousel. But I also realize you can't stay, at least not the way things have been."

"That doesn't sound very encouraging." He doesn't look at me, and I can't make myself turn to look at him.

"Before he died, Hank helped me realize that I can't carry the burden of their deaths or lose myself in the guilt. And he made me pinky promise that I'd start taking steps forward. As of yesterday, I'm unemployed." I catch a quirk in Vale's mouth, a hint of a smile. "Assuming you'll have me, I'd like to come to Seattle on a sabbatical of sorts."

Vale's hint of a smile broadens.

"I don't want to sell the cottage. I don't want to pack everything up. I just want to come and see what can be. Fair?"

"Fair." Vale takes my hand and together we sit, listening to the birds and the wind and the waves in the distance. In my soul, I feel the movement of the merry-go-round, and in my brain, I hear its happiness.

I graze the headstone with the tips of my fingers. "Tomorrow I'm going to ask them to carve a carousel into the stone and secure the globe to the base."

Knowing my baby will be protected by the magic of the carousel gives me peace. And knowing the magic of the carousel will forever be with me, gives me hope.

ABOUT THE AUTHOR

After years of pushing the creativity boundary in corporate communications, **Orly Konig** decided it was time for a new challenge and made the switch to fiction. Now she spends her days chatting up imaginary friends, drinking entirely too much coffee, and negotiating writing space around two over-fed cats. When she's not writing, she's a personal assistant and chauffer to her son which includes countless hours spent in a chalky climbing gym, or crocheting out plot points. She's a co-founder and past president of the Women's Fiction Writers Association.

The employees of Thorndike Press hope you have enjoyed this Large Print book. All our Thorndike, Wheeler, and Kennebec Large Print titles are designed for easy reading, and all our books are made to last. Other Thorndike Press Large Print books are available at your library, through selected bookstores, or directly from us.

For information about titles, please call:
(800) 223-1244

or visit our website at:
gale.com/thorndike

To share your comments, please write:

Publisher
Thorndike Press
10 Water St., Suite 310
Waterville, ME 04901